C000172834

New Yor

by

Andrew J. Morgan

Other titles by Andrew J. Morgan:

New Dawn
Vessel
Noah's Ark

Table of Contents

Chapter 1

"So how long have you been involved in the project then?"

Josh didn't have to think long about the answer. The tunnels had been his place of work for so long they felt like home. "Since 2008."

The executive beamed, his white hair and even whiter shirt gleaming in contrast to the dirty hi-vis vest and scuffed hard hat. "You've been here since the beginning then?"

"Since they broke ground."

"And are you enjoying it?"

"It's got its ups and downs, you know."

The executive turned to his assistant and nodded. "We need more workers like Mr., uh—sorry, please tell me your name again? I'm quite forgetful these days. I do apologize."

"Josh. Josh Reed."

The executive smiled. "Like Mr. Reed here."

His assistant nodded, then looked up and around the enormous rocky, cathedral-like space, which dwarfed the workers coming off shift from the tunnels. "How long did it take to dig all this out then?" he asked.

Josh took in the familiar sight, reliving in an instant the memories that had gotten him this far. "This staging area took about three months. The ground is soft up here; it's easy to dig."

"Fascinating," the executive said, his assistant nodding his appreciation. "Absolutely fascinating."

Josh's supervisor, Lionel Parker, who had been standing back in the shadows somewhat, ushered the executive forward. "If you'd like to come down these steps, we'll take the train over to the dig site."

"Ah!" the executive said with joy. "We've got trains down here already, have we? And they all said we'd never have anything running to deadline."

The executive's assistant and Lionel both laughed politely with the executive, but Josh did not. As he followed the others down the steel frame stairs, deeper into the cavernous rocky arena, he threw a glare at Lionel, who mouthed, "I'm sorry…"

On a project like this, with the size and scale and with as many unknowns as there were, every second was precious, and spending them escorting some office-dwelling executive tourist was seconds lost. Josh's team was hard at work, sure, but he needed to be there to make the decisions when they came across the inevitable next problem.

At the base of the stairs, a rudimentary platform led to a small industrial haulage engine set loose of its trucks. They boarded one by one, squeezing into the tight cab, ready to leave the calm and cool air of the open cavern and head into the tunnels.

Josh gave the train some juice; the wheels squealed, then bit, hauling its mass forward.

"So how exactly do you dig such a large hole?" the executive asked, peering out of the small, dirty windows. "The drill must be enormous!"

Lionel gave Josh a nod to tell him to answer. Josh considered pretending he hadn't seen it.

"Well," he said, wishing he were anywhere but in this train with this man, "because the East Side Access bores straight through Manhattan—"

"Right along 63rd Street," Lionel added, smiling politely.

"—there's no room to drop in a drill as big as we'd need. Normally we'd use the one big one, but space requirements have forced us to use a smaller drill to bore four separate holes that are combined to make the one big one instead."

"And what happens to the middle part, the core?"

Even from his tone, Josh could tell the executive was enthralled. "We blow the shit out of it—"

"Josh!" Lionel barked.

The executive was chuckling. "That's okay," he said. "I don't mind a little blue-collar talk when the time's right."

It was Lionel's turn to throw Josh a glare. "Well, okay then," he said.

"So you detonate it," the executive continued, "right under the city, under everyone... fascinating."

Josh allowed himself a small grin. Maybe this guy was all right. There weren't many people who found what he did interesting. "They don't even feel a thing."

"Fascinating, absolutely fascinating..."

As they passed from the main cavern into one of the four smaller tunnels, the air whipped around them. It felt immediately stuffier, warmer, like they were driving down the throat of a beast. Lights, fed by wire strung between them, rolled past one by one, ever day and yet ever night. There was no sun down here.

"You said there was easy rock to drill," the executive said. "I take it that means there's harder rock to drill, too?"

Josh was starting to regret branding this old guy as quickly as he had. "Yeah, absolutely. New York City has several bands of what we call Manhattan schist running through it. It's really hard stuff, a shale of gray quartz and white orthoclase. Millions of years of compression have turned it into one hard f—... one hard material."

"Is that so?"

"Absolutely. You can see it above ground in Central Park, great big boulders of the stuff. It runs through there, and also through downtown. That's why all the skyscrapers are built in those areas, because the ground's so solid. And we have to get through it, me and the team. It's so hard that sometimes we'll only get through a few feet in a day. The guys have to work together like clockwork to get even that much done."

"Fascinating. Isn't this fascinating, Henry?"

The executive's assistant, who Josh had now learned was called Henry, nodded. "Very much so." His tone didn't quite match his sentiment.

"Oh, don't be such a stick in the mud," the executive said. "Your salary wouldn't be quite so generous if it weren't for these boys working so hard down here."

Now Josh couldn't help but grin. He kept facing forward, watching the track as he ushered the train down the tunnel he and his team had bored, feeling a bubble of pride well up inside him. He didn't have to turn to know what kind of a face Henry was making right about now.

"Are you married, Mr. Reed?" the executive said, all of a sudden.

Josh twiddled the ring on his left hand reflexively. "I was."

"Oh, I'm sorry. A clumsy question."

"It's all right," Josh reassured him. "It was mutual. What were you going to say?"

"Well, if it's proper," the executive said, his commanding tone a little muted.

"It's fine. No problem."

"I was going to say, if I can be so bold, that it sounds like your relationship with your team in these tunnels is like a marriage: you work together through the good times, but you work even more closely through the tough. It's the only way to make it stick."

"Couldn't have put it better myself," Josh said.

"I really didn't mean any offense by it."

"None taken, really."

The train fell into quiet as Josh began to slow. They were approaching the end of the track, and he needed to focus. It was dangerous down here. He pulled up to a stop, and disembarked first.

"If you can all please keep to this gangway," he asked, gesturing to the rope-linked posts along the edge of the tunnel. He led them on, taking in the rich stench of earth and rock, feeling the damp air cling to his coveralls. It was a different world in here, even compared to the cavern, and it made him feel alive.

"It's very quiet," the executive said. "Is the drill running?"

"Not yet," Lionel said. "It's not due to start until the next shift in five minutes. We're just in time to see it."

"The guys are lining the tunnel where it was bored out earlier," Josh added. "We weld steel plates into place to maintain the structural integrity of the rock."

The tunnel curved ahead, and as they began to round it, the sound of busy, intense chatter became apparent. With it came the sight of five men hauling a curved piece of steel into place—one man on the chain pulley, two holding the steel steady, another guiding it in and the last waiting to weld. As Josh and the others walked, they watched this coordinated dance of teamwork and hard labor, an effort that seemed almost elegant in its performance. Behind, the ominous oil and dust-stained steel of the drill filled the tunnel.

"Cover your eyes," Josh warned as the welder kicked a spark bright and blue. It was the last piece of steel, right on time. "Good work, guys," Josh called out to his team. "Are we ready to roll at ten?"

The man who'd been guiding the steel turned to Josh, and they clapped hands together, gripping tight by way of greeting. "For sure. Last steel just went in."

"Thanks, Craig. Good job."

"Who are these guys?" Craig asked.

"Oh yeah, we've got some guests. Say hi." Josh gestured to his party.

"Hi."

Lionel, who was somewhere between apoplectic and terrified, took the lead. "Mr. Miller"—*so that's his name*, Josh thought—"please meet Craig Anderson, Senior Tunnel Engineer on this project, and Josh's right-hand man."

"Pleasure," the executive—Mr. Miller—said, holding out a hand.

Craig held back, glancing at Josh, who nodded him on. Craig took Mr. Miller's hand and shook it. "Pleased to meet you," he said.

"We've also got Steve Carter, Robert Jackson, Douglas Moore and Carlos Garcia," Lionel continued, each man waving in turn.

"I'm very pleased to meet all of you, and I'm also very much looking forward to seeing the drill in action," Mr. Miller said, "even if that wet blanket over there"—he pointed his thumb over his shoulder at Henry, who was actually pouting—"isn't."

"We'd be glad to show you," Craig said.

Behind Mr. Miller's back, Lionel gave two thumbs up and a nervous grin.

"We'll have to get back behind the safety line though," Josh said. "There's over a hundred tungsten carbide teeth spinning around faster than a big block Chevy on that drill, and your hi-vis vest isn't going to do shit if something goes wrong."

Craig muffled a snicker with the back of his hand.

"Sounds like some dangerous shit," Mr. Miller said, taking a step back. "I'll stand where you need me."

Craig was clearly surprised by the old man's language. "This guy's all right," he said, pointing at him. Lionel looked close to having a heart attack.

Smiles fell, and it was game time. Josh led his crew behind the safety line along with the nonessential staff, while Craig and another stayed with the drill, performing the start-up checks. The diesel engine chugged into life, loud and unsilenced, and Mr. Miller instinctively put his fingers in his ears.

"You think this is loud," Josh shouted over the rumbling idle, "you wait until it gets chewing at that schist."

Craig gave a thumbs-up, which Josh returned. He pulled the ear protection down on his hard hat before pointing to those on Mr. Miller's, which he pulled down too. A grinding whirr, then an almighty bang filled the tunnel, making Henry jump. It settled into a deep howl as the tungsten carbide teeth bit and began to chew. The rumble underfoot hummed in their limbs and swelled all around them. Such power, to grind up nature's biggest, toughest opposition only a few feet at a time. It gave Josh an immense admiration for the rock underfoot. It was his best friend, and his worst enemy.

After a while, the vibration and the drone became too much for Mr. Miller, and he signaled that he'd like to leave. Around the corner, the noise had dulled enough to remove their ear protection, and the party of four could talk again.

"Well, I have a newfound appreciation for the work you do," Mr. Miller said, offering Josh a handshake. "It's a gigantic undertaking."

"Thanks," Josh said, taking and shaking. "I appreciate the opportunity to be part of this huge project. It's one to tell my boy about when he's old enough to understand."

"I expect he'll be very proud."

Josh was about to speak again when an almighty screech filled the air, wailing and gnashing. Then it fell silent, the thrum and rumble of the drill, too. Whatever it was, it didn't sound good. The drill was only stopped if they hit something unexpected or unfamiliar, and that sounded both unexpected *and* unfamiliar.

"I'm sorry, Mr. Miller, but duty calls," Josh said hurriedly.

Mr. Miller looked concerned. "Is everything all right?"

"I sure hope so. Lionel, could you escort these two gentlemen back to the staging area please?"

"Yes, of course," Lionel replied. "If you could board the train, let's give Josh and his team some space."

"Of course, of course," Mr. Miller said. "Time is money and all that. I really appreciate your time, Mr. Reed, and thank you for showing me around this magnificent place. I'm sure Henry will be more than pleased to be finally going! Good luck to you, and I hope everything's okay."

"I'm sure it's nothing," Josh said, letting Mr. Miller and Henry board the train before turning on his heel and heading for the drill. *What bad timing*, he thought, *to have the drill come unstuck in the middle of an executive tour*. Geotech Corporation, the contractor he worked for, had fought long and hard to get this project, and he didn't want one visit from the man upstairs to put that into jeopardy. He certainly didn't want to be the one who got singled out as the reason they lost the contract. *It'll be fine*, he tried to reassure himself. Mr. Miller seemed a reasonable man.

As he approached the drill, Josh saw that the team was already getting it backed up. "Craig," he shouted over the noise, "what's going on?"

"Don't know," Craig shouted back. "Hit something hard. Could see sparks down the gap."

"Sparks?" Josh had never seen sparks before. He waited as the drill came clear of the hole, then took a flashlight from his belt and flicked it on. "Hang back," he said to the team, while he and Craig went on ahead. They cleared the front of the drill, still steaming from heat and moisture, the gnarled teeth dotting the surface like bulbous metal thorns. Inside the tunnel, the smell of dirt was thick, almost unbreathable. Water dripped from the ceiling, pooling at their feet. Veins of blue crossed grey, the scored schist worked hard into dust. Josh coughed.

The fresh tunnel, a drill's length, was only fifteen feet or so, but the lack of light meant it fell away into darkness quickly. Josh squinted, holding his flashlight ahead of him as they approached the rock face. *Although,* Josh thought, *a rock face should present rock.* This didn't. It was something else. Something that glimmered.

They stood in front of the wall that had bettered them, that had sent the drill into a shower of sparks.

"It looks crystalline," Craig said.

"Yeah," Josh agreed. He held out a hand over the material, then laid his palm on it. Cool as anything. It should be warm. He looked to the ground for spoil, found some. He picked it up, turning it in his palm. It had come away like shards of metal, splintered into curled wisps that were so light they weighed nothing in his hand.

The drill had only grazed the surface, and yet the areas untouched still gleamed anew. It was natural, but no ore.

"Any ideas?" Josh asked.

"Never seen it before in my life," Craig replied. "Some kind of native titanium perhaps? Could be an inclusion."

"Perhaps."

"There's nothing else supposed to be here; I checked the plans this morning."

"No, there isn't," Josh mumbled, partly to himself. He stared at the material, as though he could catch its secret if he stared long enough.

"You think we can go through it?"

A pause. "I think so." It must be an inclusion. A few inches thick, if that. "Yeah, let's do it."

They made their way back out of the fresh tunnel, to join the rest of the team. They looked on expectantly, hungry to push on.

"We keep going," Josh said, which was met by a small cheer.

With the drill back in place, Josh watched anxiously as the startup procedure was reinitialized. He looked at his watch; they'd stopped for thirty minutes already, thousands of dollars of wasted time. They could afford no more. They had to be on schedule. "Let's get her going," he called out. The ground shook. The teeth gnashed. The sparks flew.

Chapter 2

The metal seemed quite soft, as the drill—despite the noise and light show—moved forward with good progress. No one was expecting the great, groaning crack that shattered the air after forty minutes of drilling.

"Shut it off!" Josh shouted, waving furiously at the drill, at his team. Craig leaped into action, slapping the emergency shutoff button, grinding the drill to a halt.

Panting slightly, Craig looked at the drill, then at Josh. "Sounds like it got through," he said.

"It sounded like more than that," Josh replied. "It sounded like it was free spinning."

Craig frowned. "Did it?"

"I heard it too," Steve said, nodding.

"Me too," Carlos confirmed.

What a day, Josh thought. *What—a—day*. "Let's back it up," he said. He pulled his radio from his belt and spoke into it. "Lionel, you there?"

A crackle. "Yep. Mr. Miller's gone."

"Good. I'm going to need an evac of the tunnels. My team only. We've breached a pocket or something, so there could be gas."

"Are you sure? We weren't expecting anything like that today."

"I'm not sure, but I'd rather be safe."

"Yeah, good call. Okay, I'll get everyone out. Give me thirty minutes and I'll call back with the all-clear."

Radio away, Josh addressed the team. "You all know what might be in there, so if you don't want to take the risk, you can join the evac. If you stay here and continue, that's on you."

"Staying here, boss," Robert said, folding his arms. The others nodded.

"Well, legally we're all fine then," Josh said. "It's just the sudden explosive death we've got to worry about."

The team laughed. Josh smiled. They, like he, wouldn't give up on this job for anything. Josh didn't often feel happy, but right now he did.

"Okay, take a break," he told them. "When the message comes through, I want you all sharp."

They all took a seat on the ground, leaning up against the tunnel wall. The time passed quickly, lewd jokes filling the musty air with laughter. When Josh's radio hissed, however, the laughter stopped and the smiles fell.

"We're all clear," Lionel said, voice softened by distortion.

"Okay, guys," Josh said, getting to his feet as the others did too. "Let's do it."

As protocol dictated, the enormous drill was backed up slowly while they kept tight in behind it, sheltering them from anything the drill might release as it unplugged the hole. Inch by inch they pulled it out, Craig's hands gingerly easing the controls as Josh kept an eye and ear out for any reason to stop.

After what felt like forever, Craig stopped the drill. "Clear, boss," he said.

"All right," Josh said, breathing out at last. "I think we're good."

The relief from the team was palpable.

"Craig, with me," Josh said, drawing his flashlight and heading slowly to the front of the drill. As before, the fresh tunnel sank into darkness. The only way to see what was at the end of it was to head down there. He unclipped his radio and pushed the button. "All seems okay. We're having a look now."

"Be careful," Lionel responded.

As they edged into the tunnel, something seemed different. Before, it was halfway in when Josh had noticed the glint of the metallic face up ahead, but now it was gone. It had been replaced with… nothing.

"Do you see anything?" Josh asked.

"Nothing yet," Craig replied.

They inched forward more, delicate footsteps, ears buzzing. Josh felt his heart humming in his chest. He'd never felt like this before. Usually nothing made him feel anxious, or nervous, at least not down here. Another step closer and the hum in his chest grew, spreading to his arms and legs, and then his fingers and toes. He could almost hear it.

"Do you… do you feel that?" he said. "The vibration?"

"Yeah—I thought it was me. You feel it too, though, right?"

"Yeah, I do."

"Do you think it's traffic or something?"

Josh shook his head. "You wouldn't feel that down here, not unless there's a monster truck parade going on through Central Park. Is there any blasting going on today?"

"No, none."

"I don't know then."

Craig stopped. "You know, I'm not sure about this."

"That's fine, I'll go on ahead."

"If you're going, I'm going."

Josh stopped too, and turned to Craig. "You've got a family back home waiting for you. Kids. I don't want you coming in here if you don't think it's safe."

"You do too."

"That's—that's different."

They stared at each other, the flashlight casting a grim shadow across Craig's face.

"Fine," Craig said eventually, giving in. "But yell if you need me."

"I will."

Craig edged back out to the drill, walking into a wash of artificial light. Once Josh was satisfied that he was clear, he carried on deeper into the tunnel. The blackness at the end was ever black, the flashlight finding nothing to bounce back from. Josh squinted as he walked, trying to make out anything within, but it was useless. He was trying so hard to make out what was in there that it took him by surprise when his foot met an edge.

"Shit," he yelped, backing up. He pointed the flashlight down, to see a seam of the crystalline metal just under a foot thick lining the end of the tunnel, with nothing beyond.

"Are you all right?" Craig called out, voice reverberating.

"Yeah, fine," Josh shouted back. When his voice echoed in big, lazy repetitions in front of him, he knew something wasn't right.

"What is it?" Craig called out again, but Josh wasn't listening. The echo sounded like the space ahead was very large, larger even than the staging area at the head of the tunnel. He leaned cautiously over the edge, pointing the flashlight down, his skin buzzing with energy. A glint of metal and a dusting of rocks and debris told him that the base was about six or seven feet down. He could jump it.

"Get a ladder," he yelled back without taking his eyes away from the drop.

"A what?" Craig shouted. "A ladder?"

"Yeah."

"Okay."

Gripping hold of his utility belt, Josh sat down, legs over the edge, and shuffled forward until he was able to push himself off. The *clomp* of his feet hitting ground echoed around the darkness, bouncing around and returning from every direction.

Steadying himself, Josh raised his flashlight and looked around. What had been a buzz in his body now felt like waves of energy, as though he had become immersed in it. The air was cool, but musty. Still the flashlight fell to nothing, with only the ground in front of him, glinting and crystalline, giving him any idea of what surrounded him. *This space must be huge*, he thought, *right underneath Central Park.*

He wondered how far in it went, so he walked on, taking gentle steps and keeping the flashlight up high. The debris from the drill crunched underfoot, and he bent down to pick some up and put in his pocket. Taking a single stone, he launched it as hard as he could, listening over the beating of his heart and the thrum of the energy for its impact. Milliseconds passed, then seconds, until, in the distance, the stone skipped along the ground. The space had to be at least fifty feet across. Maybe even more.

Walking into the darkness felt like walking nowhere at all. The ground moved beneath his feet, and the flashlight scattered across the fine angles of the ground, but his position in space felt fixed. The only thing that changed was the intensity of the energy that flowed through him, a feeling which, somehow, felt comforting. It rippled and rumbled, pressing against his eardrums and his chest. It drew him on like a siren's song, a whispered question he needed to get closer to hear.

It pounded through him, and still he walked, drawing closer and closer to its source, ready to immerse himself in it and become one with its energy. He didn't even need the flashlight to know where he needed to go, and he let his arm drop to his side, walking on into the darkness, following a new sense that guided him with more precision than his mortal senses ever could.

His other senses were almost no more, his body a faint memory, his movement in spirit and not flesh. The feeling of vibration and the sound of humming filled his entire being in a way that was both completely alien and altogether familiar. He was open, vulnerable, expectant, awaiting. His time was now. It was forever. It was never.

"Boss, are you there? I can't see shit."

Josh opened his eyes. "I'm here," he said. The energy had receded, a gentle hiss in the background. He blinked, an odd sense of recollection chilling his shoulders. "I think there *is* gas in here," he shouted.

"All right, well let's get you out of there, then. Sorry I took so long getting the ladder."

So long? "That's okay." Josh turned around and made his way back over to Craig, following the moonlike hole glowing in the darkness. As he approached, Craig fed the ladder down for Josh to climb.

"You okay?" Craig asked.

"Yeah, fine, just a little light-headed."

"Does sound like gas. Probably a natural pocket."

"Let's get out of here."

They walked back out of the freshly bored tunnel to where the rest of the team awaited. Josh felt absolutely exhausted. "Right," he said, "there could well be gas in there, so I'm calling it a day."

The team groaned. No work meant no pay. "What was down there?" Robert asked.

"Nothing," Josh said. "Lots and lots of nothing." He wanted to lie down and sleep.

"All right," Craig said, giving Josh a concerned sideways eye, "let's get on out of here. Come on."

The team made audible protest, but did what they were told. As they all headed back to the train, Josh radioed in. "Lionel, we're on our way out. There's a big space down here. I think there might be gas."

"Okay, see you when you get up here."

As they reached the staging area and boarded the elevator, rising up out of the ground and into the light of day, Josh felt a little better. Less tired. Just needed some fresh air, that was all. A dull, distant headache lingered.

On the surface, he found Lionel.

"What can you report?" Lionel asked.

"There's a big chamber down there, huge, separated with a seam of native titanium or something like it. Some kind of crystalline metallic. I don't know. I've never seen it before."

"Anything inside?"

"No, just a hollow space. I think there's gas, though. I got pretty light-headed."

"Methane, perhaps?"

"Yeah, perhaps."

"Okay, well you made the right decision getting everyone out of there. I'll go call it in now. Everything will have to get sealed off and tested, so I don't know how long it'll be before your boys can get back to work."

"The guys are already pretty pissed that they'll lose out on pay," he said. "Is there anything you can do?"

Lionel, hands on hips, sighed. "I'll try. No promises."

"Thanks," Josh said, slapping him on the arm weakly.

Lionel looked concerned. "Are you okay? You seem a little… distant."

"Just the gas. I'll be all right."

"Okay, well you get yourself home and get some rest. And call a doctor if you feel any worse."

"Yes, sir," Josh said, grinning. Lionel didn't seem to see the funny side, heading off to the site offices with a frown on his face.

Josh made his way back to the team, and found them sitting around on a pile of spoil, sunning themselves. Other workers, also evacuated, grouped together around the site, doing the same.

"Right, guys, I've checked in with Lionel. He's going to see what he can do about your pay, but I can't promise anything."

"How long are we going to be up here?" Steve asked.

Josh shrugged. "Who knows. I expect they've got to get a reading on the gas and everything before they let anyone else down there."

"This sucks," Robert said, kicking a stone.

"That's the way it is," Craig replied. "Nothing we can do about it."

The heat of the sun warmed through Josh. It was nice. "Exactly. Might as well make the most of the day and head off home. I expect they'll want you off-site pretty soon anyway."

It took some doing, but eventually Josh managed to persuade the others to go home, even Craig. Josh promised to stay behind and let them know as soon as the site was reopened. Once they were gone, he found himself a soft patch of land and lay down, shielding his eyes from the sun. He dozed for a minute, until the sound of sirens jarred him awake. He sat up, and saw Lionel jogging over, the toll of senior management jiggling over his beltline.

"Josh," he said, panting as he came to a stop, "I thought you'd gone already. I've just had a call saying the police are on their way over. They're cordoning the whole site off. We've got to leave."

The sirens wailed loud and clear as multiple cars surrounded the site. "Really? The police?"

"I know, it's crazy, right? I think it's something to do with it being so built up around here. All I *do* know is that we've got to leave, now. No excuses."

Josh scanned the site, and noticed everyone else was gone. He was alone. He hoisted himself up with Lionel's help, joints stiff and grumbling, and they both headed for the exit. "It would happen on the day the executive comes, wouldn't it?" Josh said.

"It always does," Lionel groaned. "It always does."

Chapter 3

Josh and Lionel ambled across the site to broach the tall hoarding through great double gates, emblazoned on the outside with graffiti and posters. The sirens in their number were too loud to talk over, and they both waited as no less than five cars pulled up in turn, each with red and blue lights pounding the backs of their retinas. They shared a glance.

The sirens shut off, and with the lights still twirling, the officers of the law disembarked. After a huddle, most of them headed to the site, brushing past Josh and Lionel without so much as a nod, while a single officer approached. It was mid-afternoon, and the air was balmy. Josh could feel sweat beading on his scalp. He ran a sleeve across his brow.

"Good afternoon, gentlemen," the officer said, politely but firmly. "I take it that one of you is running the site here?"

"That's right," Lionel replied, stepping forward, arms crossed. "Can I ask what it is you boys need?"

The officer halted his approach, drawing a sheaf of papers from the folder he was carrying. "Everything you need to know is in here," he said.

Lionel took the papers, but didn't read them, keeping his eyes affixed on the lawman.

"We've been instructed to secure the perimeter and extract any and all personnel not related to this investigation."

Lionel looked confused. "What investigation? Are you here about the gas?"

"I'm not at liberty to say, sir."

Lionel turned to Josh. Josh shrugged, saying nothing. Lionel, to the officer, said, "What does that mean? When can we get back on-site?"

"I do not have that information, sir."

Josh, hands on hips, sighed, while Lionel held his hands up in protest. "That can't happen. *This* can't happen. We've got work to do, a schedule to keep and a budget to stay on top of. I can't have the police crawling all over this site for God knows how long, getting in the way of things. Who even told you about this, anyway?"

The officer peered into his folder, then back at Lionel. "You're Lionel Parker, correct?"

Lionel puffed up his chest. "I am."

"Then *you* did."

"What?" Josh said, turning to Lionel. Seeing Lionel's confusion, Josh addressed the officer. "What's going on here?"

The officer, pointing, said, "This man made a call informing the authorities of a situation that required intervention—"

"I called the Department of Safety and Health, not the state police!" Lionel interrupted. "You think I want all of this going on at my site? You think I want my ass handed to me by my boss for putting us off schedule? Hell no!"

"Sir," the officer said, holding up a hand, "you need to remain calm. I'm just doing my job. The Department saw fit to call in the relevant authorities, so we're here until the federal officers arrive—"

"Federal officers?" Josh repeated, shaking his head, baffled. It was all getting out of control, and so fast.

Lionel's expression mirrored Josh's confusion. "Do you mind telling me *something* about what's happening? *Federal* officers? Are you sure this isn't some big misunderstanding or something?"

The officer, taking a step back, cradling his folder under his arm, looked resigned. "I've told you, sir, I'm not at liberty to tell you anything more, and to be honest, I don't know anything more. I've just been told to come down here, secure the area and find you. That's all." The officer looked over Lionel's shoulder to another officer emerging from the site. "Ramirez," he told the man, "I need you to stay with this gentleman until the CIA arrives. They have a few questions they'd like to ask him."

"Sir."

The officer addressed Josh. "You can go."

"I'm staying," Josh said.

Lionel, to Josh, said, "It's okay, you can go. I'll hang back here and answer whatever questions they have."

"With all due respect, Lionel, I think I should stay. After all, I was the one down there, not you. I know more."

Lionel eyed Josh for a moment, then nodded. "Fine. Stay."

The officer shrugged, nodded and left, heading for the site. The officer called Ramirez stayed with them. His rank was junior, and he avoided eye contact with either of them. Josh could see that Lionel had spotted this weakness, and planned to use it to his own advantage.

"Officer," Lionel said, addressing Ramirez.

Ramirez turned, hands clasped in front of him, to face Lionel. "Sir?"

"Worker to worker, man to man, you've got to be able to tell us something about what's going on here, right? Help me out here. I don't know what's going on and I've got the CIA knocking on my door. Point me in the right direction here, would you?"

Ramirez, clearly uncomfortable, said, "I'm sorry, sir, I don't know anything, and I wouldn't be able to tell you if I did. That's my orders."

"Nothing at all? Not a single thing?"

"Sorry, sir."

Lionel, realizing the game was done, backed off. Instead, he looked at the papers he'd been given, flicking through and skim-reading.

"What do they say?" Josh asked, intrigued yet concerned.

"Standard stuff. Signed warrant, boilerplate forms, but nothing that's going to tell me any more about what's got the CIA so worked up." He passed the documents to Josh, who, upon inspection, came to the same conclusion.

"This shit's messed up," Josh said, passing the papers back.

"Damn right it is."

"You don't think we've done anything wrong, do you?"

Lionel threw Josh a stare.

"No, sorry, you're right. I don't know what it is, then. I guess we'll just have to wait and see."

They didn't have to wait long, because within thirty minutes, two blacked out SUVs arrived, hidden grille lights flashing in turn. Ramirez spotted them first, with some relief, approaching them as they pulled up. The men who emerged were inconspicuously suited and not at all what Josh had imagined they would look like. If he'd had to place them before knowing they were CIA, he'd have said accountants.

Ramirez led the group of four over to Josh and Lionel, introducing them and then vanishing as soon as he was dismissed.

"I'm agent Tom Edwards," the man leading the group said. He seemed familiar, had one of those faces everybody recognizes. "I'm sorry for this whole debacle. I'm sure we can get this resolved right away and be out of your hair."

"I hope so," Lionel said. "I've got a site to run."

"I appreciate that, Mr. Parker, and the sooner we can get our job done, the sooner you can get back to yours."

"So this isn't about gas?" Josh said, looking between Lionel and the CIA officer Tom Edwards.

"Can I ask who you are?" Edwards said.

"Josh Reed, Principal Tunnel Engineer. I assume you're interested in what we found, and it was me and my team that found it, so we may as well get to talking."

Edwards smiled, not unkindly. "Fair enough. Let's get to it then." He turned to his colleagues, who took it as a sign to disperse into the site. When he faced Josh and Lionel again, the three of them were alone. "You're both intelligent people, so I won't dance around the subject. You're right: this isn't about gas. This is about what you found. We will perform our investigation, and we may need to confirm some things with you—both of you—depending on what we find. For now, I can only ask that you stay in town and stay contactable, in case we need to follow up on anything."

"You don't need to ask us any questions?" Lionel queried.

"Not now, no, but we may need to in the future."

Lionel folded his arms. "So we've been waiting here for no reason? I get told the CIA is coming to ask me questions and it gets me worked up, you know? So I find out there's nothing to it?"

"I'm very sorry if our message got mixed up, Mr. Parker; all I required was your whereabouts and contact information. There was no need to stay on-site. You know what these local cops are like; they get a little overzealous sometimes."

"Okay then. So we can go?"

"You can go."

Edwards held out his hand to Lionel, who hesitated, then shook it. The same was offered to Josh, who shook without pause.

"Once again," Edwards said, starting to head to the site entrance, "I'm sorry to ruin your day and your schedule. If we need anything, we'll be in touch."

Josh and Lionel watched him walk away, and just before he disappeared around the hoarding, Josh called out, "What do you think we've found?"

Edwards stopped, turned and shrugged. "I don't know," he said. "That's what we're here to find out." He then continued into the site, the large doors swinging shut behind him.

"Well, shit," Lionel observed.

Josh stared at the hoarding, at the impenetrable barrier between him and what had gone from being his place of work to a federal investigation site. "What now?"

"How are you feeling? Do you want to go get something for lunch at the usual?"

"Sure…" Josh said slowly, still looking at the hoarding. Somehow it seemed unfamiliar to him now. "I'm feeling okay. Let's get something to eat. The usual."

They walked a few blocks down to a deli near 62nd and 1st, sat down outside under the shade of a tree and ate sandwiches. The walk from the site to there had almost put the whole CIA fiasco to the back of Josh's mind; he was tired and hungry, and to sit down and devour his sandwich was to melt into bliss.

"I needed that," he said, licking his fingers, all evidence of what had once been a sandwich gone.

Lionel, who was picking at his ham and cheese, looked troubled. Clearly the whole situation was taking more of a toll on him, and with good reason: he would be the one who'd have to pick up the phone and tell the boss why there were no holes being dug right now.

"You all right?" Josh asked him.

Lionel grunted. "I won't be when I let Doug know what's going on."

Josh took a swig of drink. "I'm sure he'll understand. What's he going to do, fire you for obeying a federal officer? I don't think so."

"I'm sure he'd try."

"Well, why don't you get it over and done with instead of sitting there getting yourself all worked up about it?"

Lionel slapped his half-eaten sandwich down on the table. "Yeah, you're right."

Josh stood, stretching. The sun was hovering high above, and with it burning down and the sandwich in his belly, he felt lethargic. "I'm going to head home," he said. "Call me if you hear anything."

"See you," Lionel said as he fished his cell from his pocket.

Josh tossed his trash away. As he was about to leave, Lionel, number dialed and cell to his ear, waved him back.

"Hey, man, I never got a chance to say before, but I'm sorry about the whole divorcing Georgie thing. That must be rough."

"It's okay," Josh said. "It was for the best. It's been a long time coming—more of a formality by now."

Lionel took hold of Josh's arm and jiggled it. "Well, you hang on in there, okay? I'm your friend, and I'm here if you need me."

"Thanks."

Lionel, call answered, gave Josh a thumbs-up. Josh returned it with a wave, then headed for the subway. That was the real reason he wanted to be down underground, his mind occupied and his body away from all this: he wanted to forget her, put her behind him. But he couldn't. It was too hard.

The warmth of the day and the aura of the city, once a happy feeling, held nostalgia too deep and too intense for him to cope with now. As he walked, taking long hurried strides past the ice cream shop he had taken his son Joseph to for his third birthday, he held his breath, only releasing it as he descended the steps into the gloom of the subway. His life underground and the long shifts away from home had been what had made his marriage collapse; now they were his only solace.

Into Queens and back out into the sun, he boarded a bus that took him into Jackson Heights. As they trundled down Northern Boulevard, he glimpsed—as he did every time he took the Q66— down 82nd Street to see the home he had made with his wife, where they'd had their child. It was just a flash, and then it was gone, but he savored it with a heavy heart.

Josh's apartment was a few more blocks down on 103rd, above a bait and tackle shop. It was okay, a reasonable size—after all, the money he made was good—but he kept it modest so he could make sure Georgie and Joseph were looked after. It was the least he could do. He didn't want much: a bed to sleep on, a couch to slump on, a kitchen to cook in, and a bathroom to try and scrub the guilt off in. He did that, taking a hot shower, before lying down on the couch and falling asleep to some daytime show about penguins.

* * *

Agent Thomas Edwards brushed a smear of dust from his jacket as he stepped down from the elevator cage and descended the stairs into the expanse of the staging area.

"This is quite some operation," he said to a fellow agent, following on behind. He got no response, but he didn't expect one; the apprehension was too great. He had hope—they all did—but it was too early to act on it. They needed to see it first.

Another agent awaited them at the bottom of the stairs, at the small platform where a single engine sat astride its tracks. "In here, sir," the agent said, and the three of them boarded.

"What have you found so far?" Edwards asked him, as the train pulled away, wheels chirping to find grip.

"Well, sir, I think we're looking at—well, perhaps it's best you see for yourself. I don't want to presume anything until we know for sure."

Edwards nodded. The apprehension was real. They could all feel it, as much as they could feel the warm, clammy fug that seemed to thicken the air. "How long?"

"A few minutes, sir."

They were the longest few minutes Edwards had ever encountered. As the train entered the narrower tunnel, he realized how much his jaw ached. He was biting down, and hard, and he forced himself to relax. He hadn't been this nervous since his first day of training at The Farm. Eventually they settled to a stop at the end of the tracks, and he breathed a sigh, partly of relief, and of excitement. He had to hold it in. His training told him to maintain a stoic demeanor. He straightened his tie then disembarked onto the slurry-topped concrete below.

"How much further?" he asked.

"Just around this corner. Not far."

"Okay. Stay with the train. Smith—with me."

The pair marched along the slippery tunnel, smooth brogues struggling to keep them upright. More than once Edwards almost fell, splaying his arms to stay balanced. It was embarrassing, but he didn't care. There would be something else to think about very soon.

The drill was what he saw first, and its size impressed him. He admired it as they approached it. A man in a hazmat suit awaited them. He looked anxious.

"Sir—" he began.

"In a moment, Bryant," Edwards said dismissively.

The man looked like he wanted to say something more, but decided against it. "Yes, sir."

Edwards continued around the drill, running his hand along its steel chassis. "All these years of searching," he said, "and this thing beats us to it."

"Maybe," his compadre said.

"Yes, maybe."

They entered the fresh, raw tunnel, and with no manmade footing to guide them through the rock and mud, progress was slow. At one point Edwards considered turning back to fetch some proper attire, but it was the blackness at the end that kept him moving forward. He was too close to turn around. There was no going back now.

It was hard going, and halfway down he stood still to catch his breath. His fitness wasn't what it used to be, especially since he quit field work and landed himself a comfortable desk, but he wasn't going to let that deter him. All that deskwork had led to this moment. This was it, he could feel it.

He could certainly feel something. Standing still, lungs gulping the damp, earthen air, he felt an energy in his body. A glance shared with his fellow agent confirmed that they both felt the same thing, and they pushed on, digging their heels in harder and gasping for breath until their throats were fire.

Then, they were at the edge.

"Careful, sir," Edwards's colleague warned, but Edwards waved him quiet. The energy was palpable, swimming through them, emanating from the black. It was time. He'd held back, but now he knew beyond all doubt that this was really it, what he'd spent his life searching for. Edwards allowed himself a smile.

Chapter 4

Later that afternoon, Josh awoke. He felt groggy, as he always did if he slept during the day, but all the better for it. Rubbing his eyes, he stretched, sitting up and looking out of the window. The sun was most of the way through the sky, ready to disappear behind the building opposite. He looked at his watch: he'd been asleep for three hours. Getting up, he noticed that the voicemail was flashing. He played the message back.

"Hi, Josh, it's Craig. Just calling to see what's up for tomorrow, if we'll be on-site or not, and what the deal with the pay is. If you can get back to me—oh, hang on, there's someone at the door. Anyway, get back to me. Talk soon. Bye."

Shit, Josh thought. He'd completely forgotten about calling the others. He'd been working double shifts to get the schedule back on target for the executive visit, and it had clearly taken its toll.

Hitting redial, Josh lifted the receiver to his ear. The line rang. It continued to ring. Eventually it hit the voicemail.

"Hi, Craig, it's Josh calling back about work. Sorry I didn't get back to you sooner. Look, it's probably best if I talk to you rather than leave a message. I'll try your cell."

Josh hung up and redialed Craig's cell. To Josh's surprise, the cell also rang through. There was no voicemail set up on it, so it just kept ringing. *He's going to answer*, Josh thought, every time he considered hanging up. It was at least a minute before he gave in. He then immediately dialed the number of one of the other tunnel workers. The phone rang, then went through to voicemail.

"Steve, are you there? Pick up if you can hear me. If not, call me back. It's Josh."

And then he hung up. He proceeded to dial the numbers of everyone else in the team, home and cell, and got nothing, up until the last man: Carlos Garcia.

"Carlos!" Josh exclaimed. "You're there!"

"Who's this?" Carlos replied, sounding wary.

"It's me, Josh. From work?"

"Oh, sorry! I didn't recognize your voice. Are you all right? You sounded a little tense just then."

"Yeah, I'm fine. Look, you haven't heard from any of the others, have you?"

Carlos paused. "The others? In the team you mean?"

"Yeah."

"No… should I have?"

Josh was about to tell Carlos that none of them had answered his calls when he stopped himself. It sounded stupid. He was getting worked up over nothing. They were probably sitting down to dinner with their families, or out in Central Park, enjoying the last few rays of the afternoon. A flash of a dream came back to him, the pulsing energy of the cavernous room a whisper as a headache began to form behind his right eye. "No, I was just wondering if you have."

"Oh, okay. So what's happening with work? Are we back on for tomorrow?"

"No, that's the thing. Lionel and I were leaving the site, when a load of—"

"Sorry, hang on a second, there's someone at the door."

"Okay, sure."

There were muffled sounds as Carlos presumably put the receiver to his chest. Josh could hear what sounded like conversation. It lasted quite some time, longer than Josh thought seemed normal for an unexpected sales call. He thought Carlos would have them gone and done by now. The receiver crackled, and Carlos was back. "Look, I've got to go. I'll speak to you tomorrow."

"Carlos, who's that—"

But Carlos was already gone.

Josh tried to calm himself, but he could already feel the blood pumping in his veins. It couldn't be a coincidence, could it? Craig gets a visitor, doesn't answer, Carlos gets a visitor too… can't get hold of any of the others…

"I need to sit down," Josh said to no one other than himself, and he did so. The room spun regardless.

Get a hold of yourself, he thought. *You're getting carried away.* There had to be a reasonable explanation. Of course there was a reasonable explanation, because everything was perfectly reasonable. It had just been an odd sort of day, and he was letting himself get all caught up in it. He was tired, after all, and there had been the gas, the police, the CIA... the room. There had been *something* in that room. Something he couldn't see, but definitely something he could *feel.*

"Right," he said, blinking to jerk that train of thought from its tracks. *I'll call Carlos back.* The sales caller was sure to have gone by now, and Carlos would answer the phone again, they'd have a discussion, and all would be normal.

A little unsteadily, he made his way over to the phone and redialed Carlos's number. The phone rang. And rang. And rang. Was the sales person still there? Surely not. Carlos wasn't the type to stand there and listen to their spiel with a forced smile on his face. Josh tried his cell, but it was the same story there. His blood had been pumping before; now it was a torrent through his veins.

What to do? Carlos only lived a few blocks away—in fact, they'd met at the Walmart over in Rosedale, and that's how Josh had ended up hiring him. That was back when Josh still lived at home, but it was still only a ten-minute walk from 103rd. Should he go? Would it be weird? It wouldn't be if Josh explained everything, would it? The CIA agent, Edwards or whatever his name was, hadn't explicitly told him he couldn't mention this to anyone.

Josh flopped back onto his sofa, head in his hands. It had all gotten away from him. He flicked on the TV to try and take his mind off it, but it didn't work. All he could think about was the blackness.

"Shit," he said, getting up. It was getting dark down on the street below, so he pulled on a jacket and headed for the door, grabbing his keys on the way. Then, hand on the door handle, he stopped. What was he doing? He retraced his steps back over to the phone, tried Carlos again. *He's going to answer. He's got to answer.*

There was no answer.

Before he knew it, he was out the door, down the stairs and walking the street, hands stuffed in pockets and zip done up to the top. With every footstep he doubted himself more, but he kept his eyes down, watching slab after slab of concrete sidewalk roll by, each one a little closer to putting his mind at ease.

Just stopping by, he'd say. *I was out for a walk and thought you might want to go for a drink.* Yeah. That'd do it. Carlos would be home, probably eating his dinner. Josh would apologize, they'd catch up quickly and then he'd be off, satisfied, back to his apartment, to his couch, his bed, his kitchen and his shower, and everything would be normal.

But something in his gut told him that nothing was going to be normal. He swallowed the thought back down and carried on, one slab at a time.

A car horn blared as he stepped out into the road to cross. Shuffling back, waving his apology as the car's owner scowled at him and continued on, he blinked, clearing the sweat from his eyes.

He was hot, very hot. He unzipped his jacket and let some of the cool evening air filter in. *Calm down. You need to calm down.*

He took a left onto 98th, scanning the road for Carlos's car. He thought he could see it, giving his heart a jolt. As he got closer, he could confirm that, yes, that was Carlos's car. If the car was in, Carlos was most likely in. Josh picked up his pace, relief drawing him closer. The point from him waking up this afternoon to now seemed so ridiculous all of a sudden. The sensible, rational side of him had been right all along, yet he'd still let his imagination get the better of him. He grinned at how foolish he'd been.

In through the door and up the stairs. It was always open. Latch had broken years ago, but no one cared enough to fix it. Around the old mattress propped up in the hallway. That hadn't arrived there much later than when the lock broke. It wasn't a particularly nice place. It had that smell about it: cheap soap and piss.

Then Josh was face to face with the door. Carlos's door. The door Carlos had answered that ended his call with Josh, where he'd stood and told the salesman thank you but no thank you. Where Josh was about to talk to him now and put his mind at ease. What the alternative would be, he didn't know; all he knew was that there *was no alternative.* There couldn't be.

That vast space had been so black, yet filled with so much energy.

Josh thumbed the doorbell, and a dull chime sounded inside. He listened, ears alert, waiting for the familiar sound of muffled footsteps through the apartment. He could almost hear Carlos now: *Just a sec, I'm coming!*

But he heard no footsteps. He heard no *Just a sec, I'm coming!* He heard no Carlos.

Josh rapped on the door. "Carlos, are you in there? It's me, Josh. I need to speak to you."

It had all come out at once. Josh hadn't intended to shout like that. He licked his lips and looked around, head ringing. Still no answer. His stomach tightened. He rapped again. "Carlos, come on, this isn't funny. Answer the door! Carlos!"

There was a sound, but it came from behind. Josh turned to see a bespectacled old lady peering through a crack in the neighboring door. "Can I help you?" she asked.

"Sorry," Josh said. "I was just trying to find Carlos Garcia. I work with him. You haven't seen him, have you?"

"Well," she said, opening the door a crack more. "You're not the first person to come looking for him tonight. Earlier, I heard shouting out here, so I came to see what was going on, and there were these men all dressed up in business suits escorting him away. One asked me to go back inside. How rude! Can you believe the nerve? Anyway, he went with them. He didn't seem happy, but he went without a struggle." Her eyes narrowed as she tried to make Josh out. "Are you the police?"

Josh shook his head. "No, just a friend. Did you see what these people looked like?"

"Well, my eyesight's not what it used to be I'm afraid, but I did see they were wearing those suits. You don't usually see suits like that around here! I didn't think they could be the police because the police wear those uniforms, don't they?" Then she looked worried, putting her hand to her mouth. "You don't think he's done anything wrong, do you? He's always been such a good neighbor, always helps me with my groceries. I do hope he's okay…"

"Me too," Josh said. "Thanks for the information."

"Okay then, well you have a nice evening, and if you do see Carlos, say hello from Barbara. Goodnight!"

"Night."

Barbara scuttled back inside, locking the door behind her. Josh was alone in the hallway, breathing in cheap soap and piss and feeling empty. He thought the words he had hoped he wouldn't have to think: *What now?*

Those men sounded just like the CIA agents he'd spoken to earlier. What would they want with Carlos? They'd not met him, but no doubt they knew about him. He'd have been on the roster for that shift. If it was just some questions, why did he have to go with them? And why had there been an argument? They had done nothing wrong, and he knew Carlos; he'd never kick off in a situation like that. He was calm, cool. It's what made him so good at his job.

Josh couldn't think here. He needed to go home. Feet like lead, he took himself back down the stairs, back past the mattress and through the broken door. The fresh air outside was like heaven, fumes and all. *Home. Go home.*

The walk back happened in something of a daze, guided by autopilot, barely anything registering. What *had* he felt in that room? What was that energy? What did the CIA know? Edwards had seemed sure he would find something, but he didn't seem to know what it was he'd find. A bomb, perhaps? An old government facility? A terrorist cell? A wartime bunker left buried and forgotten? There could be government secrets in there. Nuclear warheads. Maybe that's what that energy was? Perhaps they'd unearthed a secret Cold War launch platform, and the CIA had been drafted in to cover it all up. Imagine that? A nuclear weapon right under Central Park. It almost made sense. Plumes of smoke and fire billowing into the sky, blinding the people sunning themselves on their park view balconies. Soaring through the clouds, to lay waste to a country on the other side of the world. Nuclear winter, a world left in ruins.

It had to be that.

Josh was putting his key in the door before he even realized he was doing it. The door swung gently open. But wait—he hadn't unlocked it yet. He carefully withdrew the key and put the bunch in his pocket, balling up his fists and raising them, ready. Pushing the door the rest of the way open with his foot, he edged in, swallowed by the gloom. He didn't switch the light on, instead allowing his eyes to adjust as he scanned the space. Nothing seemed different. Nothing had been moved.

He swept around the edge of the room, back to the wall, around the sofa and into the bathroom, quickly ducking his head in and out again. No one. On to the bedroom, he slipped in, ready, but there was no one there. As he slipped back out again and checked the adjoining kitchen, he began to question if he'd even locked the door himself. He'd been in such a rush to get out that he struggled to remember what he'd done. Perhaps he'd gone out with the door left wide open and it had blown to.

With a sigh, he closed the door properly and switched the light on, throwing his keys and jacket on the sideboard and collapsing onto the sofa. He rubbed his eyes, trying to massage away what had become a full-blown headache. When he'd finished, and his vision had stopped swimming in a haze of green and magenta, he saw it. A picture frame, lying on the coffee table. The one that usually sat by the window, with the photo of him, Georgie and Joseph in it. He looked over at it, and saw that the frame was empty. Carefully, he picked it up. Someone *had* been here, and that someone had done this to leave him a message.

Josh stared at the space where the photo had been. He knew who that someone was, and he knew what that message was, too. They'd tried to get him, but failed. Now they had him for sure.

Chapter 5

Josh felt rage burning in him, bile in his throat, fire in his eyes. What kind of a game was Edwards playing? Was this supposed to be a threat? In a snap, Josh picked up a glass from the coffee table and hurled it at the wall, showering his television with a million twinkling shards of glass. He regretted it as soon as he'd done it, but it had taken the edge off his fury, and he was able to think more clearly.

Whatever they'd found, the CIA wanted it covered up. They were rounding up everyone involved, everyone who'd been down there, and they'd clearly stop at nothing to do it. With cold realization, Josh knew he was expendable. They'd only let him go earlier because they knew that if they needed him gone, he'd be gone, and the world would continue ticking on. He was small fry to them, a bug easily squashed.

The urge to go to Georgie was almost unbearable. It was a trap, he knew it, but he couldn't bear to let them do... he couldn't even think it. It filled him with dread. He was up, heading for the door. He would call her on the way, he decided. He'd hear her voice, she'd ask him not to call unless it was an emergency, and then he could turn back home and relax a little, knowing that this break-in picture stunt was nothing more than a scare tactic.

Walking out into the evening, down the steps to the street, cell to ear, he listened to the dial tone, then the ring. It rang long enough for his stomach to turn, and then lurch as Georgie answered.

"Hello?"

Josh cleared his throat, which was suddenly dry. "Er, hi, Georgie. It's me."

"Hello." Her voice sounded different somehow, thick.

"Is everything all right?"

"Sure."

"You and Joseph okay?"

"We're both fine."

Georgie's short answers were making the conversation difficult, but with the picture in the back of his mind, Josh pressed on. "Look, I've got a few days off while they get something sorted at work. I thought I'd take Joseph for a few days, give you a break for a while."

"Thanks, but I'm okay. I don't need any help."

Josh turned onto the sidewalk and headed for 82nd. "It's fine; I'm more than happy to do it. I'm on my way over now."

"No. I don't want you to. We're fine."

Josh was starting to feel a little put out. "Why? I want to. I'll be there in a minute."

"No, Josh, please—"

Josh hung up. Something wasn't right. They may have been divorced, but they weren't on bad terms, and Georgie's bluntness was unusual. "Come on, Lionel, let's hope you're still around…" Josh muttered to himself as he found his friend in his contacts and dialed the number.

Lionel answered almost immediately. "Now's not a good time!" he snapped, sounding almost hysterical.

"What?" Josh replied. "The CIA paid you a visit, too?"

"Someone has! I went out to get some groceries and came back to find my apartment broken into!"

"Did they take anything?"

"Not that I can see."

"They did the same to me. Took a picture of Georgie and Joseph out of its frame and left the frame on the table."

"Shit…" Lionel said. "Have you been over there?"

"I'm on my way now. That's why I'm calling you. You've got a car, right?"

"Yeah."

"I need you to do me a favor. I'm walking over to 82nd now. I need you to get over there quick. How soon can you get there?"

"Uh, about fifteen minutes?"

Josh thought it through. "Okay, I'll stall until you can get there."

"What's going on, Josh? Is Georgie all right?"

"I don't know. I called her just now and something was off. I think the CIA have been over there. I need you to hang back in your car and keep watch for me, call me if anyone comes in."

"Okay, I can do that."

Josh took a breath. He was walking fast. He needed to slow down. The air was cold and burned his lungs. "Thanks, man. I owe you."

"You don't owe me shit. This is for Georgie."

"Something's really messed up here."

"You're telling me. I feel like I've aged a month just this afternoon."

Josh felt a smile coming on. It was inappropriate, and he certainly didn't feel like smiling, but Lionel was right. He too felt like he had aged a month just this afternoon—maybe even a year. Like all the characters in all his favorite movies had a penchant for saying: he was getting too old for this shit. "You got that right. I'll see you soon. Be quick."

"I'm already walking out the door."

Josh hung up, slipping his cell phone away, forcing himself to slow his pace. It was torture, taking slow, aimless steps to turn a ten-minute walk into a fifteen-minute one, when really all he wanted was to sprint until his insides were raw to get there as quickly as he could.

He tried to tell himself that Georgie was fine—after all, she'd said so herself—but he couldn't believe it. He'd known Georgie for over a decade, and he knew that wasn't her. Not the her *he* knew, anyway. She was hiding something.

The first flicker and buzz of the streetlights popping on with deep sodium orange made him jump. A car whistled by, one of those electric types, and the adrenaline from being startled fizzed through his back and into his kidneys. He was waiting for the one car that didn't go past, that slowed down next to him, blacked out and sinister. It would stop, he would stop, they'd get out and that would be that. Another name in another secret file, scratched out with black marker. There would be no grave.

It seemed odd to see other people, out and about and acting like nothing had happened. Josh wanted to scream at them, tell them to run and hide, that the big bad wolf was coming, but then he realized that for them, it didn't matter. It had nothing to do with them. He wondered for how long he'd been drifting by people caught up in the midst of something huge, only their fearful eyes telling their true story as the rest of them blended in to their surroundings as they thought the same thoughts as he did now.

A dog barked from a high window, its call answered by another a block or two over. The wind blew cold. Night was coming.

When his phone buzzed again, nearly overdosing him on adrenaline, he was turning onto 82nd. It was Lionel.

"I'm parked a few doors down."

Lionel had come from Greenpoint, from the other end of 82nd. Josh peered down the street to see a car parked with its lights on. "I think I see you. Flash your lights."

The car's lights flashed. "You see it?"

"Yeah, I see it. Wait there for me, okay? Hopefully I'll be down in a while and everything will be fine."

"Okay."

Josh picked up his pace, jogging up the steps to Georgie's apartment. He still had a key, so he let himself in without buzzing her. Two flights of stairs, and he was at her door. His finger paused over the buzzer, he took a breath, then pushed. He heard footsteps, then the chain, then the lock. The handle turned and the door opened, only a crack. Georgie greeted him, although not with a smile.

"I told you not to come," she said in a low voice. "Go, now!"

"I'm not going until I know what's up," Josh said firmly.

"I won't tell you again," Georgie said, closing the door. Josh wedged his foot in.

"Let me in, Georgie. I know something's going on, and I want to help you."

"I don't need your help. Please go—"

There was a sound of movement further in the apartment, and a voice called out. "Who is that?"

Georgie looked back over her shoulder, fearful. "Just a sales call. I'm telling them to go," she called in reply.

The voice, Josh knew it. More footsteps. Josh stepped back, and as Georgie tried to shut the door, someone stopped her. It opened wide, and there he was, still in that suit. Edwards.

"Mr. Reed," he said, "I've been looking for you."

In his pocket, Josh's cell began to vibrate.

"I told you not to come…" Georgie said, her voice hollow. Her eyes met Josh's, and he realized then that she had been trying to warn him, but he'd not listened. He'd gone storming in like a fool, paid no attention and gotten himself caught.

The cell continued to buzz.

"I'm sorry, Georgie," he told her. "I didn't realize…"

"No matter," Edwards said, breaking him off. "You're here now, so why don't we take a walk."

The cell stopped vibrating.

"I'm not going anywhere," Josh said. "Not until I know my family is safe."

"They're fine," Edwards said, almost jovially. "See? All we want is you."

Josh, hesitant, looked to Georgie. "Is he telling the truth?"

Georgie nodded.

"And Joseph?"

"He's fine. Tucked up in bed." Her expression turned, fear becoming sadness. "What did you do, Josh? This man says he's from the CIA!"

"I haven't done anything wrong, I swear," Josh pleaded.

"He's right," Edwards confirmed. "We just want to talk to him."

"About what?" Georgie said, looking between them, the fear creeping back.

"I'm afraid that's classified," Edwards said, "and time is short. Come now, Mr. Reed; we need to be leaving. Let's not have a repeat of our visit with Mr. Garcia."

Josh hardened. He wasn't giving in that easily. "Promise me my family will be safe."

Edwards's face fell to stony seriousness. "I can't promise you that," he said, "but should anything befall them, it will not be at our hand."

Josh wasn't sure what to make of that, and by her expression, neither was Georgie, but it sounded sincere, and really, there was nothing Josh could do. "Okay," he said, relaxing his balled fists. "Let's go."

Looking back as Edwards led him from the building, he saw Georgie watching him from the doorway. She didn't have to say anything; her body said it all. Fear, anger, confusion—it was all there. And then they rounded the stairs, and she was gone.

"What's going on?" Josh demanded as they exited onto the street.

"That's a question you're going to have to learn to stop asking," Edwards said, as he led him to the black SUV now parked at the curb. "The only things you need to know are the things I tell you." He opened the door and indicated to get in. Did he look anxious? "Come on," he said. "We need to get going."

Josh looked down the street in hope that Lionel would be there to intervene, but he had gone. He had called Josh to warn him, then made his escape. Josh didn't blame him.

As he climbed in and Edwards shut the door behind him, he realized that this was no police vehicle: there was no cage, and Josh had not been restrained in any way. Edwards climbed into the passenger side and the driver pulled away.

"So what *will* you tell me?" Josh asked as they whipped smoothly down 82nd and back onto Northern Boulevard, turning east and away from Manhattan.

Edwards, without turning, said, "I suppose you've guessed that this is about the room."

"No shit," Josh said. "What is it, some Cold War bunker or something?"

Edwards let out what seemed to be an involuntary laugh.

Josh frowned. "Something funny?"

"My apologies, Mr. Reed, but that was most unexpected."

"So it's not Cold War then?"

"No."

"Government?"

"No."

Josh sat back in his seat and raised his hands in defeat. "I don't know then. What is it?"

"We don't know."

It was Josh's turn to laugh. "What do you mean you don't know? You must have some idea of its origin?"

"We have theories." Edwards's tone was a touch aloof. "This isn't the first room we've found."

"Then why don't you know anything about it?"

"Because the others were dead. Empty. This is the first we've found with—with something in it."

Josh pondered the idea of these other rooms, what they might be. "How many others have you found before this one?"

"Five."

"And what was in them?"

"I told you, nothing," Edwards snapped. His professionalism was waning, his temper showing through. He was straining under pressure. "They were empty, long abandoned."

Josh could tell from Edwards's demeanor that this endeavor had some personal connotation for him. "What do you need me for?"

"You and your team are the only ones who've been in there. For others, there have been… problems." He looked out of the window, watching as they passed by a gas station, forecourt glowing.

Josh knew he was the only one of his team who'd actually entered the room, but he wasn't going to share that—not yet, anyway. "What do you mean?"

"It doesn't matter. That's all you need to know until we arrive."

"Arrive where?"

But Edwards didn't have a chance to answer, because they were all thrown into their seatbelts as tires squealed and headlights flashed bright. The driver swerved, just missing an oncoming car that was headed straight for them. They clipped a parked truck, spinning into it and burying the nose of the SUV deep into its cabin. They'd been traveling at quite a pace, and the impact was hard.

It was over before Josh had a chance to realize what was happening. The airbags had gone off—there had been an explosion in among the crash somewhere—and both Edwards and the driver were currently untangling themselves from the great white balloons deflating around them. The air was acrid, like gunpowder.

Josh's door swung open. His ears rang. Hands grabbed him, the headlights of the car they'd avoided glaring in. He wrestled his seatbelt off as he was pulled out and dragged across the tarmac.

"Get in the car!" Lionel shouted, and all of a sudden sound overwhelmed Josh, the hiss of the SUV's destroyed engine, the blare of its horn, stuck on, the rush of blood in his head, all filling him with sound until his skull felt like it wanted to crack open.

Lionel pushed him into the car and closed the door behind him, running around the hood and jumping in himself as Edwards emerged from the SUV. He looked furious, but they didn't get to see him for long, as Lionel stepped on the gas and sent his Toyota hurtling up the street with the squeal and scrabble of tires clawing for grip.

Chapter 6

"Jesus Christ…" Josh said, blinking to try and right his vision.

"Sorry," Lionel apologized, both hands gripping the wheel hard. "I didn't know what else to do. When that SUV pulled up, I called you, but you didn't answer. I had to go. I waited on Northern Boulevard until you pulled out, then followed you around. While you waited at the lights, on 108th, I circled the gas station and headed you off. I only wanted to stop the SUV, not make it crash. I wanted to get you out of there."

"Shit…" Josh said, the two images before him almost returning to one. "I guess that makes us fugitives now or something?"

"I guess…"

Josh checked behind them, to make sure no one was following. They were okay for now.

"Look, Josh," Lionel said, fidgeting. "Don't think I've done anything rash here, okay? That driver, before I pulled away, he got out of the SUV and he made a call. I opened my window to hear it, and he was talking to someone about you. He said they were going to be as quick as they could, and that he hoped there were no more deaths."

"Deaths?" Josh repeated. His heart had only just begun to slow, and now it was back pumping at full tilt. "Whose deaths?"

"He didn't say. But I tried to call the others, and I didn't get an answer from a single one of them."

Josh's stomach turned. Carlos Garcia. Edwards had mentioned him; he'd caused trouble. Had they killed him? Had they killed the others? "Oh God…" he whispered.

"Exactly!" Lionel screeched. "You see why I did what I did now? Once that driver was back in his car, I was gone!" Lionel paused, and when Josh looked at him, he seemed ashamed. "I damn nearly left you there, Josh. I was scared. Terrified. Who are these guys to go around killing innocent people? I sure as hell didn't want to find out."

Josh patted Lionel's arm. "It's okay, bud. I'd have probably done the same. But you didn't go; you came back for me. And here we are."

Lionel nodded, tense. "Here we are."

"And we've got to get out of here, like to Mexico or somewhere."

"Mexico?"

"Yeah, like in the movies. That's where you go when you're in trouble like this, right? Mexico?"

Lionel looked affronted. "How am I supposed to know? Because I'm black I'm supposed to know where federal criminals go to hide out?"

"No, that's not what I meant…"

Lionel sighed. "Sorry, man. I know you didn't. Just stressed, you know?"

"I hear that. So, what do you think?"

Shrugging, Lionel said, "I don't know. It seems… ridiculous."

"This *is* ridiculous."

"I know, but—"

"Do you have a better idea?" Josh interrupted.

Lionel was quiet for a minute, focusing down the road. "No. I don't know." He thumped the steering wheel. "This is messed up!" he yelled.

Nodding, Josh said, "Yeah, it is, but we've got to make a decision, and quick. So… Mexico?"

Lionel was shaking the hand he'd hit the steering wheel with. He sighed again. "I suppose so. Mexico it is."

Decision made, Josh retrieved his cell from his pocket and looked at flights online. It was seven o'clock now; the next flight out from JFK to El Paso left in an hour and fifty minutes, and would get them there via Houston in just under ten hours from takeoff. It was the last flight of the day, but there was just enough time to catch it. He dialed Georgie.

"Josh, is that you?"

"Yeah, it's me."

She sounded scared. "Where are you?"

"I'm with Lionel. I—the CIA are gone. We need to go."

"Go? Where?"

"Mexico."

Georgie paused. "Mexico?" she said finally. "Why are you going to Mexico? What's going on, Josh?"

"I can't explain now, but I need you to get to JFK, you and Joseph, right now. I'll sort the tickets; I just need you to be there. It's incredibly important that you do this, Georgie, do you understand?"

"I—I don't know..." she said. She sounded close to tears. "I just want to know what's happening..."

"I'll tell you when you get there, I promise, but right now you need to get in a cab and get to the airport. I'll meet you at the American Eagle desk, Terminal 8. Can you do that for me?"

"Wh—what do I need to take? I—"

"You don't need to take anything, just you and Joseph. Leave now, okay? Don't stop for anyone."

"Okay..." She was definitely crying now.

"It'll be okay, I promise. I love you."

Those last words just slipped out, but it was too late. He was under pressure; it was an old habit. Georgie didn't say anything.

"Georgie, are you there?"

A sob. "I'm here."

"I'll meet you at JFK, right? The American Eagle desk, Terminal 8."

"Okay. The American Eagle desk, Terminal 8." She hung up.

Josh leaned back in his seat and sighed a sigh that should well have collapsed his lungs. The weight of exhaustion on his shoulders felt like it would pin him into that seat until the day he died. He hoped that day wouldn't be today.

"That's rough," Lionel said quietly.

"It's all rough."

"Nah—I mean what you just said."

Josh looked away. "What did I say?" he said, playing dumb. "I didn't say anything."

Lionel said nothing for a moment, but Josh knew he was looking at him. "All right, whatever you say. But I know what I heard, and you do too."

Josh didn't respond. As Lionel drove them out of Queens and toward JFK, Josh felt an overwhelming sadness fall on him. Everything had changed, and yet everything was still the same. He still loved Georgie, still missed her, and yet he'd let it take a thing like this before he'd tried to get her back into his life. Now he wanted to cry too, just let it flow and blame it on the crash or something, but he knew the tears wouldn't come. His emotions were like the tunnels he'd worked in for so long, buried and invisible.

"You sure we're doing the right thing?" Lionel said after a while. Josh watched the streetlights flash along the hood of Lionel's Toyota, wondering the same thing.

"What else can we do?"

Lionel's silence was his answer. If Josh had felt a year older earlier, he felt several more by now. Signs for JFK rolled overhead, and Lionel took the exit. Josh hoped the CIA wouldn't be there waiting for them. Would they know where they were going? Could they tell? The idea of going to Mexico was so ridiculous that he hoped Edwards wouldn't even consider it.

The traffic was just as heavy as if it had been the middle of the day, and they stop-started their way into the perimeter of the airport. Airplanes rumbled overhead, lights blinking, undercarriages hanging down like great, cumbersome legs. Soon, Josh hoped, they would be on board one of them, sitting behind one of the tiny points of light along its fuselage. What would they do when they arrived? He hadn't even considered it. He didn't *want* to consider it. He just wanted out. The air would taste so sweet across the border. Not like the stench of death that filled his lungs here.

"Should I head for parking?" Lionel asked as he read a sign directing them to the long stay car park.

"No point," Josh said. "We'll leave the car in the drop-off zone and just go in." He looked at Lionel, who seemed sad.

"I guess so…" was all he said in reply.

They peeled off the Van Wyck Expressway, following the signs for Terminal 8 and American Eagle. The terminal loomed over them, the gateway to their freedom, and until they had parked and got out of the car, not another word was said.

"I wonder if Georgie's here yet," Josh thought aloud. "Let's go inside and check." She wasn't. He had no missed calls, either. She would've had to wait for a cab, so she was probably still a few minutes behind. Josh could use that time to get the tickets.

They went inside, the blast of warm air as they went through the sliding doors making Josh realize how cold he was. He shivered. The large space was bustling with people, their chatter and footsteps an indecipherable hum.

"American Eagle is over there," Lionel said, pointing.

"I see it."

They headed for the desk, where they were greeted by a beaming assistant.

"How can I help you two gentlemen this evening?" she asked them.

"I need four tickets to El Paso International, three adults, one child please."

The assistant tapped the details onto her screen. "Okay, and when would you like to be flying?"

"The next one, please; eight-fifty I think."

More smiles, more tapping. "We have space for you on that flight. There's a stop-off in Houston, is that okay?"

"That's fine."

The assistant beamed. "Okay then! That'll be eleven hundred and forty dollars. Would you like to pay cash or card?"

"Card please." Josh reached into his pocket, but Lionel stopped him.

"I got this," he said.

"Why?"

"I got us into this, so I'm going to get us out of it."

Josh, sensing that *no* wasn't going to pass for an answer, let him. As Lionel paid, Josh watched through the glass as a cab pulled up outside. His heart leaped as he saw Georgie climb out, cradling a sleepy Joseph. "She's here!" he told Lionel as he collected the tickets.

"All right, I've got the tickets," he said. "Let's go meet them."

"Have a nice flight!" the attendant called out after them as they headed for the entrance.

Josh couldn't help but run over to Georgie as she and Joseph came in from the night. "You came!" he said as he flung his arms around them both, squeezing them tight.

Georgie wriggled away as best she could while holding Joseph. Her expression was not one of happiness: she wasn't pleased to see him. "I nearly didn't come. The CIA, Josh—the C-I-A! You owe me an explanation for why I'm at JFK in the middle of the night and for why you're being asked questions by the federal government! And what's Lionel doing here?"

"Hi, Georgie," Lionel said.

"Hi, Lionel."

Josh looked around, hoping no one had heard the mention of the CIA. Not only had no one heard, no one cared, sweeping past them as though they weren't even there. He ushered them all to a quieter corner of the hall, watching over his shoulder to see if anyone might be paying more attention than they should.

"It's complicated," Josh said once they had more privacy.

"Complicated?" Georgie repeated, with sarcasm.

Lionel, presumably sensing a perfectly reasonable outburst, stepped in. "We found something, Georgie. In the East Side Access tunnels. Something that had the CIA so interested that they were there within a few hours. They won't tell us what it is, but they've gone to great pains to come and find us."

"Well, where are they now?" Georgie asked. "The CIA?"

Lionel looked to Josh for help.

"We gave them the slip," Josh told her.

Georgie wasn't buying it. "You gave the CIA the slip?" she said, her anger and frustration barely held together. "You, a tunnel engineer from Queens, gave the *CIA* the slip?"

"Well, sort of…"

"Sort of?"

Lionel cleared his throat. "I intervened," he said. "I pulled out in front of the SUV they'd taken Josh in, and they… they crashed."

Georgie looked shocked. She looked between them, mouth open, cradling Joseph tight. Her eyes were wide and wild, her eyebrows contorted such that it seemed she didn't know what to feel. Josh didn't know if she was going to scream at him or ask him if he was okay. He'd never seen her like this before.

"Please understand that we've done nothing wrong," he said, trying to calm her down before it was too late.

Georgie nodded, lips pursed. "Nothing wrong. You forced a CIA vehicle off the road and escaped custody, and you say you did nothing wrong?" She stared unblinking at Josh for a while, and Josh held the stare as long as he could, hoping she could see his honesty. She must have seen something, because after a long few minutes, she sighed, the madness in her eyes fading. "Did you get hurt?" she asked Josh. "In the crash?"

"No, I'm okay. Shaken up, but okay."

"And you're sure you've done nothing wrong?"

"Positive."

She shook her head, bobbing Joseph up and down, and he shifted in his sleep. "So how did this get so out of hand? Why didn't you just go with them and answer their questions?"

Josh had hoped he hadn't needed to tell Georgie this, but he didn't want to lie to her either. "What we found..." he said slowly, trying to be tactful, "they don't want us to know about. It's something big, like, really big, and they want us gone. They—they said they'd killed the others. Took them away. I went to Garcia's house and the neighbor said she saw them dragging him off. Said she'd heard shouting before. It's messed up, Georgie, and when I got home, they'd broken in and—" He couldn't say any more. Georgie was clearly scared now, the bobbing stopped, her body rigid.

"They'd what, Josh? What had they done?"

Josh swallowed. His eyes hurt. The crash was beginning to fill him with ache. "They'd threatened you. They'd threatened both of you. They've got this big secret, and they're going to stop at nothing to protect it. That's why we've got to go to Mexico."

Standing there in tracksuit bottoms, Joseph in his pajamas, Georgie looked a mess, yet Josh loved her more now than he ever had. He was a fool to have let work get in between them, and the small glimmer of hope that came from a life together again, even if it was at the cost of leaving their home and being on the wanted list of an international agency, made him feel a twinge of happiness.

"Will you come?"

Georgie shut her eyes, as though righting her mind. When she opened them, they had a new calm. "Okay," she said, nodding. "If you think it's best, I'll come."

Chapter 7

Josh smiled. He'd always admired Georgie's tenacity. "We've got an hour before takeoff. Let's get through to the gate before the CIA puts us on some no-fly list or something."

"How long does it take to get someone on one of those?" Lionel asked. "Do they have to get a warrant or something?"

"Who knows," Josh replied. "Let's just hope the paperwork is a mile long."

They joined the line to check in and shuffled forward, the sentry scanning tickets exhibiting completely the opposite demeanor of the person selling them. Josh could feel a sweat coming on, the walk toward this man a shuffling march to his own doom.

He watched as the man, scowling, held out his hand for the next ticket, scanned said ticket, waited for the machine to go *beep*, stared at the screen for a moment—scowl intensifying—then turned his stare to the ticket's owner. Satisfied that he'd stared enough, then—and only then—would he hand the ticket back and allow the person through, waving the next person up. It was a tedious and unnecessary process at the best of times. Today it was agonizing.

Josh turned to the three others behind him, giving Georgie as comforting a smile as he could muster—which she did not return—and Lionel a look he hoped would generate the kind of strength and solidarity that would get them through, suspicions unraised. If the look Lionel returned matched the one Josh was giving, they were screwed.

Thinking it best to face forward again, Josh marched onward, one pace at a time, a funeral procession. Ticket, scowl, *beep*, ticket. Ticket, scowl, *beep*, ticket. Josh slipped into a daydream, tiredness and a creeping pain switching him to standby for a minute.

"Sir, I need to see your ticket, please."

The scowl was directed at him now. "Oh! Sorry. I was miles away there." Josh handed the man his ticket, which was snatched away from him and scanned without fanfare. *Beep*. The man stared at the screen. He didn't so much as blink. He stared and he stared and he stared, longer than Josh had seen him do for any other ticket before.

"Okay, that's fine," the man said, handing back Josh's ticket without so much as a second glance. As Josh took it, the man was already leaning around to see who was next.

As calmly as he could, Josh shuffled forward, heart beating so loud he couldn't believe the man wouldn't hear it and call him back. He had to remind himself that he hadn't actually done anything wrong, because all this tension was starting to make him feel like he had.

Once he had shuffled far enough away from the check-in desk, Josh turned to see Lionel being handed back his ticket. They were all through, although deathly pale. Josh scanned around the other passengers to see if anyone had taken any notice, but they hadn't. To be honest, they all looked as sick as he felt, if not worse. They all marched on in their own little worlds, oblivious to anything. It was a relief.

Josh grabbed a tray from the carousel and dumped his keys, cell and belt into it to be x-rayed. One by one they marched through the metal detector; one by one they were let through. Georgie set the alarm off, but it was just the buckles in her shoes. She took them off, they went through the x-ray machine, and all was fine.

On the other side, re-shoed, belted, keyed and celled, they gathered in the atrium, where the bustle of people was magnified from the hushed tension of check-in. People were laughing, shouting, running, sleeping, shopping, all at once.

"What gate are we on?" Lionel asked, looking at the departure board.

"Uh, gate sixteen, I think," Georgie replied, scanning her ticket.

Josh checked. "Yep, gate sixteen. That's concourse B. It's not boarding for another thirty minutes yet. Does anyone want to get something to eat?"

"I'm hardly in the mood for eating," Georgie said.

Lionel shook his head. "Me neither."

Josh didn't feel like he could stomach anything either, so they took a slow wander down to their gate, taking a seat when they got there. Joseph started to grumble, but Georgie soothed him back to sleep.

"He's a good kid," Lionel said, smiling.

Josh, who was also watching, said, "Doesn't get it from me. That's all Georgie. I couldn't get him to sleep for love nor money. Georgie was able to switch him off like a light. A mother's touch I guess."

Georgie, cradling Joseph and bouncing him on her lap, looked up at Josh. For a second there was a longing in her eyes, but as soon as Josh saw it, she looked down again. It made Josh feel homesick—not just for New York, but for the home he'd made and lost with Georgie.

"So what *are* we going to do when we get to El Paso?" Georgie asked both of them. Josh glanced at Lionel, and Lionel glanced at Josh. Neither of them knew.

"Well," Josh said, "as far as I'm aware we can walk through the border to Juarez, and from there we'll go as remote as we can."

Georgie patted her trouser pocket. "I brought my passport just in case."

"I only think you need that to get back in."

"I sure hope so," Lionel said, "because we don't have ours."

Josh rearranged himself in his seat. "Guess this is a one-way trip then."

Exhaustion filled him. They continued to wait in silence, while Josh took the opportunity to shut his eyes. His head was throbbing to the beat of his heart by now, and he watched colors pulse and swim against his eyelids. *What a mess*, he thought. How things had changed in the course of a single day. He thought about the executive he'd shown around just this morning—*What was his name? Mr. Miller, that was it*—and wondered what he was doing right now. Lounging in his New York penthouse suite, smoking a cigar? On the phone, demanding to know why his site was shut down? Floating face down along the East River, courtesy of the CIA? Who knew. It was all irrelevant now, all of it. Mr. Miller, the tunnel, the drilling—all of it. None of it counted for anything anymore.

In a weird kind of way, it was a weight off Josh's shoulders. He almost felt free, unwound of the commercial machine that ticked on day and night, binding him into society in the way it wanted him to be. Perhaps he'd enjoy this new life; a slower pace, his friend and his family by his side, hot sun and cool shade, warm sand between his toes…

"Josh, wake up!"

Josh started, finding himself slithered halfway down his seat. Peeling his face from the faux leather and wiping the drool off his cheek, he slid up again, taking a moment to consider where he was and what he was doing there. "What's going on?" he slurred.

Lionel was rigid, staring past Josh and along the concourse. Georgie was too, occasionally looking to Lionel, concern pulling her lips thin. Joseph was dozing in his own seat, slumped against Georgie, her coat over him.

"I don't know…" Lionel said. Josh sat up and started to turn to see what had spooked Lionel, but Lionel held up a hand, signaling for him to stop. "Don't!" he whispered.

"What is it?" Josh whispered back, the old headache rising anew. He desperately wanted to turn around, could feel the breath of this apparition on the back of his neck. He was taken for a moment to his childhood, hiding under the bed sheets, hot as hell, not daring to move.

"Suits," Lionel said. "They're asking people questions." He paused, mouth stuck on a word. "You can look now, but be quick."

Josh turned as discreetly as he could to see three men in suits, walking and stopping, talking to people, expressions drawn, responses stony. They moved from group to group, sometimes stopping for a few seconds only, sometimes talking for a minute or more. Occasionally they were handing something out, something which was received with apprehension. "Shit…" Josh said, turning back to Lionel and Georgie. "What are we going to do?"

"We can't exactly run, can we?" Georgie squeaked, panic in her voice. "Where would we go?"

Lionel was nodding. "You're right. There's nothing we can do except sit here and wait it out. We can't get by them, and the other way's a dead end."

Josh scanned the space, looking for an answer. There was the shop across from them, selling newspapers and candy and such, the vending machines and— "We could hide out in the restrooms," he said. "They might not look in there."

Lionel and Georgie checked them out. "Don't you think they'll look in there?" Georgie asked.

"I don't know, but I don't know what other option we have."

"Josh is right," Lionel said. "There is no other option. Georgie, you go first with Joseph. They probably won't be looking for you—not yet, anyway. Then Josh and I will go together."

"Don't you two want to go first, before they get close enough to recognize you?"

Josh shook his head. "I'm with Lionel, you should go first. I want you to be safe—"

"And I want *you* to be safe!" Georgie interrupted, face reddening. "Like you said, they're probably not looking for me, but they're looking for you!" She sat up, peering down the concourse. "A few more families and they'll be here, so you need to go, *now*, both of you." She looked between the two men, her eyes pleading. "Okay?"

Josh was about to respond when a shout made them all start.

"Hey!"

It was one of the suited men, broken away from the rest of the group, who had all turned to see why he was shouting. "Hey!" he shouted again, before breaking into a jog toward Josh and the others.

"Oh shit…" Lionel said.

Oh shit was right—there was no time for them to hide in the restrooms now. In a few seconds the man would reach them, and… he went sailing by. The group watched him as he caught up with another passenger and placed a hand on the man's shoulder to stop him. The man turned to face the suit, and the suit handed him something.

"You dropped your passport," the suit said.

The man, at first confused, pulled out his headphones and took the passport. Then his face broke into an embarrassed smile, and he bowed and nodded and thanked the suit.

"Could have been a bad day for you," the suit said. "You hang on to that a little more carefully."

The man, still nodding and smiling, pocketed his passport and continued on his way. The suit turned, and Lionel, Georgie and Josh all whipped forward again. But it wasn't quick enough—he had seen them. Although Lionel and Georgie now had their backs to the suited man, Josh could still see him, and he was looking their way. Josh kept his eyes forward, staring at nothing, chest thumping and gut wrangling. The suit walked slowly toward them, Josh willing him to keep on walking, but he seemed to slow further as he approached, turning as he came level. Josh looked up at him, and he was standing there, hands on hips, examining them.

"Have you heard the good news?" the man said.

This took Josh by surprise. "What?" He looked at Lionel and Georgie, who had broken their aimless stares to also look at the man addressing them.

"Have you heard the good news?" the man repeated. "About Jesus Christ, our Lord and savior? How he sacrificed his life so you could have yours?"

Relief flooded through Josh with such tenacity that he almost fainted. The room spun a while as he gathered himself together. "No thank you," he said. "We've had just about enough good news for one day already."

"Okay," the man said. He reached into his jacket pocket. "Here, why don't you take this." He handed Josh a leaflet, on which was written *For God So Loved the World* above a picture of a dove with an olive leaf in its beak. "Give it a read; it might just save your life."

Josh took the leaflet, still a little disorientated by what had just happened, gave the man a forced smile and watched him walk back to the group. "Jesus…" he whispered, turning the leaflet over but not really reading it. He looked up at Lionel and Georgie, both of them appearing as stunned as he felt. Josh laughed, and at first the other two stared at him, but then they started laughing too. It was ridiculous, hysterical and terrifying, and they were all exhausted. The only option was to laugh.

Joseph stirred, and they all got control of their mirth. "That was close," Lionel said.

Georgie pulled her coat back up over Joseph, and they all relaxed a little in their seats. "The sooner we're at that border," she said, "the better."

Not long later, the speakers overhead announced the boarding of their flight, and they gathered themselves up and joined the quickly forming queue. The rush of cool air from the gangway as the crew opened the doors out to the plane was very welcome. In less than ten hours, they would be free.

Chapter 8

Pulling the belt tight, Josh tried to relax in his seat, but he knew they weren't quite out of the woods yet. They had a two-hour long stop-off at Houston before changing to a connecting flight to El Paso—more than enough time to get caught. Hopefully the CIA had no idea what they were up to, given how out-there this plan to escape to Mexico was. At the thought, a stomach-lurching reality check dropped: the CIA was killing people to keep them quiet, so getting caught was not an option.

"I guess we'll need to change our names," Josh said quietly. The plane was almost empty, but he thought it better to keep his voice down anyway. Georgie, who was in the window seat, with Joseph between them, turned away from the window, where lights flashed and glowed from the darkness.

"I suppose," she said. She looked tired. Her response seemed numb. Josh was sure the reality of the situation would kick in again tomorrow and that he'd have a whole lot more explaining to do. For now, sleep deprivation and shock were enough to keep her calm. It was probably for the best. Joseph, who had awoken when they had boarded, turned restlessly in his seat. Georgie soothed him, and he cuddled up to her. He too was quiet. He'd never been a loud kid.

"Maybe we can think about that tomorrow," Josh said. "You get some sleep."

He leaned across and pulled the window blind shut. The cabin lights were dim, and Georgie, coat rolled up and wedged between her head and the fuselage, yawned. "I don't think I'll be able to get to sleep," she mumbled, shutting her eyes.

"Try," Josh said. Georgie said nothing, so Josh turned to Lionel across the aisle. "How are you holding up?"

Lionel laughed softly. "As well as can be expected. You?"

Josh shrugged. "Same. Okay. Headache's almost gone."

"Good, that's good." Lionel shook his head slowly, staring into the distance. "What a day, huh?"

"What a day."

They said nothing for a moment as a flight attendant brushed past. The hum of the air conditioning built as the pre-flight whirrs and clicks began.

"What are you going to do once we get there?" Josh asked. "You're welcome to stick with us."

Lionel scratched his leg. "Truth be told, I haven't really thought about it. I suppose it wouldn't be right of me to hang around with you guys too long—"

"You can stay with us as long as you like," Josh said, cutting him off.

"—so I'd probably find my own place, you know. Nearby, so we can keep in touch."

Josh smiled. "I'd like that."

"Listen, we'd better get some cash out when we land in El Paso, as much as we can."

Josh realized the thought hadn't even occurred to him. Could he even use his cards in Mexico? "Why don't we get it out in Houston, in case they try and freeze our accounts later? Shit, they might have even frozen our accounts now…"

"I don't want them to see account activity until we're in El Paso, so we've got time to get clear."

Josh laughed. "Are you sure you've never done this before?"

Shaking his head, frowning, Lionel muttered, "Damn racist…"

"I'm joking! Jesus, Lionel, lighten up."

"Pfff."

The aircraft jerked as the pushback tug guided them away from the terminal. Once they were squarely on the taxiway and moving under their own steam, Josh had a thought. "How did you buy the tickets?"

Lionel, eyes now shut and seat reclined, said, "Cash."

Josh sat up. "You had *eleven hundred dollars* in cash on you?"

"Yeah."

"Why?"

Not moving, Lionel opened an eye and gave Josh a sideways look. "I'm gangster, that's why," he said. "That what you want to hear, honky?"

"You're such a dick," Josh said, sitting back and reclining his own seat. They both laughed.

Wheels up, Josh managed to actually get some shut-eye. His dreams were distant but restless, punctuated with moments of semi-awake dozing when his neck or back or arms began to ache. It was around five hours to Houston and one hour back on the clock, which would put them down in the early hours of the next day. He knew he needed to get some sleep now so he'd be able to function when they landed.

As the hours passed, the dreams became more vivid. He was in the tunnel, but he was on his own. Then he was in the room. It was black, but he could feel the energy. He could feel it as he had the first time, but with a new sense that guided him with more clarity and precision than any of his mortal senses ever could. Somehow, through his dreams, he felt more able to interpret the energy in that room now than he could back when it had happened. What had been a bombardment of stimuli then made more sense now, like his brain had needed the time to filter through and sort it out. Messy, tangled strands had been ordered into straight, even filaments, and he could feel so much more through them.

There had been a presence. Life.

But it was more than that. It wasn't life as in the existence of something, it was life as in the journey of some*one*. A path traveled, leading to that moment. A tunnel, leading into the moments to come. A circle, joining the ends together. Like this moment, this presence, had a *memory*.

Josh jolted awake, the dream still clear in his mind. But now it made no sense to him at all. He rubbed his eyes, willing the dream and its stupidity away from him. He needed a clear head. He needed to be able to think without nonsense like that clouding his judgment. Looking over at Georgie, he saw that she was ungracefully sleeping, mouth agape and arm wedged between her head and the armrest. He smiled. He liked to see her like this; it was so personal, so intimate, and it felt like home. Home, he realized, was wherever his family was, and right now they were with him. Despite the odds, he felt at peace.

Lionel, too, was asleep, although the grace with which he had wedged himself upright lacked much of the personal connection Josh had with Georgie. Lionel snored, smacking his lips and rolling about in his seat, making it shudder under his weight.

The dream was almost gone now, which made Josh more at ease.

"Good morning, ladies and gentlemen," the loudspeaker announced softly to the cabin. "We will begin our descent into Houston very shortly, so if you could all fasten your safety belts, return your seats to the upright position and fold your tray tables away please. Thank you for flying with American Eagle."

Josh did as he was instructed, then leaned across to jab Lionel awake. "We're landing soon," he said, as Lionel blinked his way back into consciousness. Then he turned his attention to Georgie, who was stretching and yawning. Josh held his breath as he saw on her face that she didn't understand where she was—then the realization as it all came back to her. Her shoulders slumped.

"What time is it?" she asked, groggy.

"One in the morning," Josh replied.

Georgie sighed. "At least I don't have to go to work."

Josh helped her wake Joseph, who'd fallen asleep again and slipped down so his head rested on Georgie's arm.

"Where are we going?" he mumbled, rubbing his eyes.

"We're going to Mexico," Josh told him, clipping his belt around him while Georgie sat him upright. Secured, Joseph slumped back onto his mother.

"I don't want to go to Mexico," he said sulkily. "I want to go home…"

Josh looked at Georgie, whose face was sad. Josh felt a pang of guilt over dragging them both into this. He needn't have done it. He'd been selfish. What he'd chosen to do he'd done because he thought he was protecting them, but now, in the early hours of a new day, he could see it was because he didn't want to lose them forever. "I'm sorry," he said, to Georgie as well as to Joseph. Joseph grumbled, so Georgie, breaking eye contact with Josh, soothed him quietly.

"It'll be okay," she said. "We'll have fun, right?"

Joseph nodded, still sleepy. "Okay," he said.

"Good boy."

The cabin crew took their seats as the plane's nose dipped, banking right to enter the landing pattern. The thought of touching down gave Josh an unwelcome squirt of adrenaline, making him feel a little nauseous.

"Nearly there," Lionel said. Josh looked over at him. Lionel was properly awake now and sat up, bags under his eyes and a wry smile on his face. "We might actually do this."

"I sure hope so," Josh said.

The thump as tires hit tarmac came sooner than he'd expected, and before long they were gathering themselves up and leaving the plane.

"Have a nice day," the flight attendant said as they stepped out the door.

"Thanks," Josh said. "You too."

They hurried on through to the main concourse as fast as they dared, finding the gate for the plane that would take them through to El Paso.

"It's not on the board," Lionel said. "Too early yet."

"Well, I'm starting to get hungry," Josh said. "Shall we get something to eat?" He didn't really feel like eating, but he knew from the welling nausea that he needed to.

"Sure," Georgie said. "What about you, Joseph? Are you hungry?"

Joseph, being held by Georgie, buried his head in her chest. "No," he said.

Georgie cuddled him tight. "Well I am, so let's go get something."

They settled for the least unappealing food emporium that was still open, a fast food place serving breakfast burgers and hash browns. They sat at their table, eating the greasy food in silence, tiredness weighing them all down like a wet blanket. Josh was still secretly grateful that Georgie was too tired for round two, although he was starting to wonder if she'd just accepted their fate and gone with it. The decision to bring her may have been a selfish one, but she had come willingly, and that pleased him. He hoped that he was still as important to her as she was to him.

"Gate's up," Lionel said, wiping his mouth with a napkin and pointing. They all looked. "Gate A11."

They finished up and made their way to the gate, this time with no hassle at all. The airport was almost deserted, with only the sound of the floor mop to listen to. As they walked down to the gate, Josh leaned to Lionel and said, "I don't want to speak too soon, but I think we've managed to get away with this."

"Well, forgive me if I don't celebrate until I'm on Mexican soil," Lionel said in return. "And then forgive me if I don't celebrate at all, because this is all one big shitty mess."

"You're right—sorry."

Sleep crept up on Josh once they'd taken a seat in the waiting lounge at the gate, and he jolted suddenly awake as his head dropped. "Can't keep my eyes open."

"Not long until we board," Georgie said.

Lionel looked at his watch. "Few minutes."

Josh sat up and rubbed his face, trying to keep himself awake. He looked at the time: three-forty-five. Through the big windows looking out at the runway, Josh saw the first glimmers of morning staining the night sky purple. He checked his watch again, then realized he needed to put it back an hour. While resetting his watch, he said, "Sun comes up early here, doesn't it?"

"Closer to the equator I suppose," Lionel replied, also looking.

They stared a while, watching the glow march slowly on, changing hue as it moved. It painted the gleaming aircraft rolling to and from the runway in a beautiful wash of deep lilac. It was almost relaxing.

The announcement for their flight gave Josh another dump of adrenaline, but this time he was pleased for it, giving him the energy to haul himself up out of his seat and help Georgie with Joseph. "I'll carry him," he said, and Georgie, at first making to take Joseph back, let him.

"Sure," she said. Joseph wriggled at first, but a little bouncing soon calmed him.

There were even fewer people on this flight than the last, maybe ten or fifteen in total, and they all joined the queue for a final ticket check before boarding. If they were going to get stopped, this was where it would be. Josh looked down the concourse to see if there was anyone coming, but there was no one. They reached their turn in the queue and the attendant smiled at them—especially at Joseph— checked their tickets and let them on. They were through. They were free.

Trying not to show his excitement, Josh ushered their group onto the plane. They took their seats in apprehensive silence, Josh watching the door for that last-minute burst in, the moment when everything went wrong, but when the cabin crew sealed the cabin and the plane was backed away from the gate, he almost squealed with happiness. He looked to Lionel, who was also showing signs of delight, and to Georgie who—still looked tired. It was understandable. Her situation was different. Josh gave her a smile and she returned it. He leaned over and squeezed her hand, which she looked down at but did not pull away. "Thank you," he said. She didn't reply.

When the wheels left the ground as the plane thundered down the runway, Josh let out a sigh of relief, drowned out by the roar of the jets. It was the first day of the rest of his life. The first day as a free man. He couldn't have been happier.

Chapter 9

Josh leaned back in his seat and smiled. He didn't really know why he was smiling—after all, his life as he knew it was over—but he was. In three hours, they would come in to El Paso International, they'd get a cab to the border and they'd be free. Whatever it was buried deep beneath New York, it would be gone forever. The CIA, Tom Edwards—all of it—would be in the past.

The sun was marching up above the horizon, and above the thin scattering of clouds, it looked to be the onset of a beautiful day. Josh had always loved the heat of the desert, but having moved to wherever the work was, he didn't get to experience it much. He was glad to be coming back to it. If he shut his eyes and tried hard enough, he almost felt like he was going on vacation.

He knew this euphoria would be short-lived, that the thrill of escaping would soon wear off, but he chose to enjoy it while he could. What they would do, where they would go—he had plenty of time to think about that later. Eyes shut, he let his shoulders loosen, clasped his hands over his belly and promptly fell asleep.

When he awoke, he did so like he had been asleep for a full twelve hours on the most comfortable mattress ever made. He felt renewed, invigorated. He checked the time; they had around an hour left. Georgie and Lionel were both asleep, while Joseph was keeping himself occupied with some toys. Josh stroked Joseph's cheek, which Joseph took no notice of, busy with his own quiet mutterings.

Georgie's window blind was down, so unclipping his seatbelt, Josh slipped out and into the empty row of seats in front. He peered out of the window to see that the sun was high above, burning down as if it were near midday. He checked his watch again—it was five-thirty in the morning. He looked around for a member of the cabin crew, but he could see none. Ahead, the cockpit door was open. Standing to return to his old seat, where he planned to wake Lionel, he noticed that other passengers—who weren't sleeping—were also looking out of their windows. From the passengers who were both awake and with someone else, urgent whispers emanated. The pit of Josh's stomach turned cold, and he slid along the empty row of seats and shook Lionel awake.

"Lionel, there's something weird going on," he hissed.

Lionel, clumsy from sleep, seemed to take several attempts to understand what Josh was saying. In the end Josh climbed over him, pulled up the window blind, pointed and said, "Look!"

Giving him a disdainful glance, presumably at being woken, Lionel shuffled along the row of seats heavily and glanced out of the window. His expression was a journey of thought: annoyance, curiosity, confusion, then worry. He checked his watch, then looked to Josh. "I don't understand…" he said.

"Me neither."

"It's five-thirty, right?"

"Right."

"Then why's the sun already going down?"

Josh blinked. "It's coming up—isn't it?"

"No," Lionel corrected. "It's going down, over there. In the west. We're going south, yeah? Then that's the west."

Pushing past Lionel, who grunted in protest, Josh had another look out of the window. Sure enough, the sun was dipping low in the sky, tinting the clouds red. "What…?" he whispered. Then he realized that he could actually *see* the sun moving, sinking down toward the horizon. In minutes, it would be gone.

He dropped into the seat next to Lionel, barely able to breathe. Georgie was still asleep; he decided not to wake her, not yet. He needed to find a crewmember first. Then he remembered that the cockpit door was open, so he leaped up and started marching down the aisle toward the nose.

"What are you doing?" Lionel called out after him. Josh didn't respond.

The passengers who were awake watched Josh as he stormed through the plane, but he took no notice of them. As he approached the open door, thick with armor yet hanging loose on its hinges, he saw that the cabin crew was huddled in with the flight crew. The faces he could see looked worried. One lady saw him, approached him.

"Please remain in your seat, sir," she said, blocking the way. She sounded less confident than she probably intended. There was definitely a waver in her voice.

"What's going on?" Josh demanded. "What's happening?"

"Please, sir, go back to your seat," the lady said. Another turned to assist, trying to shepherd Josh back out.

Josh held up his hands; he didn't want a quarrel. "I just want to know what's going on, that's all."

"Sir—"

"We don't know what's going on," a deeper voice said from further into the cockpit. The cabin crew parted, allowing Josh to see a man sitting in what he assumed was the captain's seat. The man, dressed in pilot's uniform, had twisted in his chair to address Josh, and looked anxious.

"The sun, it—" Josh started.

"I know," the captain said. "And it's accelerating. The plane's fine, except communications are down so we've lost all contact with ELP—sorry, El Paso International."

Josh could feel his legs starting to quiver. "Have you been able to contact anywhere else?"

The pilot shook his head. "No."

"Can—can we still land okay?"

The pilot paused, then said, "We should be fine."

The cockpit was silent for a while as the sun sank completely, casting them all into darkness. The co-pilot flicked the cabin lights on, which blinked into life above them.

Josh ran a hand over his head, trying to think. He had an answer, but he didn't want to believe it. "The room…" he whispered.

"What's that?" the captain asked.

"Oh—nothing," Josh said. He realized there was nothing more he could achieve in the already crowded cockpit, so he made to leave. "Thanks."

"We'll keep you updated," the captain called out after him.

By the time he had made his way back to Lionel, the sun was already rising again, casting a wash on the cabin's ceiling.

"What did they say?" Lionel asked, visibly worried.

"We've lost contact with El Paso," Josh said, lowering himself into the seat next to Lionel. His own voice sounded distant. "They don't know what's going on. But I think I do."

"The room…" Lionel said in a hushed whisper. It was like he'd read Josh's mind. "But… how?"

Josh shook his head slowly. "I don't know." He looked out of the window; the midday sun was almost peaking. "I don't know."

"Should we tell Georgie?" She was still fast asleep, huddled up under her coat.

"No," Josh said. "Let her rest. She'll need it."

"You're probably right."

Another passenger, an older lady wearing pearls and a woolen sweater, approached Josh and Lionel. "Excuse me," she said. "I saw you went to speak to the pilot; can you tell me what's going on please?"

Josh was speechless for a moment, unable to take his mind away from the room to articulate a response to the lady's question. "Uh…" he said.

"The captain doesn't know," Lionel told the lady. "No one does."

"Oh," said the lady, looking disappointed. "Okay, well, thank you."

She headed back to her seat, telling others along the way that the captain didn't know. They took the news in silence, all unable—like Josh—to process how they should react to the situation.

Josh was about to speak again when a shout went up at the front of the cabin. He and Lionel craned to see what was going on, when a suited man in his thirties stood up and stormed into the cockpit.

"What's going on?" the man yelled, hands on hips.

Josh couldn't hear what the response was.

"Don't tell me to calm down!" the man yelled. "I demand to know what's going on!"

Another quiet response.

"I don't believe you!"

The man made to walk forward, but was pushed back against the throng in the cabin. The plane lurched.

"Sir!" Josh could hear the captain's voice now, loud but firm. "Please take a seat or I will be forced to restrain you!"

The captain pushed through to go face-to-face with the man, who was smaller than he was. The man, cowering slightly, backed up and showed himself to his seat quietly. Watching him, the captain addressed the cabin, talking loudly rather than using the loudspeaker. "Please all remain calm. We're trying to get more information on the situation and will update you as soon as we know anything. At present we are all perfectly safe and scheduled to touch down as expected—so long as you *all remain calm*." He made an emphasis on that final point, glaring at the man in the suit.

Once he was assured that everyone was staying quiet and in their seats, he retreated back into the cabin, pulling the door shut behind him.

"Jesus…" Lionel said.

Josh heard movement to his side; Georgie was waking up. "What time is it?" she groaned, pulling up her blind a crack. The sun had dipped out of sight again, but when it shot back into view, Georgie sat bolt upright. "The sun…" she said, looking at Josh, eyes wide. "What's going on with the sun?" She looked back out of the window, the sun moving fast enough to trace a shadow smoothly around the cabin.

"We don't know," Josh said, "but I think it might have something to do with what we found."

"Oh, God…" Georgie said, frightened eyes searching Josh's. "What did you find that could do *this*?"

"I—I don't know…"

"You don't know? What do you mean you don't know?" She sounded scared. Josh *felt* scared.

"It—it was just this room. I thought it was empty. But there was this—this energy, I don't know."

Lionel shifted. "You didn't say anything about any energy before."

"I thought it was gas or something. Now—now I don't know. I just don't know."

Georgie looked back out of the window again, as if unable to believe her eyes or ears. Every second that passed, the sun was moving faster, doing a lap of the Earth in less than a minute.

"How long until we're due to land?" Lionel asked.

Josh checked his watch. "About thirty minutes now." To Georgie he said, "Look, Georgie, we'll figure this out, okay? The captain said we're fine to land, so once we do we can get where we're going and figure this out from there."

"But—but the CIA," Georgie said, voice thick with fear. "Maybe you should go back, go and speak to them? Maybe you can help them fix this?"

"How?" Josh said. "How am I supposed to fix this? I don't know—" He stopped himself, realizing that his voice was getting louder and more high-pitched, distressing Joseph. Georgie cuddled Joseph close, and he calmed a little.

"I don't know anything about this, okay?" Josh continued, voice under control. "I just found this room, the CIA turned up, and that's all I know. They should be able to handle this, not me. I don't want any part of it."

Georgie, pleading, said, "But you're *already* a part of it! Don't you think you could be of some help? Don't you think you should at least *try*?"

Josh sighed. He knew Georgie was right. He glanced at Lionel for support, but Lionel said nothing. "Okay," he said. "As soon as we land, I'll contact Edwards."

"You promise?"

"I promise."

The loudspeaker crackled overhead, and the captain spoke—although he lacked composure. "We're beginning our descent now. We've still got no communications, but the pattern seems clear. I want you all to find a window and take a look outside, and come straight to the cockpit if you see another plane, okay? We're going to open the door again, so please remain composed and we should get down just fine."

The door promptly opened, and the cabin crew emerged. They hurried down the aisle, directing people as calmly as they could to find their own window.

"I'll go to the row in front," Josh said, getting up. Once he was positioned, he pressed up against the thick Perspex, looking out into the distance. He wondered what kind of a panic might be going on down below. The sun was looping so fast around the Earth now that it was like a light bulb being flicked off and on again over and over, and was beginning to make him feel quite sick. "Do you see anything?" he said to Lionel through the gap between the seats.

"Nope. Light's hurting my eyes though."

"Me too."

The sun was really accelerating, looping faster and faster. Josh had to pull away for the sake of his stomach and his head, the blur of the sun strobing through the window. He had no idea how the captain was going to land in these conditions. The nose dipped and they slowly banked, drawing the ground closer. The sun streaked rings across his retinas, which pulsed with flashes of day and night, and he had to pull the blind back down. He heard Lionel do the same.

"Final approach," the captain told them, his voice strained. "Please make sure your seatbelts are fastened."

The cabin crew had vanished again, so Josh darted back to his seat to help Georgie buckle a struggling Joseph in. They were all frightened; Georgie's hands were trembling. Her blind was still open a crack, and Josh could see the ground coming in fast.

"I'm sorry," he told her, and she tried to give him a smile, but it came out tearful and scared. They held hands across Joseph, Georgie's hand squeezing harder every time a new whirr of flaps or undercarriage rumbled through the fuselage.

"I should have stayed with you," Josh told her. "I'm sorry I abandoned you."

"It's okay…" Georgie whispered, tears running down her cheeks. She wiped them away with her free hand.

Outside, Josh could see that the landing was imminent. He braced himself, holding Georgie's hand tight. "I love you—"

A shout went up in the cockpit as the nose hit hard into the ground, jolting the plane, slamming Josh forward in his seat. He hit the back of the seat in front of him, but had no time to think about it as the scream of tearing metal ripped at his ears, the fuselage twisting and buckling. The rest of the plane thumped down, pivoting about the collapsing nose section, throwing the cabin into darkness. The plane rumbled and squalled as it slid forward along the ground at tremendous pace, shredding apart around them. Flames burst in through a tear in the side, rushing through the cabin in an instant, engulfing them all. The pain was immediate, making the sound of the cabin collapsing on top of them distant.

Only a few seconds had passed since the plane had made its first contact, and already Josh knew that this was the end.

Chapter 10

Darkness isn't dark until you're dead. Then the flames come. They wrap around you, like a cloak. They slough your skin and melt your bones. The sound—you don't hear it, you *feel* it. A light. A blur. Agony.

Then the darkness is real.

Even in the darkness, the room spun. The energy was still there, the last living trace tingling in his fingers. He pinched them; he was real. He took a breath. His lungs filled. His ears pricked.

"Boss, are you there? I can't see shit."

Josh opened his eyes. "I'm here," he said. The energy receded, a gentle hiss in the background. For a moment he didn't remember, and when he did, he didn't believe it. *I think there* is *gas in here*, he wanted to say.

But he didn't.

"All right, well, let's get you out of there, then," Craig shouted. "Sorry I took so long getting the ladder."

So long? "That's… okay." Josh turned around and made his way back over to Craig, following the moonlike hole glowing in the darkness. Before he approached, he stopped, waiting for the dizziness to abate.

"You okay?" Craig asked, feeding down the ladder for Josh to climb.

"Yeah, fine, just…" Josh paused. "Just a little light-headed," he added finally.

"Does sound like gas. Probably a natural pocket."

"Let's get out of here."

Josh climbed out of the room, and wandered behind Craig back through the fresh tunnel toward the rest of the team.

"Are you all right?" Craig asked again. "You seem quiet. Gas got you feeling sick?"

Josh snapped from his thoughts. "Huh? Oh, yeah, probably."

"Maybe you should see the doctor?"

"Yeah, maybe…"

They said nothing more until they reached the rest of the group, who awaited their return expectantly. They stared at Josh and he stared back, saying nothing.

"Well…" Craig said, talking for Josh, "seems like there could well be gas in there, so I suggest we call it a day."

The team groaned. "What was down there?" Robert asked. Craig looked to Josh.

"Nothing," Josh said. "And something."

The awkward silence that followed was broken by Craig, who said, "All right, let's get on out of here. Come on."

The team made audible protests, but did what they were told. As they all headed back to the train, Craig radioed in. "Lionel, we're on our way out. There's a big space down here. I think there might be gas."

"Okay, see you when you get up here."

Josh wanted to be sick. Perhaps it was the gas? Perhaps he just needed some fresh air. As they reached the staging area and boarded the elevator, rising up out of the ground and into the light of day, Josh felt a little better. Less tired. Just needed some fresh air after all. A dull, distant headache lingered.

On the surface, he found Lionel.

"What can you report?" Lionel asked.

"There's…" Josh started, but stopped. He could feel panic making his insides tremble. He wanted to ignore what he knew was true, blame it on the gas or something like that, but he couldn't. "I'm sorry," he said, "I have to go." With that he stumbled away, leaving Lionel confused, watching him leave.

"Josh!" Lionel called out after him. "Are you all right?"

Josh ignored him. The dizziness was coming back, the world spinning, the flames licking at his flesh. How it had burned, how the pain had *become* him. There was something else there, something that itched in his mind but could not be reached to scratch. Footsteps thumped behind him and a hand clapped on his shoulder as Lionel caught up with him, keeping him upright as he staggered onward.

"Josh, maybe you should come and sit down, okay?"

Unable to speak, Josh let Lionel lead him to the temporary office building at the edge of the site, where he took a seat while Lionel went to call an ambulance. Once Lionel was gone, Josh was up again, stumbling his way out of the building and on toward the entrance. Through the gates and onto the street, he headed for the subway, for home.

The cool darkness of the subway calmed his nerves a little, leveled his head. He needed to focus, to think about what had happened and make sense of it. But when he did, his head seared with pain, the flames rising and the ground trembling.

When he exited the subway, a couple of missed calls from Lionel appeared on his cell, but he ignored them. Putting everything to the back of his mind as best he could, he boarded a bus to take him back to his apartment. As they passed by 82nd, he pressed the bell, causing the bus driver to lurch the bus to a halt. Josh jumped up and ran down the aisle, squeezing past other passengers to get off.

"Don't leave it so late next time," the bus driver reprimanded him as he jumped off. The doors shut behind him and the bus pulled away as he pointed in the direction of Georgie's apartment. He ran there as fast as he could.

Letting himself into the building, he staggered up the stairs, tripping, scrambling his way up to her front door. He pressed the buzzer and rapped as hard as he could, his knuckles stinging.

"Georgie!" he yelled. "Georgie!"

There was no answer. He rang and knocked a few more times, until he was sure she wasn't there. Back against the wall, he slid to the floor, lungs heaving, heart thrumming. She would be back soon. He would wait. He tipped his head back against the wall and shut his eyes.

Flames flashed and flickered behind his eyelids, burning his retinas. His body, it felt... thin. Stretched. Spread too far, like it didn't fit right. He wanted to cry, to ease the fire in his eyes, but he had no tears. He was drained.

"Josh..." a voice said. Josh opened his eyes. It was Georgie, at the top of the stairs, with Joseph. "What are you doing here?"

"Daddy!" Joseph squealed. Georgie held him still.

"Hey, Joseph," Josh said, scrambling up to his feet, swaying clumsily. "Georgie, you're... I was waiting for you."

Georgie, keeping her distance, pulled Joseph closer. "Shouldn't you be at work?" she asked. She looked on with disgust as Josh struggled to stay standing. "Are you... are you drunk?"

Josh was appalled. "Drunk? I'm not drunk! I just need to talk to you."

Georgie shook her head. "Now's not the time, Josh. Maybe later, when you've sobered up."

"I'm not drunk!" Josh shouted, making Georgie jump. The disgust became fear. "I'm sorry," Josh said. "I didn't mean to shout. I just need to talk to you. It's very important. Please."

Georgie considered him for a few moments, hesitating. Finally, she said, "Okay, but let me take Joseph in first and put him in his room. We can talk out here."

Josh nodded. It was the best he was going to get, and he knew it. He moved aside to let Georgie by, who watched him as she unlocked the door and let herself in. Once inside, Josh heard the bolt and chain slide into place.

"Shit…" he said to himself. She wasn't going to come back. She was probably calling the police, in fact. He'd have to go. Waiting a moment more, he then decided to leave, turning for the stairwell. As he made for the stairs, the bolt and chain slid once more, and he spun to see Georgie standing in the doorway, arms folded.

"This'd better be good," she said. Her face was no longer harsh; if anything there may have been some sympathy there. Josh walked back toward her, slowly, leaving enough distance to let her feel safe.

"The CIA…" Josh said. "They—they're going to be looking for me."

Georgie's expression turned to one of disbelief. "The CIA?" she repeated. "What did you *do*?"

"No," Josh said, shaking his head. "Not yet. *Soon*."

Even more confused, Georgie repeated, "Soon? I don't understand what you mean, Josh."

Wringing his hands with frustration, trying to fight the fire burning in his head, Josh croaked, "Soon, Georgie, soon. The CIA… they're coming for me. I—I found something, something powerful, something they didn't want me to find. We have to go, Georgie, now, before it's too late and everything—" Josh stopped himself, if only to cease the white hot pain behind his eyes. As they cooled and his vision returned, he saw Georgie making to shut the door. "Please, Georgie, no! You've got to listen to me!"

"You're drunk, Josh," she said as the door swung shut.

Josh leaped forward and threw his arm in the gap, crying out as the door pinched it against the frame.

"Josh, what are you doing?" Georgie yelled, opening the door again to see Josh stagger backward, cradling his arm.

"I can prove it…" Josh said, tears pricking his vision. "Come with me and I'll prove it. Please. I'm not drunk."

Again, Georgie was faced with a dilemma. "I can't leave Joseph," she said.

"Bring him with us."

"Are you sure it's safe?"

Josh nodded quickly. "It will be if we go *now*."

Georgie still wasn't convinced, so Josh approached her, hunched forward, holding his throbbing arm against his chest. She backed away, and Josh stopped.

"Please," he said. "Please. Trust me. I know I've not been there for you in the past, but I'm here for you now, and I need you to trust me. Please."

Georgie hesitated. "You're telling the truth?"

Nodding, Josh said, "Yes, one hundred percent."

Shifting weight from leg to leg, Georgie sighed. Then she dropped her arms by her sides. "Fine. Let me get Joseph." She receded back into the apartment, leaving the door ajar. Josh waited, anxiousness boiling in his gut. They needed to go. They needed to already be gone.

When Georgie returned, she had Joseph. "If it turns out you're lying," she said sternly, "I'm gone. You'll never see me or Joseph again, do you understand?"

"Yes."

"Come on then, let's get this over with."

She followed Josh down the stairs, out into the street. They walked down to Northern Boulevard, where Josh hailed a cab. They all climbed in; Josh told the driver to head down to Manhattan, 63rd and 3rd.

"Where are we going?" Georgie asked.

"The East Side Access," Josh told her. "You'll see why."

As they left Queens and entered Manhattan, reaching the site, Josh signaled the driver to pull over.

"This is still on the clock," the driver told him.

"That's fine," Josh said. To Georgie, he said, "Watch."

At first, Georgie seemed confused; then the sirens began to ring out. Soon, a group of police cars were forming up outside the site entrance, where Lionel appeared to meet them. They could not hear the conversation Lionel had with one of the officers, but Josh didn't need to. They talked for a while, then the officer left for the site, leaving Lionel with another.

"I don't get it," Georgie said, voice low. "What's happening?"

"Watch," Josh said, staring out at the scene. They watched for a few minutes more, until two black SUVs arrived. The men who got out looked like accountants, but Josh knew who they really were.

"CIA…" Georgie breathed.

Josh nodded. "CIA."

"Hey, what's going on here?" the driver asked. "I don't want to get involved with no CIA espionage shit. You can get out if you think that's gonna happen."

"No," Josh said, "we can go. Please take us back."

"Okay," the driver said. "But that's it, right? No more federal government shit?"

"No more."

"All right."

They headed back out of Manhattan, back into Queens and toward Jackson Heights. As they were about to pull onto 82nd, Josh asked the driver to pull over. The driver grumbled, but agreed; the fare was mounting up, after all.

"Georgie, will you come and get some lunch with me? There's something else I want to show you."

"I've already eaten, Josh. I've done what you asked, and I want to go home. The driver's right—I don't want to be involved with any of this either."

"Thank you, ma'am," the driver said.

"Stay out of this please," Josh said back to the driver. "Georgie, please. It's the last thing I'll ask of you. It will all make sense, I promise."

Georgie considered Josh's proposal, then nodded. "Fine. But no more, okay?"

Josh smiled. His head was feeling better. "Thank you. Driver, please take us to 103rd, Lou's Pizzeria please."

"Sure thing."

The driver dropped them off at Lou's Pizzeria on 103rd, and Josh paid the man. "You better watch your back," the driver said in parting before driving away, shaking his head. Josh chose to ignore him, following Georgie and Joseph into the restaurant. He chose a table by the window, overlooking the bait and tackle shop, above which was his apartment. The stairs that led up there were visible from the pizzeria.

They sat down, and Josh passed Georgie a menu.

"Why are we in a pizza place opposite your apartment?" she asked.

"You'll see," Josh said, watching out of the window. "It might take a while, but you'll see."

"A while? How long is a while?"

"I don't know."

Georgie sighed. "You're paying for this pizza, right?"

"Of course."

"Fine, I'll have three slices of Hawaiian then."

Josh gave their order to one of Lou's finest, and soon they were digging in. Josh didn't think he'd have much of an appetite, but once he started eating, he realized how famished he was. He could feel his energy returning, the blood flowing back to his face, the tingling in his extremities fading away.

"So what do they want?" Georgie said between mouthfuls of pizza.

"Don't worry, I haven't done anything wrong," Josh said. "You enjoying your pizza, Joseph?"

Joseph, tomato sauce all around his mouth, nodded enthusiastically.

"Don't worry?" Georgie said in disbelief. "You somehow knew the CIA would be coming to your site, and you think I shouldn't worry? How *did* you know, anyway?"

"It's hard to explain. I'm not entirely sure why myself."

"And what do you expect to happen here, at Lou's Pizzeria of all places?"

"I don't know for sure."

Georgie dropped her slice back on her plate. "Then *why* are we sitting here? This pizza—" She cut herself off, leaning closer to whisper. "This pizza's awful. You know it is."

"Joseph seems to be enjoying it."

"Joseph is three years old. He enjoys most things."

Josh sighed. He needed to buy some more time, but he knew he wasn't going to get away with dodging Georgie's questions for much longer. "They're going to come to my apartment, they're going to break in, and they're going to steal a picture of us."

Georgie almost spat her mouthful of pizza out. "*What*?" she said.

Josh said nothing, looking down at the table.

"First—if that *is* true—how do you even know that? And secondly, why would they do such a thing?"

Josh looked around, knee bobbing, trying to think of the best way to phrase what he needed to say next. "They want to—to—"

Not sure how best to put it, Josh ran his index finger across his throat. Georgie shook her head.

"No, Josh. This is ridiculous. I don't know what's wrong with you, but I suggest you see a doctor, a good one." She stood up. "I'm going now, okay? Please don't follow me, and please don't try to contact me either."

"Georgie, please," Josh said, also standing up. "All I ask is another hour, two at the most, then you can go. That's it. If nothing happens, I'll never contact you again. I'll get help. I'll do whatever you want. Please, I'm begging you."

Georgie, eyes narrowed, stared at Josh. She saw something, some honesty, some truth, because she sat down again, albeit slowly. "You really believe this, don't you?" she said.

"I do. I—I have to. And I need you to believe it, too. Otherwise…" He trailed off.

"All right—two hours, and that's it."

"Two hours. Thank you."

The next hour and a half passed with small talk, and Josh even began to enjoy himself. He'd always loved Georgie's company; she had a way of making him laugh like no one else could. She was smiling, eyes bright and cheeks flushed, as she told Josh about a friend of hers.

"I couldn't believe it," she said. "You could see the string poking out of her shorts and—ugh, I can't even say it!"

"That's awful," Josh said. "Did anyone tell her?"

"How can you?" Georgie exclaimed. "What do you say? *Excuse me, your ripcord's showing?* You can't just say something like that to someone!"

Josh shook his head. "No, I suppose not. Wow, though. Just wow."

"Tell me about it."

A silence followed, but it wasn't uncomfortable. As the afternoon grew late, the shadow cast by the buildings opposite left only the glow of the table lamp to see by in the dingy pizzeria. Georgie was beautiful to Josh anyway, but with this light she was stunning. "I miss this," Josh said.

Georgie nodded. "Me too."

Joseph, who'd been drawing with crayons, leaned up against Georgie. "I'm sleepy," he said. Georgie cuddled him, stroking his hair.

"That's okay, baby. We'll be leaving soon."

Josh looked at his watch; only fifteen minutes until the agreed deadline arrived. Joseph moaned, burying himself deeper into Georgie's chest. "I wanna go home!" he said, voice muffled.

Georgie looked at Josh. "I'm sorry," she said. "I should take him back."

Josh wanted to fight for those last fifteen minutes, but there was no point. "All right then. Can I get you a cab?"

"No, that's okay," Georgie said, standing and picking up Joseph, whose bottom lip was starting to tremble. "It's a short walk."

"Okay, if you're sure. Here, take my coat. It's cold out."

"Thank you," Georgie said, letting him drape it over her shoulders. She turned to face Josh; they were close. He could feel her warm breath on his face. "Listen," she said, "whatever's going on, I hope you get it sorted out. I didn't mean what I said earlier; I still want you to be in my life, and Joseph's life especially. If you need anything, let me know and I'll do my best to help you out."

"I appreciate that," Josh said. He put his arms around her and gave her and Joseph a quick hug. "I'm sorry about today. I—I need to take a nap or something, that's all."

"Okay. Well, I hope you feel better."

Josh went to the counter to pay the bill, and as he was collecting his change, Georgie called to him.

"Josh! Come here, quick!"

Josh turned to see two black SUVs pulling up outside his apartment.

Chapter 11

"Georgie, get back from the window," Josh whispered urgently. He pulled her back and sat her down, where they watched on as four men—all dressed in suits—exited the vehicles and ascended the stairs to Josh's apartment. Two kept watch at the top of the stairs, while the other two carried on around the side to his front door.

"Oh my God…" Georgie mumbled. Josh looked at her. Her face had gone pale and her eyes were wide and scared.

"What's going on?" the guy at the counter said.

"Don't worry about it," Josh told him, not turning around.

"Are you guys in trouble or something?"

Josh faced the man. "No trouble," he said. "It's just a… a misunderstanding."

"Okay," the man said. "But I don't want any problems here, you understand?"

"I understand."

Josh turned back to the scene, watching and waiting as the men did their work. It seemed like hours before the two who had entered returned; Josh's limbs ached from staying so still. Once they had all boarded their SUVs and driven away, he finally allowed himself to breathe. "See?"

Georgie looked at him, speechless and terrified. She was shaking her head slowly. "Josh..." she whispered. He wasn't sure if she was angry with him, scared for him or what, but he knew he had no time to lose.

"Follow me," he said, getting up and leading her by the hand to the street. The guy at the counter eyed them until they were gone.

Josh led her, as she carried Joseph, across the road and to the stairs. She didn't resist; she seemed almost catatonic, shock preventing her from doing anything other than what Josh wanted her to. He led her up the stairs, pushed open the unlocked door, and switched on the light. Everything was untouched, as he expected, everything except—

"The picture frame..." Georgie said, pointing. She approached it cautiously, sitting down on the sofa, placing Joseph down next to her, and picked it up. She held it gingerly, as though it might crumble to dust. "The picture frame..." she repeated, showing it to Josh.

Josh nodded grimly.

"How—" Georgie was having trouble talking. "How did you know?"

This was it. The moment he said it aloud was the moment he committed himself to believing it, the moment he made himself admit that he was having a breakdown, losing his mind or whatever.

But he knew. He *knew*. This was real. "Because I've done it all before."

Georgie, frowning, made to speak, but couldn't. She tilted her head; Josh knew what she meant.

"I've—" He took a breath. "I've gone back in time. I've done all this before. I know what happens next."

Still struggling to speak, all Georgie managed was, "How?"

"It's why the CIA is after me. The tunnels—there's a room. There's something in there. Something they're desperate to keep secret."

For a moment, Josh thought Georgie was going to be sick. She was very pale, and teetering in her seat.

"Are you okay, Mommy?" Joseph asked, poking her.

"Yes, baby," she said, holding him, eyes distant. "I'm okay."

"Are you sure?" Josh said. She looked at him like she had never seen him before, wary.

"How can I possibly believe you?" she said quietly.

Josh's plan wasn't working out. He'd known that she, like himself, wouldn't believe it was true, *couldn't* believe it was true. She was slipping away; he had to get her back before it was too late. "The picture, Georgie," he said, gesturing to it, still in her hand.

"You could have had it here on the coffee table already."

Panic was making Josh frantic. "Okay, well, they came when I said they would."

"If you knew they were looking for you, it was just a matter of time as to when."

Josh had run out of ideas. "Please," he begged. "Please believe me!"

Georgie, standing and scooping up Joseph, said, "How can I believe you, Josh? Time travel? You expect me to believe that? You've gotten in trouble with the CIA and the best lie you could come up with is *time travel*? I was right: you need to see a doctor, Josh. This is ridiculous."

She went to leave, but Josh blocked her. "You can't go back home, Georgie."

"Get out of my way."

"You can't go back!"

Georgie tried to push him, but he stood firm. "Josh, get out of my way!" she screamed.

"Okay," Josh said, stepping aside, "but if you go back they'll—they'll be waiting for you."

Georgie, already marching past, stopped. She turned slowly. "What?"

"They're at your apartment now. They're waiting for you. The picture—it was a message to me. They knew I'd come to you if they threatened you, so that's how they knew they'd get me."

Georgie had nothing to say. Her expression was stern. Then it fractured, breaking into sorrow. "Oh, Josh…" she sobbed. "What have you done?"

"I'm telling you the truth."

Eyes reddening, she shook her head. Then she turned on her heel and left. Josh, still standing there, considered running out after her—

but he couldn't. He knew he had to let her go. He couldn't drag her into this, *shouldn't* have dragged her into this. The only way to protect her was to stay away. He'd already gone too far. "Shit," he muttered to himself.

Retreating to the sofa, he flopped down, picking up the empty picture frame. There they'd once been, the three of them. He could remember the photo like it was still there; they'd been so happy. Now they were torn apart. He tossed the frame back down, angry. Not just angry, frustrated. Trapped. He remembered a promise he'd made to her; it came with the burning of flame and the agony of fire. He'd promised to contact them, the CIA. Hand himself in. Talk to them.

He clenched his fists. Handing himself in would be suicide. He looked at his watch: it was five-fifteen. The fire, that had been later. He couldn't remember exactly when, but it had been later. The next day, perhaps. He had time.

Pulling out his cell, he rang Lionel. He'd be out getting his groceries about now, perhaps not even left yet. Bobbing his knee, Josh waited for Lionel to answer. The line clicked.

"Josh," Lionel said. "What's going on? You ran off on me back at the site. Are you okay?"

"Hey," Josh replied. "Yeah, I'm fine. Are you at home?"

A pause. "Yeah, why?"

Josh took a breath. "I need you to do me a favor."

"Sure…"

"The CIA paid you a visit at the site today, right?"

"Yeah, they did. Have they contacted you, too?"

Josh thought about his answer. "Sort of. Anyway, they're going to visit you soon, while you're out getting your groceries—"

"How'd you know I was going to get my groceries?"

"Don't worry about that for now, please. Just listen."

"Okay…"

"I want you to go out as you'd planned, but I need you to do something first: I need you to leave a note with my name and cell number on it. Put it somewhere obvious like on the TV or something, a place where someone will easily see it."

"Hang on, are you saying the CIA are going to *break in* to my apartment?"

"Yeah. They did the same to me."

Lionel was silent for a moment. "Maybe I should stay back, wait for them—"

"No!" Josh interrupted. "No. You do not want to do that, okay? Trust me."

Again, Lionel was silent.

"Lionel, you there?"

"I'm here."

"Will you do this for me?"

"I guess."

"Good. Once you've done that, come and meet me and I'll explain everything, okay?"

"Where shall I meet you?"

Josh thought. "Central Park. By the entrance to the zoo."

"Why Central Park?"

"Because I want to go down there again and find out what all this is about."

Lionel sighed. "This doesn't seem like a good idea, messing around with the CIA. Are you sure about this?"

"Hey, you trust me, don't you?

"Sure, I guess."

"Then yeah, I'm sure."

"Okay. In that case I'll see you at Central Park soon."

Lionel hung up. This was the best way to do this; Josh could confront Edwards about the whole thing, then ditch his cell and stay safe. That way he'd still have the upper hand, know what was going on. Then… then he could try and uncover the secret of the room.

It was as good a plan as any. Lionel would be writing the note about now, then be preparing to leave. Josh needed to leave, too. Georgie had cast off his jacket when she'd left, so he grabbed it, put it on and exited his apartment. No cabs—only public transportation. He would be harder to track that way, if anyone were still looking for him.

The bus came after ten minutes, and he boarded quickly, checking the street to make sure no one saw him. It was half-empty, and he found a seat toward the back. All he could do now was wait, bobbing his knee furiously.

"You seem anxious," said an old lady sitting opposite him. "Are you all right?"

Josh smiled, without emotion. "Fine, thanks."

"You'll worry yourself into an early grave if you keep on like that."

Josh smiled again, but said nothing. The thought of death didn't help ease his nerves at all.

Once he reached his stop, he hopped off the bus and headed for the subway. He checked his cell to make sure he'd not had a call, then dipped into the subway entrance. Lionel would probably take a taxi into Manhattan, so he'd be there before Josh; hopefully he didn't have to wait too long. It would take Josh about forty minutes in total to get to Central Park, fifteen more than Lionel. Josh decided to call him when he got off the subway at the other end.

Bursting out into the late evening sun, Josh whipped out his cell, hitting redial. There was ringing, but Lionel did not answer. Josh skipped a little quicker toward Central Park, trying Lionel again, but still he got no answer. There had also been no call from Edwards.

"Shit…" he muttered, pocketing the device. He broke into a full run, negotiating block after block until Central Park came into view. The trees cast long shadows across the path, the golden evening sunshine sparkling through the leaves, and he shaded his eyes to see ahead as he approached the zoo. To his relief, Lionel was there—but that relief faded quickly when Josh realized Lionel wasn't alone. Suits, four of them. Not a member of public in sight. Josh stopped in his tracks, horrified. How had this happened? Was Lionel too late? Did they catch him as he was leaving? Did Josh make him stay at home a little too long? Did… did Lionel sell him out?

"Mr. Reed," the suit he identified as Edwards called out.

Frozen to the spot, Josh said nothing, his lungs heaving from exhaustion and terror.

Edwards approached him. "Mr. Reed, we just want to talk."

Josh spun around, breaking into a run, almost tripping over himself. Two more agents rounded the exit, blocking him. He scanned the park, looking for another way out, but it was too late. He was surrounded. He turned to face Edwards, who was almost on him, Lionel following behind.

"Sorry, Josh," Lionel said. "But this is the federal government, man. I'm not going to mess with this shit. You got to talk to them."

"But—" Josh squeaked. "But Carlos—Craig—Robert—all of them! He killed them, Lionel, don't you see? He killed them!"

Edwards, looking around, said, "I hope you don't mean *me*, Mr. Reed, because I haven't killed anyone."

Two agents approached Josh from behind and restrained him. He struggled fruitlessly. "Liar!" he shouted. "Liar!"

"No, Mr. Reed, I'm not a liar. Whoever told you *that* is a liar, but not me."

Josh looked at Lionel—it was *him* who'd told him, but now, this time, it was different. He stopped struggling, and the agents let him go. "Who then?" he panted. "Who died?"

"Did someone die?" Lionel said, anxious.

Edwards addressed them both. "Yes, I'm afraid someone did die. One of ours. They went into the tunnels to investigate, and…" He trailed off, expression somber.

"So you didn't kill anyone?" Josh asked.

"No."

"Then—then where are the others? Carlos, Robert? Craig?"

"They've gone to Langley, the CIA headquarters, for research. Don't worry, they're quite safe. We're trying to put a picture together of what's going on, and we need to talk to anyone involved in this site." He indicated to his fellow agents, who started to lead Josh out of the park. "But there's a lot we need to do, so please, let's go."

"And my family?" Josh said, resisting. "What about them? What about the picture?"

"They're safe. I apologize for taking the picture, but it was the most efficient way to secure you after you… disappeared." He reached into his jacket and retrieved the photo, handing it to Josh. Josh took it and slipped it into his pocket.

"Now please," Edwards almost begged. There was a desperate fire in his eyes. "We *need* to go."

Josh considered Edwards for a moment, but couldn't see any reason for the man to lie. "Where are we going?" he asked eventually.

"Down," Edwards said.

"Down?"

"Into the tunnels."

Chapter 12

Josh didn't understand. "Why?" he asked cautiously. "Why do you need me?"

Edwards gestured to the exit of the park. "Walk with me and I'll tell you." To the other agents he said, "Please escort Mr. Parker to Langley." Lionel made to protest, but Edwards cut him off. "Thank you, Mr. Parker, but we need you with the others. Anything we can learn from you will be vital in our research."

Lionel looked to Josh pleadingly, but Josh nodded.

"It's okay," Josh said. "I'll be fine. Go."

Without another word, Lionel went with the two agents, looking back at Josh over his shoulder as Josh and Edwards stood and waited. Once Lionel was gone and they were alone—save for two other agents shadowing them from a distance—Edwards said, "What I'm about to tell you is classified. I tell you what I tell you for the benefit of the mission, and no more."

"Okay," Josh said. They started to walk, also heading for the exit.

"This isn't the first room of its type we've found."

"The others were empty," Josh said without thinking.

Edwards slowed, eyes flashing. "What makes you say that?"

It was confirmation of what Josh believed—that he had indeed relived time. Despite the constant reminders, he still couldn't quite believe it. But his temporal journey was unknown to Edwards—at least, that was how he made it seem—and so he needed to backtrack quickly, protect his hand. "A lucky guess."

Edwards stared at Josh for a moment, Josh unsure how he was going to react. Then Edwards smiled an unkind smile, one of distrust. "Of course," he said. "A lucky guess indeed."

Edwards picked up his pace as they threaded the path back to the exit. Josh hurried to keep up. All at once he felt uneasy; Edwards had full government backing to get what he wanted, and clearly nothing was going to stop him.

"What happened to the person who died?" Josh asked carefully.

"You don't need to concern yourself with that," Edwards said, slightly ahead of Josh and not turning around.

Josh stopped, folded his arms. Time to dig in his heels. Edwards clearly needed him, so he was going to make the most of it. "I'm not going another step further until you tell me."

With exasperation, Edwards also came to a halt. Sighing, he approached Josh, stopping closer than Josh found comfortable. "You see those two men over there, those agents?"

Josh looked, and saw. They returned the look, without emotion.

"They will carry you to that room and throw you in if you don't comply. Now—" Edwards paused for a second, composing himself.

He was clearly on edge. "Now, I don't want that to happen. I want us to work together, *solve* this together. If I have to force you to do something, that isn't going to be as productive, and goodness knows where we'll end up. So let's do this the right way, okay? You know that makes sense, don't you?"

Josh briefly considered making a break for it, but he knew that he'd simply run in to more agents outside the park. There was no way out, and he decided he'd rather be in control of himself than have two federal agents push him about. After all, he had returned to the park to investigate the room for himself. "I'll do it," he said, "if you tell me why your man died."

Edwards twitched. "Fine," he said, backing up a step. "For the benefit of the mission. When we first approached the room, we felt an energy. Perhaps you also felt it?"

"I did."

"When we sent an agent in to investigate it, however, he was immediately destroyed, burned into cinder by a flash of light. He had no chance."

Josh swallowed. "I'm sorry to hear that."

"It was a defense mechanism, Mr. Reed, a protective device to stop the wrong people entering. But you—you've been in there. It's in our report, confirmed by the site log. You're the only one who has."

"And that's why you need me?"

"Precisely."

Josh realized that although he had agreed to cooperate, he didn't feel quite so comfortable following it through now. "How do I know the same won't happen to me? Something could have changed since I went in."

Edwards was getting twitchy again. Josh could see that he wanted to get moving, but was also trying to hold his impatience down to keep Josh talking. Josh would exploit this as much as he could get away with, if it meant staying alive.

"You won't. The room, it's—" Edwards paused, seemingly unable to put his thoughts into words. "It's *yours*, Mr. Reed. It answers to you."

"Why? How?"

Edwards said nothing.

"I take it you're not going to tell me."

"Once we've confirmed that you can indeed enter the room, I promise to tell you. But not before. I have done something for you already; now you must do something for me."

Josh was running out of stalling tactics. "So now I go back in?"

"That's right."

"And there's no other way to do this?"

"No."

Josh looked back at the two agents, arms crossed and faces crosser. "Okay," he said slowly. "I guess I have no other choice, then."

This pleased Edwards. Together they walked in silence from the park, where more agents gathered outside, turning the public away.

Escape would have been impossible after all. The room beckoned to him, and he was powerless to ignore it.

He barely recognized the site. Inside the entrance was a military checkpoint, guarded by men armed with automatic weaponry. He would have had no hope of breaking in. If he was honest with himself, he was foolish for thinking he even could.

Further into the site were vehicles mounted with satellite dishes, but they weren't press; they were all CIA, presumably sending data back to Langley for study. Cables, thick as an arm, were routed from every direction into one coil, threading down the pit and into the tunnels.

"We've tried every kind of delivery system we can think of," Edwards told Josh as he saw him looking at a row of bomb disposal robots. "If it's flesh, it gets vaporized; if it's electronic, it ceases to respond. We've lost three multi-million dollar robots to that room."

For all the equipment, the site was sparsely populated. It was something of a high-tech ghost town. "Where is everyone?" Josh asked.

"This is the highest level of clearance," Edwards said. "Only the people who absolutely need to be here are here."

They entered the elevator cage and plummeted down into the tunnels. In the great staging area, agents busied themselves viewing data that streamed in from cables writhing deep into the tunnels. On the far side was a makeshift hazmat station where two agents were being hosed off in their bright yellow hazmat suits, having returned from an expedition.

"We don't send people down there unless we have to," Edwards said as the elevator came to a clattering halt. "We don't want to take any more unnecessary risks."

"What about me?" Josh asked as they headed down the steps to what had been the temporary train station, and was now an equipment delivery hub.

"This is necessary," Edwards replied. He led them to a unit in the middle of the chasm where cleaned hazmat suits hung on a railing. "We're going to get outfitted first, and then we'll be heading down into the tunnel. We've got some equipment we'd like you to take in there with you."

"I thought electronic equipment doesn't work in there?"

"I said it doesn't respond," Edwards said, hauling a hazmat suit off the railing and handing it to Josh. "Here, try this on."

Josh took the suit. It was heavy, clammy. "What do you mean it doesn't respond?"

Edwards was now clambering into his own suit. "The remote vehicles we sent in became unresponsive minutes after entry. We couldn't get them back. So we sent one in with a rope tied around it so we could pull it out again."

"And?"

Edwards raised his eyebrows before pulling the suit up onto his shoulders. "What we found was quite remarkable. Do you need help putting your suit on?"

Josh looked at the suit. "I'm not going to wear it," he said, handing it back. "I don't see the point."

"Are you sure?" Edwards said. "I strongly suggest that you do."

"Was the man who got fried wearing one of these?"

Edwards said nothing for a moment, then took the suit back. "Fine. Don't wear the suit." He returned it to the rail, then picked up a facepiece for himself.

"So what was so fascinating about the robot?" Josh asked.

"The data," Edwards said, voice muffled by the facepiece. "It was all there. The room simply prevented it from leaving wirelessly, like a defense mechanism. It's the material that stopped the signal, that crystalline metal—it's organic. It's in the rooms we found before, and it's here, too, Mr. Reed." The excitement in Edwards's voice was building, his face alight with joy. "It was dead in the rooms we found before, but here it's—it's alive."

Josh frowned. "Alive? How?"

Edwards, grinning, said, "There's a lot of questions we don't have the answers to. But all that could change now. The data that came back from the robot was fascinating—and there's so much more to see. We've waited a long time for answers, and now we're finally going to get them. *You're* going to get them."

He indicated for Josh to follow as they headed to the train. It was stationed across the chasm and at the entrance to the tunnel leading to the room. There was another sentry point there, where agents in hazmat suits stopped them.

"Sir, he needs a suit," one of them said to Edwards.

"It's okay," Edwards said. "Step aside."

"But, sir—"

"I said step aside."

The agent did as he was told. "Yes, sir."

They passed through the checkpoint and boarded the train. It was hot, hotter than Josh had ever known it to be. He could see that Edwards was already starting to sweat in that suit.

"Are you ready?" Edwards asked.

"As I'll ever be."

The train moved forward, into the tunnel. They weren't too far in when Josh felt a familiar vibration in his skin. "The energy," he muttered to himself, looking at his hands.

"What's that?" Edwards asked. "I can't hear you very well."

"I said I can feel the energy," Josh repeated. "It's stronger than before."

"Yes, you're right. We've detected readings rising exponentially over the last few hours. Whatever's in that room is expanding."

As they headed further into the tunnel, the vibrations became stronger and stronger until they became almost too uncomfortable to bear. The train was buzzing and clattering as its joints and fixings hummed with the energy, while Josh's own vision began to blur. The train slowed, pulling up at the end of the track.

"It's just you from here on in," Edwards said, voice raised over the vibration. He opened a container on the floor and retrieved some items which he handed to Josh. "A flashlight," he said. "And a video camera. This camera is better than the ones on the robots. We've got the data; now we're hoping to get a better view of what's actually in there."

Josh took the items. "So you just want me to go in and film?"

"Yes. Your report when you return will be more valuable than any other data we can gather from outside."

"Okay, I think I can handle that," Josh said. He sounded calmer than he felt.

"Great. Well—not a moment to lose."

Josh took that as his cue to go. Pocketing the flashlight, he headed down the tunnel, pushing through the wall of energy. *What am I doing?* he wondered to himself. As the tunnel straightened out and the drill came into view at the end of it, he stopped. Edwards couldn't see him from here, so he leaned up against the wall, staring at the end of the tunnel, biting down on his own teeth to stop his jaw from buzzing. All he wanted, more than ever before, was to be with his family. How had he ended up in this mess? Why was he down here? Why was he the only one who could go into that room?

With a sick feeling in his gut, brought on by more than just the energy, he knew his choices were limited. He couldn't stay where he was, and he certainly couldn't go back. The only way for him to go was forward. Swallowing the nausea back down again, he set off toward the room, fighting every breath, forcing every step. Small, loose stones moved across the ground, and rising dust fogged the air. He coughed, drawing more dusty air in, causing him to cough even more.

Eventually he was able to gain control over his breathing, and standing tall, eyes streaming, he pushed on. Closer, he could see that screws on the outer shell of the drill had vibrated loose, and in some cases had fallen out completely. An inspection panel at the rear hung ajar, every nook and cranny peppered with debris.

Josh's hands and feet were turning numb and his fingers were pale; he knew he'd have to be quick. He entered the fresh tunnel on the other side of the drill, the last passage between him and the room.

He could see that the CIA had made a vague effort to support the bare tunnel, but some of it had caved in. Josh climbed over mounds of rock and dirt, sweat pouring from him, the heat and the vibration sapping his energy at a colossal rate. By the time he reached the edge of the tunnel, he wanted to collapse, but by now it was his own intrigue that spurred him on.

The room, the portal through time, was right in front of him. There was a ramp laid down from the edge into the darkness— presumably for the robots—so it'd be easy to get out if he needed to. If he could. He noticed that the vibration had become so strong that it no longer seemed like vibration; if anything it felt like he was floating, his mind separate from his body, hovering in the air. All he needed to do was take one more step forward and he'd be in. Hopefully he wouldn't be fried.

He pulled the flashlight from his pocket, turned it on and pointed it into the darkness.

Then he stepped in.

Chapter 13

The flashlight was powerful, but the beam didn't seem to reach far. Josh took his second step into the room, entering it fully. He held his breath, waiting for the burning flash of electricity to turn him to dust. None came. He took a third step, dancing the flashlight all around to try and get a feel for the scale of the room. He looked down over the edge of the ramp, and his blood froze as the light caught a shape. It was the agent who'd entered, his yellow hazmat suit melted to his body, burned and blistered and fused into one congealed mess. Josh looked away, his stomach already delicate. He turned his attention to the inside wall, tracking the flashlight along it and up to the ceiling.

But the ceiling never came. The flashlight played and danced along the shimmering crystalline material, glinting with almost holographic veracity, but as he went higher with it, it soon weakened and rolled off to nothing. This room was at least twice as high as the staging area. The top surface couldn't have been buried much more than fifty or so meters below the surface—maybe less.

And then he had a thought: perhaps that was why Central Park was where it was? The skyscrapers were built on areas of the tough Manhattan schist, he knew that, but perhaps engineers had tested this ground before, found this material and decided not to build on it, creating the park instead? How close they could have been to unearthing this place, choosing instead to ignore it because it wasn't the schist they knew and trusted.

He continued on slowly, the ramp bowing under his weight. At the bottom, three robots sat motionless, their batteries long run down. They were eerie to see under the flashlight, their metal parts shining and their plastic and rubber ones dull. Josh turned on the camera and started recording as he sidestepped around them. He kept alert, still pointing his flashlight every way, searching but not knowing what he was searching for.

Floating forward, carried by the energy, he walked into the glow of his flashlight, revealing more and more of the room. At first it seemed like the crystalline material would go on forever, but as the energy amped up even more, something began to emerge from the shadows. The reflection of the flashlight caught, shimmering back. Josh focused the beam, drawing himself toward it, drifting on the wave of energy.

It was a sphere, large, reflective and bright, but it wasn't convex as he was expecting, but *concave*. Three stories tall, it reflected the world back in on itself, flipped upside down. Josh circled it. It was like staring into the mouth of a great chrome creature, insides frozen, then swirling, then frozen. Josh swallowed.

This was what Edwards was looking for. This was the reason he himself had died and come back again. This was his second chance.

Cautiously, so very cautiously, he approached it. As he did, he could feel its power rise, but it wasn't uncomfortable any more; it was familiar, warming—hopeful. It was a hot shower, soothing him—not just his mortal body but his soul as well. Josh felt like it knew him, understood him. He could trust it, and it him.

He stood beneath it as it towered overhead. The footage he'd already got would give Edwards everything he'd need and more, but he realized he could go one better: he could try and push the camera into the sphere, get a glimpse of what was on the other side.

Would that even be possible? Perhaps he could test the sphere first. Pointing the flashlight in all directions, he searched for something he could throw, but there was nothing. The ground was uneven, but none of it was loose. Then he remembered the gravel he'd picked up earlier. He patted his pocket—it was still there. Its presence was unnerving; it felt like a lifetime had passed since he had last entered this room, yet theoretically it had only been a few hours.

Feeling for a good-sized fragment, he rolled it between his fingers as he backed up a few steps and took aim. Then he hurled the stone, hard, right into the epicenter of the sphere. There was a ripple as the stone disappeared beneath the glossy surface, a pulse of energy that rolled through Josh like a wave, and then—nothing. No clatter as it flew out the other side and returned to the ground, nothing at all. Silence. Just silence and energy.

Primed, Josh took the video camera in a one-handed grip, then approached the sphere. Its chrome surface swarmed above him, ready to swallow him up. Josh's chest, deep and distant, sent flushes through his body that made his mouth dry and his hands clammy. He adjusted his grip to get a better hold of the camera's smooth, plastic body.

Inches away, he considered backing down. His calm had gone, fear and doubt eating it away in great tearing chunks. What kept him moving forward was his desire to know, his *need* to know. He was in here not for Edwards, but for himself. He needed to know the truth. He needed to know that what had happened to him was real.

Slowly, carefully, he pushed the camera at arm's length into the surface of the sphere. At first the sphere resisted, tension in its skin, but with more effort the tension broke, gently sucking the camera in, the hum of energy growing as the lens pushed deeper. Josh held it there, heart thumping. He didn't know how long to shoot for, but he felt like he needed to keep the camera there for as long as possible, as still as possible.

After a time, he retracted the camera from the silvery wall. It took a little effort, particularly in the last few moments where the suction of the sphere clung on to the device, but it popped out with a tug. Josh staggered back a few steps. The camera seemed fine; he looked up at the sphere, and it was unchanged. One minute frozen, the next, a swirling mass. His heart was calming, and he licked his lips. It was time to go. He did not want to outstay his welcome.

He walked back to the exit ramp, guided by the flashlight to the bright hole in the wall through which he'd entered. Having the sphere to his back made him nervous, but at the same time he felt sad to be leaving it behind. It made him feel… special. Outside of this room he was no one; inside, he was unique. As he hit the foot of the ramp, he turned around to see it one last time, but the flashlight just wasn't powerful enough to pick it up this far away.

With a sigh, he scaled the ramp, thumbing the stop button on the camera. Once he was out of the room, he decided to take a look at the footage. Excitement crept up in him, anticipation at what he'd see. He danced over the uneven ground and out into the fluorescent light of the reinforced tunnel, slowing to watch the clip back on the camera's folding screen. He fast-forwarded the footage until—there it was. The intensity of the sphere hadn't been captured by the camera under the beam of his flashlight, but its immense size was apparent. So too was the strange concave illusion. He could see the beam of the flashlight skipping over the sphere's surface, pinprick sharp as the sphere remained still, smeared and tubular as it distorted. Watching it over, Josh got chills. He held his breath as the camera jerked, knowing that he had just thrown the stone. He couldn't see the stone, but he could see the ripple in the sphere's surface. He also saw something that he'd missed at the time: the sphere seemed to glow brighter for a second. It could have simply been the flashlight moving, but that didn't seem right. It was as though the sphere had emitted a flash of its own light. Energy he couldn't see with his eyes that had been picked up by the camera, perhaps.

Then came the moment he'd been so desperate to see. The camera wobbled as he readjusted his grip, then the view filled with silver as it probed toward the concave outer skin. When it hit, all went black, and for a moment Josh was bitterly disappointed. But then, as he knew he was pushing the camera in deeper, pushing through the resistance, something spectacular happened. The screen lit up in a rainbow of color, swirling and strobing, bands of rich reds, greens and blues slipping up and down with such intensity that it flashed completely white in places. It was a kaleidoscope of patterns and colors, a world unrecognizable to the visible spectrum. Staring hard at it, Josh thought he could make out shapes—people perhaps—but with a blink it was gone. The screen was black again, empty. Noise danced in the shadows.

But then there was a light. A single, bright, moonlike light that danced across the frame, then froze in the top right. Josh paused, and zoomed in. It flickered between frames, bright and without detail, but Josh felt sure he knew what it was. It was somehow familiar, yet he could not put his finger on it.

He played on, and within moments the light had disappeared, the rainbow pattern jumping into view again, swirling fast as the camera was withdrawn. Then it was back in the room, silver sphere reflecting back, upside down and heavily distorted. Josh hit stop.

Making sure he had a good hold of the camera and its precious footage, he headed back through the tunnel, following the curve around to the station. The energy, compared to its strength in the room, felt almost weak now, even though it was still flowing through him. But that thought fell by the wayside as he realized that the train was gone, and so was Edwards.

"Hello?" he called out, but there was no response. A cold chill ran through him; something wasn't right. As he continued on, the fluorescent tubes above began to dim, and after a few seconds, had gone out completely. It was so dark that Josh couldn't see his own nose, so he switched the flashlight on and followed its glow. The construction company had probably switched off the power, knowing the takeover was going to be long-term. The CIA agents would need to bring their own generators down.

It would be a long trip back to the staging area on foot and in the dark, but there didn't seem to be any other option. On he trudged, muddy, slippy ground glossy under the harsh flashlight. The tunnels felt so different like this; larger, emptier. Walking toward the black was not an unusual thing for a tunnel engineer to have to do, but under the circumstances, and despite the humidity, Josh's blood still ran cold. He would be glad to be out of there.

The sound of his own feet splish-splashing through the muddied concrete got him into a rhythm, pacing him along as the meters rolled by. There couldn't be much longer to go.

And there wasn't. He could hear the echo of his footsteps getting broader before he saw the edge of the tunnel as it breached the staging area, and he could see before he'd even arrived that the power was out there, too. As his footsteps were the only thing he could hear, he presumed that the agents had all been evacuated until power could be restored. Although he felt a little peeved at being left behind, Josh understood why they'd done it: he was used to being down here, had done the emergency drills. They had been drafted in from an office, as green to the underworld as they come.

In the staging area—an enormous space that seemed even more huge with the lights out—Josh could see a faint wash of light peeking in from the elevator shaft on the other side. The elevator itself would probably be out of action, but there was an emergency ladder that ran alongside it, so he pointed himself toward the shaft and made his way over there. Equipment lay abandoned around the place; the evacuation had been quick, unexpected. A hazmat suit peered out from a muddy puddle. Josh looked away; it gave him the creeps.

At the foot of the ladder, he pocketed the flashlight, but had to leave the video camera behind. It was too bulky; he'd need to get a bag or something to carry it up in.

The climb up the long elevator shaft was an effort, but the bright white light above kept Josh pushing on. Occasionally he'd lean back against the cage to catch his breath and let the burning in his palms and the cramp in his forearms recede. As he progressed, the distances got shorter and the breaks got longer, and before the last push, Josh wasn't sure he was going to make it at all. He needed to get fitter, he decided. He probably wouldn't pass the evacuation testing next year if he was still in this state.

But push on he did, and soon Josh was outside, blinking in the sun. After the darkness of the tunnels, it took him a moment to regain his vision as he shielded his eyes and looked around. As sight returned, he saw that all the CIA trucks had gone. The sentry post was abandoned, the gate to the site ajar. Around the site, plants had overtaken the mud and rubble, as well as equipment left behind by the agents, growth that swamped the landscape until it was unrecognizable. Weirdest of all, though, was the sound. This was Manhattan, one of the busiest hubs in the world, a place where silence was unheard of.

Yet, right now, silence was all Josh could hear.

Chapter 14

Josh looked right up at the sun, as if expecting to look down again
and see everything as normal. But it wasn't. It should have been
evening—his watch agreed—but it was clearly early afternoon. The
site should have been neat, with agents occupying the area, but it
wasn't.

A bird tweeted; the day was calm. At first Josh was fixed to the
spot, not knowing what to do next. His mind hissed with static,
unable to comprehend the situation. A breeze chilled him, and he
realized he wouldn't be able to stay there all day, so he decided he
would see what was going on outside the site, see if he could make
sense of what was happening.

He clumsily picked his way across the uneven ground,
occasionally stumbling over a bushel of grass or a piece of
equipment hidden by foliage. The hinges on the gate had rusted stiff,
but Josh was able to pull it open enough to squeeze out.

The street beyond was quiet, with no sign of life other than the
singing of unseen birds. Cars were parked, shutters were open, but

there was nobody there. Cracks in the road gave way to blossoming greenery, the sidewalks in an even worse state of repair. Vines crawled up the buildings either side. A tree had forced its way up through an area to Josh's right, the roots lifting through the slabs and spreading up into a canopy that cast a cold shadow over him. That tree had to be at least thirty years old—maybe older.

Rust had eaten away at shop fronts and cars, their shapes still recognizable but their condition unsalvageable. There was an aged stillness to it all that Josh found unsettling. He pulled out his cell and saw what he was afraid to see: he had no service. He tried dialing Georgie anyway, and then Lionel, but the calls wouldn't connect. As far as he could tell, he was the only person in Manhattan, a thought that put lead in his belly.

He walked toward the subway for lack of any other ideas, peering in through the still intact windows of the cars as he passed them. To his surprise, their interiors tended to be in a reasonable condition— bar the bleached fabric and light dusting of mold—and Josh wondered if they were still drivable despite their appearance. He tried the door of one; it was locked. The next car was open, but with no keys. The third car, parked up on the sidewalk at an angle, had its door open, its interior in a far worse state than the first two. It still had its keys hanging from the ignition, however, so Josh gave them a twist. Nothing. Battery had probably given up a long time ago.

He was getting hungry, so he stopped at a small convenience market to see if they had anything that might still be good. He used his flashlight to illuminate the space, warm and musty and dark. The shelves were still full, although cardboard packaging sagged, fruit and vegetables were nothing more than black slime, and bags of bread were swollen with gas. Josh rummaged through, picking his way across the dusty floor, holding his nose to keep back the smell of decay. The newspapers and magazines—or what rotten fragments were left of them—looked unchanged from when Josh had seen them last. There was even a headline he recognized. People must have left in a hurry.

There were some cans of fruit toward the rear, and Josh grabbed a couple, retreating back outside. He was glad to be out of there: it gave him the chills. The cans had pull-tabs, so sitting down on a wall, he peeled the lid back on one and ate greedily from it, tipping the contents into his mouth. He drank the sugary syrup too, draining the can of its last drop and setting it beside him on the wall. He pocketed the other can for later.

Feeling better, energized, he was able to turn his thoughts to his situation. Being in that room, it had pushed him forward through time… or had it held him back? His brain hurt thinking about it. Whatever had happened, Manhattan must have been evacuated a long time ago. Perhaps if he crossed over the Queensboro Bridge and onto Long Island, he'd find more answers.

With a renewed vigor, he headed east toward the bridge, navigating his way through the overgrown and uneven streets. Shop windows, filled with ageing goods, doors still open, passed by, as did empty apartments with windows dark and fronts crawling with ivy. Progress was slow, the sidewalk crumbling and the roads clogged with abandoned cars.

As he walked, afternoon settled in fast, the shadows lengthening in front of him and the sky turning golden. But something was wrong. When he'd emerged from the elevator, the day had appeared to be breaching afternoon—now, only about an hour later, the afternoon was almost gone. Time seemed to be moving… too quickly.

He continued on, a rumble of panic deep in his gut picking up his pace. Walking faster, occasionally checking behind him, he noticed something peculiar through the valley of high rise buildings: the sun was visibly slipping through the sky, down toward darkness. The air began to cool, and he shivered; soon it would be night.

The sun… he thought. *Something is wrong with the sun…*

The flash of a memory made him twitch.

Josh sprinted the next block as fast as he could, striding over cars in leaps and bounds, pumped with the energy from the fruit and the adrenaline coursing in his veins. Slipping ever faster, the sun vanished into night. Josh stopped, lungs heaving for oxygen. He stared dumbfounded at the star-speckled sky, rich and bright without the city lights to wash it out. "It's when I move," he wheezed to himself. "The sun moves when *I* move."

The room. The sphere.

Josh's thoughts were halted by the sudden flash of a memory: he was on a plane, looking out of the window, the sun leaving streaks across his retinas. But the memory was hazy, and he couldn't piece it together fully. He thought hard, digging as deep as he could, searching for an answer that teased him with its proximity. The more he thought, the more his throat closed up, a lingering sense of death and fire prickling his brow with sweat despite the cold night air.

He shivered again, this time partially from fear. Dark shadows loomed, their contents invisible. With no idea what creatures had become the new owners of the night—and not wanting to know—Josh jogged on, against the burning will of his lungs, until the sun picked up ahead of him. Morning light gave him the chance to think again, and he continued on, walking slowly around cars as he did.

On the plane, the sun hadn't always moved quickly. It was normal at first. The sphere—perhaps drilling into the room had caused its power to leak? The energy was stronger when he had gone back to it. Perhaps that energy distorted time somehow—made the sun move faster? But how? And why?

He continued on to the Queensboro Bridge, the sun looping over him and out of sight a few times more. During the moments of night he ran to bring the sun back up again, and soon he was exhausted. Traffic, frozen in a rusting stasis, built up as he got closer. Soon the cars were mounted up on the pavements as well, doors flung open. An old shoe, rotten and sagged, stood propped up against the curb. Its owner must not have had the time to retrieve it.

Careful not to cut himself on any of the rusted metal, Josh climbed up and over the cars that blocked his path. His muscles ached and his stomach pined for something proper to eat. He wouldn't last much longer. As he arrived at the Queensboro Bridge, the sun having completed a few more laps and sitting somewhere around late afternoon, Josh saw that it was a logjam of cars. He considered negotiating his way through, but he knew it would take him hours, and he'd have no way of running through the night.

As he stood to contemplate his next move, he noticed something else. If he stayed where he was, time seemed to move normally. He tried walking back toward Central Park, back toward the sphere, and still time seemed to move normally. It was walking *away* from the sphere that accelerated time. A horrible thought hit him: how far was the sphere's reach, and how far ahead in time would he have to travel to get there? Years? Decades? *Centuries?* Would... would Georgie and Joseph still be alive?

The thought made his stomach knot. He had to turn his mind away from it, for now at least; to dwell on it would be his undoing. Right now, his survival was paramount. To start, he would occupy himself with figuring out what he was going to do next.

The last twilight rays shone across the East River, and Josh could feel the weight of sleep clawing him down. He could try and make it back to the site, but the thought of clambering over all those cars made him want to die. If he hadn't had to climb the ladder out of the staging area, he'd probably have been all right, but he had, so he wasn't.

Continuing on wasn't an option, either. Even if he wasn't about to pass out from exhaustion, he had no idea how far he'd need to travel before he reached civilization, or even normality.

A snap: *El Paso, that's where I was flying.* The memory bloomed in full, rich color, but carrying a disheartening message: if it had been like that in El Paso, he'd have to travel two thousand miles at least.

The other option was to go back to the site, back to the sphere. Really, it was the only option. Anything else filled him with a hollow sense of despair. But first—sleep.

Picking his way along 2nd Avenue, Josh scanned for an appropriate place to spend the night. Buildings and rooms wouldn't be scarce, even unlocked ones, but Josh wasn't thrilled with the idea of fumbling his way through a dark apartment block in the middle of the night, and preferred the idea of locking himself in something like a truck.

The ideal candidate was parked half a block away in a line of traffic. It was a big semi, hauling an open trailer loaded with spoil. It could well have had something to do with the East Side Access. In fact it was very likely. With darkness nearing, and feeling the cold and fear settling in, Josh hurriedly climbed up to the cab and swung the door—which was thankfully unlocked—open.

It wasn't too bad inside: the interior had no mold and only smelled a little. Shining his flashlight in the back, he saw that it was empty, so he pulled the door shut and flicked the lock. Then he checked the other door to make sure that was locked, too. From this vantage point, he could see quite far around himself, the last hint of day picking out the cars in front and behind with a deep, almost black, purple. As long as he stayed where he was, night should be as usual.

The back quite conveniently had a small cot already made up—one reason why he'd chosen the semi—and he retreated into it and pulled the curtains shut behind him, before having a closer look at his temporary accommodation. The walls had posters up on them: a band that probably played music far heavier than Josh would have enjoyed, judging by the fonts and color palette, as well as several topless pin-ups. They caught Josh off-guard; that was the last thing he wanted to think about.

With nothing else to do, Josh dug out a blanket from the box under the cot, wrapped himself up in it, lay down and tried to go to sleep. At first he struggled to keep his mind from swirling with thoughts of his family and everything that could have happened to them, but soon exhaustion got the better of him and took him into unconsciousness.

He awoke in the pitch black a while later, his stomach hurting. In his sleepy confusion, at first he couldn't work out why his stomach ached, but then he realized: he was hungry. Awake, he sat up and retrieved the other can of fruit, which he ate quickly. His hunger, although not satiated, was reduced, and he climbed back into his cot. Just as he got comfortable—if a little cold—he needed the bathroom.

"Shit," he said, sitting up again. With the flashlight shielded to avoid light escaping the cab, he looked around for a bottle or something he could go in, but couldn't find one. He'd have to go outside. "Shit," he mumbled again.

Flashlight off, he searched up and down the street by the light of the moon to see if there was anything else out there. As his eyes adjusted to the darkness and detail began to resolve itself, he convinced himself that he was alone. Quietly, he unlocked the door and opened it, climbing out onto the step. He did his business from there, the spatter of urine on the cold street below painfully loud in the quiet of night. He willed it to come out faster, until finally—finally—he was finished. He zipped up and was about to retreat into the cab when he heard a noise.

It sounded like snuffling, the padding of paws, too—big paws. Without another moment's hesitation, Josh retreated into the cab, pulling the door shut as quietly as he could and locking it behind him. He stayed down and out of sight for a while, until eventually building the courage to look out of the window. Peering in the direction that the noise had come from, he watched the shadows, but he could see nothing. Opening the window a crack, he listened for the sound again. After a moment of held breath, he heard it, and looked for the source, searching for movement. Then he saw it.

Haggard and thin, the big creature wore a coat of fur that was patchy in places. It lumbered along, sniffing in cracks and gaps, searching for food. Occasionally it would stop, licking the side of a car or a patch on the sidewalk. It was a bear, full grown and padding along 2nd Avenue, and Josh was stunned. He was even more so when a cub, small and frail, tottered along out of the shadows after its mother. It wobbled unsteadily, it too looking malnourished.

Josh watched the pair as they wandered down the street and around the corner. He didn't breathe until they'd gone. Window wound back up, he retreated to his cot, pulled the curtains shut and fell quickly into an exhausted, dreamless sleep.

Chapter 15

The curtains did a good job of keeping the morning sun out of the cab, and by the time Josh woke up it was already blooming midway up in the sky. He felt surprisingly refreshed, and even more surprisingly, he felt calm. He knew what he needed to do.

The sun bleached the cabin as he pulled the curtains back fully, and he stretched out the tightness in his muscles from climbing that damn ladder. He would have to go back down it again, but that would be easier, thankfully. The pit of his stomach rolled with nervousness at the thought of approaching the sphere again.

First, he needed to find some food. His stomach growled at an alarming volume, and he could feel the onset of cramp beckoning his body to fall into spasms. Being well-rested, he also needed to be well-fed before attempting the climb into the pit again, or else he risked falling and dying, or worse—falling and getting seriously injured. He would lie there in agony while the crows slowly pecked the flesh from his bones, and that would be how he ended. He shuddered.

Scanning the road from the cab, Josh could see no sign of the bear and its cub. At first he thought he might have dreamed it, but a rather anemic and dehydrated heap of droppings on the sidewalk below indicated otherwise. Saying farewell to his small fortress, Josh hopped down from the cab and pointed himself back toward the site. As he'd expected, time seemed unaffected as he drew closer to the room.

A good night's sleep meant a fresh mind, and he thought as he walked, hoping to bring sense to this otherwise senseless situation. He remembered a documentary he'd seen about space-time, and how the universe was connected. The video had shown a big, elasticated sheet, representing space, and the tutor had dropped ball bearings of various sizes onto it. The sheet had sagged and the ball bearings were drawn together. The tutor had explained that the dips in the sheet, the visual representation of gravity, had also been dips in *time*, that areas of high gravity also had a big impact on the way time worked, too. Just like a black hole, he remembered.

Perhaps that's what this sphere did. It somehow affected space-time, plunged deep into its fabric. The closer he got, the more distorted time became.

The room—the crystalline material, Josh realized. *That was supposed to contain it.* When Josh had cracked the room open, the effects had spilled out, expanding across the world. What was clear was that this—this *sphere*—was not here by accident. Edwards had said there had been other rooms, although they were dead, lifeless, destroyed. Why was this one different?

The other question Josh mulled over as he trundled down 61st, looking for that convenience store, was—why him? Was he the first to ever go in there? Did his presence somehow activate the sphere? The room wouldn't let anyone else in, or so Edwards said. It was connected to him somehow. But why?

And what about its creator? What had happened to them? Who were they? There was the possibility that the sphere was government-owned, funded, constructed, whatever. But Edwards, he'd denied it, and Josh believed him. He seemed too worked up about it to be lying.

What about the Mayans, he thought, *didn't they have advanced technology or something?* After a moment's hazy wondering, he came to the conclusion that the Mayan theory was probably just something misremembered from a late-night B-movie he'd drunkenly watched.

The thoughts got wilder and wilder. Josh had never really given much consideration to the possibility of alien life, and for all he had cared, there was none, but now… now he had to face the very real possibility that this sphere was not of earthly creation.

So many questions. Would he ever get answers? Would he wake up in the hospital and find that this was all just some comatose hallucination? He tried to think back further, to when they'd first discovered the room, tried to remember if he'd fallen, banged his head. Gas, there was gas… or what he'd thought was gas. All of a sudden his brain didn't seem to have untangled quite as much as he'd hoped. What he did know for sure, however, was that he was hungry, and that he had arrived at the convenience store.

This time he figured he'd take more supplies, just in case. He found an old shoulder bag behind the counter, dusted it off and shook out the spiders, then began to fill it with cans of this and that, boxes of crackers and other items he assumed would still be edible. He also found some extra batteries for his flashlight, but none of them worked.

Figures, he thought. The possibility of the sphere doing absolutely nothing when he stepped into it lurched his stomach, which then did a double loop-the-loop at the thought of how much more time would have gone by during his period back in that crystalline room. The epicenter, that's where the space-time tunnel bored its way back to the past. The room, the area immediately surrounding it, that was the precipice, the edge of the waterfall over which time plunged. Ten minutes by it had advanced him several decades; he could not afford to lose that much time again. It was a one-way trip.

Josh was so hungry that he ate in the store, despite the smell and the dust. The crackers he ate were dry and stuck to his throat, but they went down okay with some more canned fruit. He ate to be full—but not too full; he had to walk and climb after all—zipped up the bag, slung it over his shoulders, and exited the store.

He froze.

Across the road, on the sidewalk, was the bear. Under the clear light of day, Josh confirmed what he thought he'd seen yesterday, that it was gaunt and haggard. Hungry. He could not see the cub. The bear watched him, then snorted. Josh backed up a step, which made the bear move one pace toward him. Josh froze; so did the bear.

Was it going to attack? Did it have the strength? He was well aware that he was a walking slab of meat to this bear, which considered him with a sideways eye like it meant to put him in its stomach. It snorted again, and took another lumbering, ponderous step forward. Josh backed away, through the shop door. It was a single door, probably too narrow for the bear to enter. It took another step forward, leaning to sniff in Josh's direction. If the bear got any closer, he'd be trapped. If the bear was hungry, it would probably wait him out, guarding the entrance until Josh finally had to leave.

Easing the door shut, Josh slid the bolts top and bottom, just in case. Then, scrambling his way back through the store, negotiating a spilled basket full of decimated goods, he found the rear entrance and tried it. Locked. *Shit.* There were stairs to the next floor, but that was no use. The front really was his only way out. Quietly, he made his way back again. The bear was at the front door, stood on hind legs, sniffing at the vent above.

"A bear in Manhattan," Josh whispered to himself. "What next?" He laughed, taking himself by surprise. What next indeed. He looked around; if the bear was hungry, he could give it food, or at least something tastier than him. He picked up the basket, emptied out the waste, and went about gathering items he thought the bear might like. Meats, cheese, fruit—they were all out of the question, but there were some packaged treats that seemed okay. Probably not the healthiest choice for it, but beggars couldn't be choosers, and right now, Josh didn't exactly have the luxury of choice. Once the basket was full, he found a clear space and emptied it all out. Then he opened the packaging and started loading the basket with the unwrapped food.

It wasn't enough. He gathered some more items from the higher shelves, reaching for the surplus, when, perched on a stool, he missed his footing, grabbing at the shelf and pulling it and its contents from the wall. He and they came crashing down, the shelf landing on his leg. He yelped in pain, which in turn made the bear slap its weight against the glass. It roared and pounded, the entire store front buckling under its weight.

Wincing from the pain, Josh scrambled up, quickly checked his leg—it was bruised, but didn't seem broken—gathered up as many boxes as he could and hobbled over to the basket. He tore the packaging open, scooping out the sweet snacks and loading the basket with them. The bear roared again, but dropped to all fours, peering in through the window at him.

Basket full, Josh heaved it up and took it around the back, to the stairs he'd found while investigating the back door. He went up a flight, into the darkness of the second floor hallway, heart pounding in his ears. It wasn't particularly noisy downstairs, but it was eerily quiet up here. The only light he had to go on was whatever escaped through the cracks below the doors along the hallway, which were all shut. Not wanting to risk wearing his flashlight down unnecessarily, he let his eyes adjust while he tried to get his bearings. The stairs had twisted him around, so it took him a moment to think which way would take him to the front of the building. He hobbled down the hallway, trying to take shallow breaths as he kicked up dust, heading for the door at the end. *That should be the one.*

The handle was cold, and Josh turned it slowly. He didn't know why he was being so cautious, but he felt he ought to anyway. Easing the door ajar, light flooded out, and he blinked to readjust. Then he entered fully, and looked around the room. It was a bedroom, neatly made, nicely decorated—or had been—with a chair in the corner. In that chair were the remains of a person. They had not fully decomposed, years of sun and dry air mummifying their skin into a parchment-like sheath over their bones. Some fragments had torn away, but on the whole they were intact, covered with dusty, stained clothes and an apron.

The storeowner. Must have stayed when everyone else left. Josh wondered how many others might have stayed, why they hadn't joined the exodus. On closer inspection, he saw a pill bottle on the floor beside the body, covered in dust. They'd taken their own life. They couldn't bear to leave it all behind, except to move on to death. It made Josh feel sad to think that someone had needed to make that decision. An image of Georgie flashed in his mind.

He broke away from the corpse—and his thoughts—turning his attention back to his current predicament. The window was easy enough to open, if a little stiff, and he looked down onto the street to see that the bear had taken to lying down outside the front of the store. It was leaning against the door; was it doing that on purpose? Did it know it was trapping him? He didn't really want to find out.

From the basket he picked out a small cake, something to get the bear started. He took aim out of the window and threw, hoping to land it near the bear—but not *too* far away. Instead, he hit the bear smack on its head, and the bear skipped back and let out a startled roar. The cake fell off, but the bear didn't notice it, too busy searching out the mysterious attacker. It roared again as Josh selected another cake, taking better care in his aim this time, factoring the weight of the treat into his throw. It sailed downward, landing in front of the bear, catching its attention.

Cautiously, the bear approached it, sniffing. It got within inches, snuffling loudly enough for Josh to hear from his lofty vantage point—and then it turned away.

"Oh, come on…!" Josh groaned to himself.

The bear, a few steps away from the cake, turned back. It considered the cake from a distance, sniffing the air, pawing at the ground. Josh willed it nearer with his mind, holding his breath and staring unblinkingly until—at last—it edged a little closer. Its neck was stretched right out to get a good scent without walking any further, and then Josh heard it smacking its lips. It roared, bucking onto its hind legs, as if challenging the cake. The cake did not respond, so the bear calmed, then edged another step closer.

"Go on…" Josh commanded breathlessly. "Eat the Goddamn cake…"

Another step closer, then another, and the bear was on top of the cake. In a sniff and a swallow, the cake was gone. Then it noticed the first, and gulped that down too. Josh reacted quickly, taking advantage of the bear's hunt for more to eat. He hoisted the basket onto the window ledge and started hurling the contents out into the street, trying to create a trail away from the shop. The bear was cautious again, but soon was eating as fast as Josh could throw. Josh realized that he wasn't going to have enough time to run back downstairs and get out if the bear continued eating so quickly.

There was only one thing left to do: Josh picked up the basket, leaning it into his shoulder, took a breath and launched the entire thing out of the window. It didn't go far, but it went far enough, and it landed with a smash and a clatter, spilling its contents everywhere. The impact made the bear jump, but the smell emanating from the sweet, mushy pile was too great for it to ignore. It skipped the rest of the trail and went straight to it. This was it—this was Josh's opportunity to get out.

Ignoring the pain flaring in his leg, he bolted from the room, along the hall and down the stairs, snatching up his bag along the way. He ran for the exit—almost throwing himself to the floor as he slipped on a loose can—jumping straight for the bolts and flinging the door wide open. His leg was fire, but he gritted his teeth and went for it, the bear with its back to him. He ran as hard as he could, not turning around. The bear cried out, but it wasn't a roar, it was a long, mournful sound—but still Josh did not look back. He ran until he reached a blockade of cars mounted on the sidewalk, and quickly climbing over them, he took the opportunity to glance back over his shoulder.

The bear had not made chase; it had been joined by its cub, and both of them were eating from the basket. For now, Josh was in no danger, so he reduced his run to a quick walk, trying to keep the weight off his leg, and continued on toward the East Side Access.

Chapter 16

The walk back, slowed by the pain in his leg, took Josh a lot longer than he'd hoped. He had to stop occasionally to let the pain ease off, but he finally made it back to the site. It was a relief to get there, but he still had the ladder climb to make. He gritted his teeth, stepped on to the first rung with his good leg, then heaved his bad one on too. It was painful, but it was bearable. Holding his weight on his good leg, he shifted the bad to the next rung down, then hung his weight from his arms while his good leg caught up. The pain while he swapped legs was immense, but he did it. One down, a million to go. It may as well have been. He looked down. It was a long way into the darkness, and his head swam.

He repeated the process a few more times over, skipping himself down one rung at a time, and soon his arms were straining against his weight. He couldn't keep it up. His hands were bordering on cramp, and if that set in, he'd be done. There was only one option, and that was to lean on his bad leg and go down alternate rungs, rather than one at a time. He took a few quick preparatory breaths, then lowered himself to the next rung, leaning on his bad leg. He cried out, the pain shooting needles up his thigh, but he was okay. *It's just pain*, he told himself. *I can push through it.*

And push through it he did for the next rung, and the next, and the next. His head was light from the agony, which had become constant, and he let himself climb on autopilot until—

"Shit!"

His hands slipped on a rung, and he tumbled backward, fingers clawing at the air. For a brief second he was weightless, silence ringing in his ears. Then he crashed back against the cage, chest pounding fit to burst, gulping oxygen like it was the last he'd ever breathe. The cage had saved him. All of a sudden, everything felt very real. Clarity had come to him in an instant.

He steadied himself on the ladder, taking a firm hold, and instructed himself to pay more attention. The adrenaline dump had reduced the pain enough to get moving again, and he focused on his rhythm, making sure he kept hold of the ladder at all times. As the heat and pain began to build again, he realized he only had about a floor left to go, and he hurried down the last few rungs, cramp and pain forgotten. To touch down on solid earth was a blessing, and he collapsed to the ground, sitting in the mud, catching his breath and letting the agony fade a little. A cool draft blew down the shaft, and he let it evaporate the sweat from his brow. It was a small relief, but a welcome one nonetheless.

When he felt ready to go on, he took a can of fruit from his bag and drank the juice, leaving the fruit behind for later. Then he remembered the camera he'd left at the foot of the elevator shaft, and stuffed that into the bag as well. Zipped up and ready to go, he flicked on the flashlight and headed into the darkness. Unable to see the right tunnel from there, he picked his way across, looking for equipment and other objects that he recognized. There was that hazmat suit in the puddle; he was going the right way.

Soon he found himself at the sentry point, and the tunnel loomed ahead, a dark hole in an already dark cavern. Somehow it seemed blacker than black deep down inside.

Fighting every instinct not to enter, Josh pushed on, heading into the depths. The slippery ground made it hard to keep steady, and the constant sliding made his leg ache badly. But there was no going back—only forward. Every time he felt a wobble as his soles lost grip, he righted himself and redoubled his efforts. He'd get back to that room, back to the sphere. The alternative didn't bear thinking about. He certainly didn't want to spend a night or two down here while he waited for his leg to ease up, and he definitely didn't want to be wandering God knows how far across America to find civilization—if it even still existed.

Step by step he trudged through the tunnel, listening. At first he wasn't sure if it was just his imagination, his blood rumbling behind his ears, but then he was sure—he could feel it, the energy. He was getting close. By the time he reached the end of the track, he could feel that detachment, that numbing vibration that separated his mind from his body.

Josh tried his best to push the nervous bile back down his throat. The tunnel rounded, and soon Josh's flashlight picked out the drill. It was rusted and old, a relic. That was not a concern for him, but what lay beyond was. The tunnel that extended from the drill into the room had partially collapsed. Josh took a spade abandoned near the drill and approached the collapse. He prodded it gingerly, listening for signs of any further structural failure, and when there were none, started digging. Praying the collapse was only a few feet deep, he stuck the spade in at the top and started to pull material out. As he did, more spilled in from a pocket above the tunnel, and for at least thirty minutes he was clearing fresh spoil as it was added to the pile.

God, thirty minutes, he thought, checking his watch, catching his breath. He tried not to think how far into the future he'd been slung, focusing on the digging instead. But he was hot, doubly so because of the work, and it was making him sweat profusely and his leg throb. It was hard going.

What made things worse was that the flashlight, wedged into the wall, seemed to be getting dimmer. *Did it just flicker?* Panicking, Josh redoubled his efforts; he knew he didn't have much time left before all he'd have was darkness.

Continuing to dig, he finally cleared all the new spoil and actually started to tunnel through. He burrowed as high as he could in the hope that much of the tunnel's ceiling was still intact. The CIA's attempts to support it clearly hadn't worked, but he hoped that not all of it had failed. He would crawl through, that would save time, so the tunnel would only need to be narrow.

By the time he was reaching in with the spade as far as he could, he was still not through. There was only one thing for it: he'd have to clear the rest by hand. He clamped the flashlight between his teeth, tied his bag to his ankle and climbed head first into the hole. The spoil was a mixture of damp earth and hard, fragmented schist, so it simultaneously soaked through his clothes and dug into his skin. It scratched and clawed at him as he shuffled in, the tunnel barely wider than he was, arms stretched out in front, dragging himself along. It was hot, musty, damp. Close. The flashlight, in his mouth, spilled light everywhere but where he wanted it, but he did his best to guide himself forward. There wasn't really enough room to lift his head anyway, so he had to work by feel alone.

He scooped the dirt out with his hands, as much as he could manage. He tossed fistfuls toward himself, trying to spread it out thin so he could still fit past. It splattered his face. He continued scrambling through, fingers burning wet as mud and blood became one.

It will be over soon, he told himself.

He could only clear as far as he could reach, kicking himself forward to start digging again. Every time he did, his leg cried out, but by this point he was in pain all over, and he didn't really notice. He just wanted to be out, or be dead. One of those two would happen, he'd make sure of it. The end couldn't be far.

Then he heard a rumble. He paused, holding his breath to listen. It swelled above the vibration, and then it died away. It was distant, but it was enough of a warning for Josh to get a move on. He scrabbled at the spoil as fast as he could, grinding his fingers away at soil and rock. The rumble sounded again, louder, closer. He could feel earth falling around his legs. A chunk dropped down somewhere behind him—he was trapped. He couldn't dig backward, so he hoped he could still go forward. His neck ached, his arms ached, his legs ached, his chest, knees and hands stung from multiple scratches, and he felt like he was going to vomit. *Dear God, please don't let me vomit…*

When his fingers pushed through and felt air, he almost cried. He had spent much of his life in tunnels, but all that experience felt like nothing compared to this. He wriggled and thrashed to get out, banging his head and arms and legs, writhing free of the tunnel and spilling down onto the ground below. Somewhere in the fracas, he had lost the flashlight; it was pitch black. Another rumble sounded, and the small tunnel closed up for good. The flashlight was gone. He could see nothing.

Standing carefully, he picked up his bag and felt his way forward step by step, feeling out with his foot for the ledge, and then the ramp. When he found it, relief overwhelmed him. He shuddered, the energy growing stronger in him. It seemed to draw away his pain, leave the damaged flesh and bone behind. He stepped onto the ramp, walked slowly down it, and by the time he had reached the bottom, the pain was gone. The sphere, he could see it, but not with his eyes—with his soul. Where his mortal senses interpreted his surroundings through electric impulses, the sphere connected with him directly, a sense so clear and pure that there was no doubting it.

Josh walked toward the sphere, at first timidly, eventually striding with confidence. He lowered his hands, no longer feeling his way, letting the sphere guide him.

He almost fell when he hit something hard, and cold. He clung onto it to steady himself, feeling a mix of smooth metal and squidgy rubber.

"The robots," he said to himself. He negotiated his way around them, and continued to the sphere. He was close, so close. The energy shuddered through him. He followed its wake, right to its origin. The sphere, it was right there. He had arrived. Without sight it was more beautiful and spectacular than before, a warmth and light that spoke to him, and only him. Without fear he stepped in, and what he thought was darkness became nothing.

Chapter 17

"Don't forget, we've got a party to go to on Saturday."

Josh looked up from his laptop. Georgie was changing Joseph, who was gurgling contentedly. "What's that?"

"One of the other kids at daycare is having a party on Saturday, remember?"

Josh thought back. He did remember. *Shit*. "I said I'd work on Saturday."

Georgie didn't seem to miss a beat. "Okay, sure," she said.

"Is that okay?"

"Sure."

Josh returned to his laptop. He was planning a surprise trip for the three of them to Niagara Falls for their seven-year wedding anniversary. Georgie had always wanted to go, but until now, Josh had never been able to find the time.

"You did promise," Georgie said, buttoning up Joseph's romper. She picked him up, bobbing him up and down while he sang and gurgled.

Josh thought he'd been let off too easy. "Did I?"

"You know you did."

He did. "I'm sorry," he said, closing the laptop and putting it to one side. He stood and approached Georgie, who turned her shoulder to him. He put his arms around her and Joseph. "I'll make it up to you, I promise."

"Will you?" Georgie said cynically.

"Of course I will." He kissed her on the temple. "You'll see."

"Okay."

"All right then. I have to go and get ready for work now."

"Okay."

Josh had a shower and got himself dressed, leaving Georgie with Joseph. The uneasy guilt that followed him around was still there; the only thing that overshadowed it was the looming deadline to finish excavating the staging area and start the first tunnel of the East Side Access. Four weeks they had left. Four weeks. It seemed like they needed four months. The big boss was pulling in all the overtime he could get; flooding had slowed progress right down, but they all knew that excuse was never going to fly when the rest of the project got held up. Over in Queens, the contractor coming in from the other side was actually *ahead* of schedule. Josh was well aware that being shown up by them was a surefire way to hand the entire job over to their team.

He would have to swallow the guilt down and get on with it. Four more weeks of overtime, then it was back on schedule. He'd take

Georgie and Joseph to Niagara Falls, they'd have a great time, and everything would go back to normal.

Normal. He didn't even remember what that was any more. Ever since Joseph had been born, it seemed like his life had lost meaning. He was happy and everything, thrilled to be a father, but all of a sudden his coworkers, his job, all of it seemed somehow—pointless. But he had to do it. He had to keep working. For his family.

Georgie would be back at work soon, but he didn't want her to be; he wanted her to be able to stay at home and enjoy her time with Joseph. She didn't much like her job—she was an HR manager—so Josh convinced himself to work hard, work the overtime and build their savings so she could quit permanently. She'd mentioned starting a small flower arranging business; perhaps she'd be able to do that from home.

Dressed, he grabbed his keys and gave Georgie and Joseph a kiss goodbye. Georgie passed Joseph to him and he cradled him in the crook of his arm. Truth be told, he still got butterflies every time he held him. He was so small, so delicate, and it made Josh nervous. What if he dropped him, or held him wrong, or—

"He really loves you," Georgie said, smiling down at Joseph, who was staring at Josh.

"Does he? All he seems to do is shit and eat."

Georgie chuckled. "Of course he does. You're his daddy."

Josh looked at Joseph, and Joseph looked at Josh. *You really switched things up*, Josh thought. He was in limbo, unable to feel at home being a father, unable to enjoy his work and his friends like he used to. Everything was distant, and he didn't know how to fix it. Did Georgie know how he felt? He hoped not. He didn't want to let her down.

So he worked. Hard. If he couldn't be a father, he could still be a provider. Everything they ever wanted, both of them. He could give them that. Josh handed Joseph back. "And you're his mommy," he said.

Georgie took Joseph and kissed him on the nose. Joseph was still staring at Josh. "Say bye-bye, Joseph," Georgie whispered to him. With a free hand, she wiggled Joseph's arm so it looked like he was waving goodbye.

"Goodbye, Joseph," Josh said. He leaned in to give Georgie a kiss. "And goodbye, you. I love you."

"I know," Georgie replied.

The Saturday came and went, and the next, and the next. In a week, Josh planned to surprise Georgie with the trip to Niagara Falls. It was all booked and ready to go, flights, hotels, everything. He couldn't wait to tell her. He'd nearly let slip a couple of times, but thankfully he'd managed to stifle himself before she'd caught on. She was clever, though; he'd have to be careful if he didn't want her to piece the puzzle together.

With some hard graft and a lot of luck—the drill had hit a pocket of softer material within the schist—Josh's team had pulled the schedule back on track, and Josh was relieved that he'd be able to take the time off with his family. Perhaps he'd get to bond some more with Joseph.

"Niagara Falls, huh?" Lionel said, taking a slurp of coffee. The sun beat down as they took their lunch break topside at the usual.

"Yeah, Georgie's always wanted to go."

"She's never been? It's pretty amazing."

"No, she hasn't. Neither have I. I'm looking forward to it."

Lionel, waving his sandwich, said, "How long are you going for?"

"Four days."

"You flying?"

"Yeah."

"Coach?"

"First class."

Lionel, mouth full, nodded. "Nice…" he mumbled.

"It's our anniversary, so I wanted it to be special."

Swallowing, Lionel said, "You could have taken a week if you wanted to."

Picking at his own sandwich, Josh said, "Yeah, I know. But we've got too much to do here. I don't want to let the team down."

Lionel snorted. "What, you think you're irreplaceable? You're an ant, boy. I could get a hundred just like you"—he clicked his fingers—"in a snap."

Josh laughed. "I know," he said. Then he felt—empty. "But I—I want to stay on top of it, you know, keep focus."

Lionel put his sandwich down and placed a hand on Josh's shoulder. "You still worried about Joseph?"

Josh shrugged. It made him feel small to admit it. He'd mentioned it to Lionel when Joseph was born, casually asking for advice, hoping that Lionel wouldn't make a big deal of it. And he hadn't. He'd reassured him, told him it would all come in time, all the usual stuff. That had been nearly a year ago. He'd hoped Lionel would have forgotten all about that by now.

"You don't have to carry this all by yourself," Lionel said, sitting back. "I'm your friend—talk to me."

"It's fine," Josh said.

"Is it?"

"Can we talk about something else?"

Lionel sighed. "If that's what you want." He returned to eating his sandwich, in silence.

Grinding his teeth, Josh stubbornly ignored Lionel. He took a great, snatching bite of his own sandwich, chewed it and swallowed. What did Lionel know? He was divorced, had been for years. Kids were teenagers now. Things were different for him back when they were young. His was a big family; they'd got lots of support, while Josh—his family was all the way out in Maine, and they barely ever saw them. Georgie had no family, so it was just them. Just the three of them, in their apartment, all the time. No air, no time to breathe. He couldn't bear it.

The subject didn't come up again.

On the day of the flight, Josh could feel a cold coming on. Work was exhausting, and on his first day off in God knows how long, it was like he'd let his guard down and the bugs had just walked themselves right in. He downed some pills, the last in the packet. "Remind me to get some more cold medicine at the airport," he called out to Georgie, who was out in the kitchen frying up pancakes.

"Sure," she called back. "You feeling unwell?"

"Got a cold coming on."

"Oh, baby," she said. "Hopefully the fresh air at Niagara will do you some good. Clean out the bad city stuff."

Josh could hear the frying pan clang and pancakes being loaded onto plates.

"Breakfast's ready!" Georgie announced.

Josh pulled on his socks, rubbed his face and went to the kitchen, greeted by the smell of maple syrup and a beaming Georgie. He'd told her about the trip that morning when they'd woken up, and she'd screamed. It was a hell of a way to start the day.

"How long have you had this planned?" she said, laying his plate down, still grinning.

"A while," Josh said, picking at the pancakes with his fork. He took a bite; the flavor, although good, was dulled by his throbbing sinuses. Great.

Georgie was looking at the tickets, her own pancakes untouched, when her eyes widened. "First class?" she squeaked. "These must have been really expensive."

"Steve knows a guy at the airline. Got us a discount."

Georgie looked fit to burst with happiness. If there was one thing Josh knew she liked, it was a bargain. "Thank you," she said. Her eyes filled.

"Happy anniversary."

Georgie leaned across the table and squeezed his hand. He could feel her quivering. "I only got you a card," she said. Her lip trembled, too.

Josh squeezed back. "You gave me a son," he said. "That's the best present anyone can have."

Georgie smiled a watery smile, and nodded.

"Anyway, cheer up," Josh said. "We're going to Niagara Falls!"

Georgie beamed again, eyes red and shining. "I love you," she said.

"I love you."

They got the cold medicine at the airport like they planned, and all loaded up with pills, Josh reclined his leather seat and shut his eyes. His head was beginning to throb, and he hoped it would clear by the time they landed in around an hour. Georgie was bouncing Joseph on her knee, jiggling Josh's leg, so he moved it.

"Sorry," Georgie said, moving her own leg.

Josh didn't open his eyes. "That's fine."

"Are you feeling okay? How are your sinuses?"

"I've just got a headache. I'm trying to sleep it off."

"Okay, sorry."

"That's okay."

Josh jostled awake when the plane touched down. He stretched—his headache had gone. They had a cab waiting for them just outside the airport, ready to take them to their hotel. As the driver loaded their suitcases, Josh's cell rang. It was Lionel.

"I've got to take this," he said, wandering away for some privacy. He answered. "Hello?"

"It's Lionel."

"What can I do for you, Lionel?"

Lionel sighed. He was struggling to say whatever it was he needed to say. "We've got some guys off sick. We need you."

"I'm on vacation."

"I know, I know, and I'm sorry, but work has ground to a halt and I can't do anything until you're here. You'll get a big bonus on this, if that helps?"

Josh took the cell away from his ear. He looked over at Georgie, who was wrangling Joseph into the cab. He'd slept on the plane and was full of energy, bawling his eyes out and twisting and thrashing.

"Come on!" Georgie called out to Josh. Josh returned to his call.

"I'm sorry, Lionel, I don't think I can. I would normally, but—you know…"

"Okay, sure, I understand," Lionel said. "But…"

"But what?"

"But we've still got the big boss on our asses from the delay on the staging area. I can't afford to lose more time, not when we've just got it back."

Josh folded his arms. "That's not fair."

"You think I don't know that? You think I want to be having this call? I'm telling you how it is—you're the one that needs to make the decision."

Josh screwed up his face while he thought. "How much is the bonus?"

"Five thousand."

That was a lot of money. They really must be desperate. "How long do you need me?"

"It could be one day, it could be all four."

"So I could come down one day and get back for the rest of my vacation?"

"Maybe. Depends when the other guys come back in."

"What's up with them?"

"Colds."

Colds should clear up enough in one day. Josh could get there, work a day, and be back in Niagara with Georgie and Joseph in no time. The five thousand would pay the vacation off several times over. It would mean that Georgie could stay at home, not have to go back to work. "Okay, I'll do it."

"You don't want to check with Georgie first?"

"Nah, she'll understand."

"Okay, if you think that's best. When will you be here?"

Josh looked at his watch. "I'll get the next flight back. A couple of hours, three at the most?"

"Okay, see you then."

"See you then." Josh hung up. Then he took a deep breath. He approached the cab. "Georgie," he said, trying to smile. "I've got some bad news…"

Chapter 18

"Boss, are you there? I can't see shit."

Craig's voice. Josh opened his eyes. "I'm here," he said. "I think—" He stopped. Something was different. Something that itched in the back of his brain.

"Boss?" Craig shouted.

It was like a tick gnawing in his head. He knew there was something he was supposed to remember. "Gas," he said eventually. "I think there *is* gas in here." The tick gnawed further, an unreachable tickle that needed to be scratched.

"All right, well let's get you out of there, then. Sorry I took so long—"

"Getting the ladder…" Josh muttered to himself.

"What's that?"

Josh snapped from his daze. "What? Oh, nothing." How did Josh know what Craig was going to say? Why was this familiar? He headed for the moonlike hole glowing in the darkness, instinctively swerving around—what? What was he swerving around? For some reason, his senses expected to feel cool metal, soft rubber. But why? It made no sense, yet his fingers tingled with the anticipation.

"You okay?" Craig asked him as he approached the ladder hanging off the edge of the moonlike hole.

Josh blinked, then began climbing the ladder. "Yeah, fine, just a little light-headed."

Craig helped him up. "Does sound like gas," he began.

Probably a natural pocket, Josh thought.

Craig peered into the blackness. "Probably a natural pocket."

Josh felt a headache coming along, dizziness following close behind. "We need to get out of here," he said, stumbling toward the drill, leaving a concerned-looking Craig at the entrance to the room.

"Josh?" Craig called after him, striding to catch up. "What's going on?"

"I don't know, but we need to get out of here. All of us. Now."

Craig took a moment to respond. "O—Okay, boss, whatever you say. I'll get the team evacuated." Lifting his radio from his pocket, he called back to Lionel to tell him what was happening. Josh kept on walking, back through the tunnel to where the rest of the team awaited, and by the time he got there, he felt absolutely exhausted.

"What's happening?" Steve asked.

Josh didn't respond. Breezing past, he was heading straight for the train.

"Hey, wait up!" Craig shouted from somewhere behind. Josh stopped. His mind felt like it carried on moving forward, latent momentum that made him want to sick his guts up. The others came running over, and he felt an arm on his back as he leaned forward to right himself.

"Hey, man, are you okay?" Craig asked him, leaning close. Josh stood tall, pushing him aside.

"I'm fine," he said. "I'm fine. Come on, let's go."

All right," Craig said, sounding unconvinced, "let's get out of here."

The team made no audible protest; Josh could feel their attention was placed his way, out of concern. "I'm fine, really," he tried to reassure them, but the silence and ashen faces he got in return were clear to understand. They rode the train without another word, heading for the tunnel exit.

When they arrived, Josh disembarked first, and Craig jogged to catch up. "What's going on?" he asked.

"Nothing," Josh said, taking big strides up the stairs to the elevator shaft.

Craig grabbed him by the shoulder and stopped him. They faced each other, eye to eye, and Craig signaled to the others to hang back. "It's not nothing," he said, staring at Josh, unblinking, until Josh had to look away. "Come on, Josh. Tell me. Something happened in there, didn't it?"

"I don't know. It's…" Josh began. His stomach turned again as his mind raced with electricity.

"It's what?" Craig said, gripping Josh's shoulder hard.

Josh sighed. He may as well say it out loud. Perhaps it'd help. "There's something in there."

"In the room? Like what? An animal or something?"

Shaking his head, Josh said, "No, like an object. A—a portal."

Slowly, Craig released his grip, stepping back to consider Josh. He seemed unsure. "Are you messing with me?" he asked. "Are you messing me around?"

Quietly, Josh said, "No."

"What kind of… portal?"

These words Craig spoke, Josh didn't remember, but the ones before… he remembered *them*. He also remembered something else, something deep in his gut, a built-in knowledge he couldn't explain, like being able to breathe, or understanding how to digest food. It was there, in him, like it had always been there: he had traveled through time. "It's a portal into the past," he almost whispered. "To now."

If Craig had thought Josh was trying to play a trick on him before, he definitely did now. "This isn't funny, Josh. I was seriously worried about you. You can't—" He cut himself off, face falling. Josh hadn't laughed, or even smiled, and Craig must have realized that he wasn't lying. "Maybe you should see a doctor," he said, looking Josh up and down. "The gas must have made you sick."

Josh didn't want to argue, so he just nodded.

"Okay, let's get you out of here," Craig said, leading Josh by the arm and waving the others to follow. As they stepped into the elevator, light trickling in from above, Josh caught a look at the long, caged ladder stretching way up high. His stomach fluttered with déjà vu.

As the elevator began its ascent, Josh went to adjust the straps on his bag, when his heart skipped a beat as he realized it was gone. *Wait a minute*, he thought. *What bag?* He didn't have it with him now, but he remembered having it at some point before. There was stuff in it, cans of fruit, a—a video camera.

A video camera?

The elevator cage shuddered upward, bathing them in more and more light. The air started to turn fresh, and it helped to clear Josh's head. The others were muttering between themselves, probably about him, but he had tuned them out, too busy picking at the scab forming over the tick's burrow.

He remembered another time, in the future. Before he'd come back. After now, many years after now. But before. His head thumped. The memory was laced with static.

"Let's go and see Lionel," Craig said to Josh as the elevator came to the end of its journey. "You guys," he said, addressing the rest of the group, "you can hang back here while I take care of Josh."

They muttered agreement and took seats on rock and grass.

"Come on," Craig said, and Josh followed. They said nothing until they arrived at the site offices, where Lionel came out to greet them.

"What can you report?" Lionel said.

"There's a big chamber down there," Craig said. "Huge, separated with a seam of native titanium or something like it."

"Some kind of crystalline metallic," Josh said. "I don't know. I've not seen it before."

Lionel listened while Craig gave Josh a look of disbelief. Josh had known what Craig was going to say, and had beaten him to saying it. He knew, because it'd happened before. Not quite like this, but close enough.

"Anything inside?" Lionel asked.

"No…" Craig said, breaking his attention away from Josh to resume the conversation with Lionel. "Just a hollow space. I think there's gas, though. Josh seems pretty light-headed."

"Methane, perhaps?"

"No," Josh interrupted. Both Craig and Lionel looked at him.

"Then what?" Lionel said.

Before Josh could talk, Craig stepped in. "Josh isn't feeling too well. I think the gas is affecting him. He needs to see a doctor—"

Looking irritated, Lionel said, "Well is there gas or isn't there? I need to know!"

"There is," Craig said sternly, staring at Josh to keep him quiet. "Josh needs an ambulance."

"I'm fine," Josh said.

"You're not."

Lionel, hands on hips, said, "Okay, okay. Craig, thank you. That will be all for now."

"But—"

"I said *thank you*," Lionel repeated, cutting in.

Craig looked between them with a disapproving expression. "Fine. But keep an eye on him." To Josh he said, "You're not well.

I'm saying that as a friend. Go to a doctor or something." Then he turned on his heel and left.

Lionel, who trusted Craig almost as much as he trusted Josh, looked to be mulling the strange conversation over. "What's all this about?" he asked Josh. "Are you sick or are you not sick?"

"I'm fine," Josh insisted. "It's—it's not what he thinks."

"And what does he think?"

Josh shrugged. "He thinks there's gas down there, I guess."

Sitting on the edge of his desk and folding his arms, Lionel asked, "And what do *you* think?"

"I—" Josh began, then stopped. He knew how Lionel would take it—the same way Craig did. "What if I told you I knew what was going to happen?"

Confused, Lionel blinked. "I'm sorry, what?"

"What if I could tell you what was going to happen, you know—in the future?"

Lionel didn't seem to be able to comprehend the question. "I'd say you were bullshitting me. Why, what are you getting at?"

Josh took a quick breath. All or nothing. "I can tell you what's going to happen. Today. The future."

Standing, Lionel picked up the phone on his desk and began to dial. "That's it," he said. "Craig was right. I'm calling an ambulance."

Josh leaped across the room, snatched the receiver from Lionel's hand and slammed it back onto its cradle. "No!" he shouted. "No. Give me a chance to prove it first."

Taken aback, Lionel said, "I really think you should see a doctor…"

"I'm fine," Josh said. "I told you. And you can't force me. But I'll give you this: let me have a chance to prove myself, and if I'm wrong, I'll go to the doctor."

Lionel considered the offer. "How long do you want?"

"A few hours. Three at the most."

They stared at each other for a while, Josh pleading, Lionel with suspicion.

"Okay…" Lionel said. "I'll let you have a chance. But for the record, I think you've gone batshit crazy."

"I know you do, and I understand why, but we've been friends a long time and I need you to trust me."

Lionel resumed his arms-folded position, looking at Josh with narrow eyes. "All right then, Madame Reed, what have you got for me? Lottery numbers, I hope."

"It's not like that," Josh said.

"Oh, of course it's not."

"Give me a minute."

Lionel gestured for him to take that minute. Sitting down on the desk opposite, Josh shut his eyes. What he saw was a churning storm of information, rushing by so fast he couldn't understand any of it. Somewhere in there was the truth, the key, the reason he was there.

"It's been a minute," Lionel said.

"Shh!"

A light, dim at first, sparkled in the melee. Josh tried to pin it down, but it winked in and out of sight as he attempted to close in on it. Every time he thought he was near, it would wink out and he'd have to start the search again. There was no direct path; perhaps he could try something else.

The room, that was where everything was focused around. Deep below New York, it held the answers. The light winked brighter. The light was the answer. The light was the room. But how to get to it?

They had dug, had found the room. Josh had entered the room. It was familiar. He had not spent more than a handful of minutes in there, yet somehow he felt like it had been his home for a lifetime.

"Two minutes."

"Lionel, shut up."

Did he travel somewhere from that room? No, that wasn't right. He'd traveled *back* to the room. His mind flared, filling him with pain. He flinched.

"Are you all right?" Lionel sounded concerned this time.

"Fine."

There had been fear. Who or what had he been afraid of? An animal? The light winked brighter still. A—a bear? No, that couldn't be right. But it was. A bear. He could see it. Gaunt and matted. Phantom pain twinged in his leg.

But that was not where the fear came from. The light dimmed, the information speeding by so fast it burned the backs of his eyelids.

"Josh, whatever you're doing, I think you should stop."

"I'm nearly there…"

The zoo in central park, the pizzeria across the road from his apartment, Georgie's front door, the picture frame… they all flashed by, glimpses of things he knew brought that same fear, that same primal urge to run. But what was he running from?

A suit, brown.

"Josh, I'm phoning the ambulance."

Neat hair.

"Just a minute…"

Plain features.

"No, Josh, now."

He looked like an accountant.

"One more minute, I swear…"

The light exploded into brightness, outshining everything else. He stared into it, mentally shielding himself from its power, clear and bright and certain. The man's name was Edwards.

"The CIA is coming," Josh said. He opened his eyes. Lionel had the receiver in his hand and his fingers ready to dial, frozen in mid-air.

"The CIA?" he repeated.

"Yes."

Lionel slowly replaced the receiver, not taking his eyes off Josh. "What makes you say that?"

"When Craig reported the evacuation, you called the Department of Safety and Health, didn't you?"

"Well, yeah…" Lionel said uncomfortably, "but that's procedure, not a prediction."

"They passed on the message higher up, right the way to the top. The CIA wants what we found. They're on their way."

Lionel went to speak, but couldn't.

"I know it's hard to believe," Josh said, "and I barely believe it myself, but in a few hours a load of police cars will show up, looking for you. Then the CIA will follow."

Lionel was shaking his head. "You've got to be kidding me…" he said.

"I'm not."

"And how exactly do you know this?" There was suspicion in Lionel's voice, but also curiosity.

"I've—I've done it before."

"Done what before?"

"This," Josh said, gesturing all around him. "I've done all this before."

Lionel still didn't seem to follow.

"I've come back in time," Josh said. His stomach turned saying it. "I've already lived this."

Lionel sat motionless on his desk, a dumbfounded expression slapped across his face. "How am I supposed to believe that?" he said, almost in desperation. "Why are you doing this to me? Do I look stupid?"

"You don't have to believe what I'm saying. You'll see it soon enough."

"In a few hours, right?"

"Right."

Lionel huffed, standing up. "Well, I've got a whole load of paperwork to do because of this nonsense, so if you'll excuse me, I'm going to be getting on with that in the meantime."

"Sure."

"And you," Lionel added, pointing at Josh, "are to stay there, you got it? Don't you even think about moving."

"I won't."

Lionel eyeballed Josh one last time before rounding his desk and sitting down. "Good," he said. For the next few minutes he slapped paperwork about, hacking at his keyboard and scratching with his pen. Josh could see Lionel was annoyed, but he realized it wasn't because Lionel was cross with him, but because he thought Josh was trying to take him for a fool and didn't understand why. It was understandable. They'd been friends for years—Lionel was godfather to Joseph—and now it seemed like Josh was abusing all that over a stupid joke.

But he'd done what he needed to do. And now they'd have to wait. What would happen when the CIA came, when the man called Edwards came? He wasn't sure.

He thought of Georgie while he waited, wishing he could go further back in time; there was so much he'd do differently. He almost found it hard to believe he'd let them go at all, but the person he pictured doing that seemed so different to the one he was now. Now he'd sacrifice everything for them.

The phone rang, jarring Josh from his thoughts. Lionel picked it up.

"Hello? Yes, it is. Uh huh. Okay. Right, right." He listened for a while, before saying, "Okay then, we'll see you soon." Then he hung up. He didn't say anything more for a moment, staring into space. Then he looked up at Josh, as pale as an African American could be. He opened his mouth to speak, and his lips crackled with dryness as they separated. "Well," he said, his voice strained, "It looks like you might be right."

Chapter 19

Before long, sirens wailed over the site. After the call, Lionel had sent the others home. Josh stayed with him. As they waited outside the site gates, Josh told Lionel, "Whatever happens, go with it. Pretend I never said anything."

Lionel, uncertain, nodded. The sirens in their number became too loud to talk over, and they both waited as no less than five cars pulled up in turn, each with red and blue lights pounding the backs of their retinas. They shared a glance.

The sirens shut off, and with the lights still twirling, the officers of the law disembarked. After a huddle, most of them headed to the site, brushing past Josh and Lionel without so much as a nod, while a single officer approached. It was mid-afternoon, and the air was balmy. Josh could feel sweat beading on his scalp. He ran a sleeve across his brow.

"Good afternoon, gentlemen," the officer said, politely but firmly. "I take it that one of you is running the site here?"

"That's right," Lionel replied, stepping forward, arms crossed. "Can I ask what it is you boys need?"

The officer halted his approach, drawing a sheaf of papers from the folder he was carrying. "Everything you need to know is in here," he said.

Lionel took the papers, but didn't read them, keeping his eyes affixed on the lawman.

"We've been instructed to secure the perimeter and extract any and all personnel not related to this investigation."

Lionel glanced at Josh. Josh gave him a small nod. *Go with it.*

"What investigation?" Lionel asked the officer. His voice wavered. "Are you here about the gas?"

"I'm not at liberty to say, sir."

"What does that mean? When can we get back on-site?"

"I do not have that information, sir."

The immense feeling of repetition made Josh's skin crawl. It felt unreal; the quicker he could break the loop, the better, but for right now, it had to continue this way.

Lionel held his hands up in protest. "That can't happen. *This* can't happen. We've got work to do, a schedule to keep and a budget to stay on top of. I can't have the police crawling all over this site for God knows how long, getting in the way of things."

The officer peered into his folder, then back at Lionel. "You're Lionel Parker, correct?"

Lionel puffed up his chest. "I am."

"Then you'll know it was *you* who informed the authorities of the situation here—"

"I called the Department of Safety and Health, not the state police!" Lionel interrupted. "You think I want all of this going on at my site? You think I want my ass handed to me by my boss for putting us off schedule? Hell no!"

"Sir," the officer said, holding up a hand, "you need to remain calm. I'm just doing my job. The Department saw fit to call in the relevant authorities, so we're here until the federal officers arrive—"

"Federal officers…" Lionel repeated, glancing at Josh. If he had any doubts about Josh's prediction, they would now surely be gone. To the officer—and to Josh, subtly— Lionel said, "Do you mind telling me *something* about what's happening? *Federal* officers? Are you sure this isn't some big misunderstanding or something?"

The officer, taking a step back, cradling his folder under his arm, looked resigned. "I've told you, sir, I'm not at liberty to tell you anything more, and to be honest, I don't know anything more. I've just been told to come down here, secure the area and find you. That's all." The officer looked over Lionel's shoulder to another officer emerging from the site. "Ramirez," he told the man, "I need you to stay with this gentleman until the CIA arrives. They have a few questions they'd like to ask him."

"Sir."

The officer addressed Josh. "You can go."

"I'm staying," Josh said.

"He's staying," Lionel reiterated.

The officer shrugged, nodded and left, heading for the site. The officer called Ramirez stayed with them. His rank was junior, and he avoided eye contact with either of them. Josh could see that Lionel had spotted this weakness, and planned to use it to his own advantage.

"Josh," Lionel hissed, nodding Josh closer. They turned their backs to Ramirez, who didn't seem to care. "You've got to tell me what's going on here. I've played your games, you've had a good laugh, and now shit's getting real. Talk."

Josh knew he still had some convincing to do, but at least now the foundations had been laid. "In that room is a portal. A time portal."

"Bullshit—"

"No, Lionel, it isn't." Josh held Lionel's frustrated and angry stare until Lionel had to blink. "I'm telling you the truth, I swear to God."

Lionel grunted, but did not interrupt.

"It's like a—a time well. I think the hole we drilled—well, its effects are leaking out, spreading. I'm the only one who can go in there, go back in time."

Lionel's lip twitched. Josh could see that he was poised somewhere between wanting to believe Josh, and thinking that Josh had gone completely off-the-wall crazy. "So you've—" His voice crackled, and he had to clear his throat. "So you've come back in time? That's what you're saying?"

A memory flashed in Josh's mind. "I was here, in Manhattan, but it was decades into the future. Everyone was gone. The city had been abandoned."

"*What?*" Lionel said in disbelief, shifting his weight from foot to foot.

Josh nodded. "The only people I saw were dead."

Lionel teetered.

"Maybe you should sit down?" Josh suggested, helping Lionel keep his balance. Lionel pushed him away, almost as though Josh's touch burned.

"I'm fine," he said.

"You're not fine."

"No, well… I'll be fine."

A pause. Then Josh said, "Do you believe me?"

Lionel shrugged. "I don't know. How can I?"

"Why would I lie?"

A bead of sweat ran down Lionel's brow. "I don't know."

"Then believe me," Josh urged. "The man from the CIA— Edwards—will be here soon. He looks like an accountant. Face is real familiar. He'll tell you he's sorry about the whole thing, and that we weren't supposed to be held back. If you ask him about what we've found, he'll tell you he doesn't know."

"And then what?"

"That's when we leave. Or when we left. This time will be different."

Lionel looked confused. "Different? How?"

"This time I know more than he does." The rumble of tire on tarmac caught their attention. "Remember," Josh added, "go with it."

Two blacked-out SUVs pulled up, hidden grille lights flashing. Ramirez had spotted them first and was approaching them as they pulled up. The men who emerged were inconspicuously suited, just as Josh had described. Ramirez led the group of four over to Josh and Lionel, introducing them and then vanishing as soon as he was dismissed.

"I'm agent Tom Edwards," the man leading the group said, "and I'm sorry for this whole debacle. I'm sure we can get this resolved right away and be out of your hair."

"Edwards…" Lionel mumbled.

"Yes, that's right," Edwards said, his expression quizzical. "I appreciate that you have a site to run, Mr. Parker, and the sooner we can get our job done, the sooner you can get back to yours."

It was Josh's turn to take the lead. "I know what this is about," he said, looking between Lionel and Edwards.

"Can I ask who you are?" Edwards said.

"Josh Reed, Principal Tunnel Engineer. I assume you're interested in what we found, and it was me and my team that found it, so we may as well get to talking."

Edwards smiled, not unkindly. "Fair enough. Let's get to it then." He turned to his colleagues, who took it as a sign to disperse into the site. When he faced Josh and Lionel again, the three of them were alone. "You're both intelligent people, so I won't dance about the subject. You're right: this is about what you found. We will perform our investigation, and we may need to confirm some things with you—both of you—depending on what we find. For now, I can only ask that you stay in town and stay contactable, in case we need to follow up on anything."

Lionel was staring into infinity, dumbfounded by the whole ordeal. Josh spoke for him. "We're not going anywhere. You may not realize it now, but you need us more than you think. It's in there, Edwards. What you're looking for is in there."

Studying Josh, Edwards held his tongue, deliberating his response. Then the smile returned. "And what do you think we're looking for, Mr. Reed?"

Josh had to pick his words carefully. He wanted Edwards to take him seriously, but didn't want to show his hand just yet. Edwards couldn't be trusted—that much was clear. "Something you've been trying to find for a very long time."

Edwards stared at Josh for a while, then at Lionel. His decision was made. "Okay, Mr. Reed, Mr. Parker, I think I've used up more than enough of your time." He gestured for them to leave, then started for the site entrance himself. "We will be in touch if we need anything further."

As Edwards walked away from them, about to disappear into the site, Josh called out, "You've sent one of your men in there. He'll die if you don't stop him."

Edwards stopped, and when he turned to face them, his expression was dark. "Be careful with what you say, Mr. Reed. Threatening a federal officer is a serious offense."

Josh had never seen Edwards like this before. He knew the man was ruthless, but he was also calculating, and this brief exposure of his inner self gave him the chills. "It's not a threat. The room, it's—it's not like the ones you've found before. It's alive. It's protected. I'm the only one who can go in there."

Edwards was clearly torn. It was apparent that he couldn't believe Josh knew anything, but he also couldn't ignore what Josh had just said. "Tell me how you know this," was all he asked.

"You—you told me."

Taking a few steps toward Josh, Edwards said, "What do you mean, *I* told you?"

"The room."

"What about the room?"

This was a pivotal moment, Josh knew it. The words were loaded in his mouth, ready to fire, but once he pulled the trigger, there was no going back. "It's a portal," he said slowly. "A portal through time."

Chapter 20

Edwards appeared to have frozen; even his expression was ice. Josh swallowed, throat dry, waiting for Edwards to respond. Perhaps Edwards already knew? He didn't seem to; there was surprise in his locked down expression. Did Edwards believe Josh? Perhaps not. Regret ballooned, and Josh's throat would not moisten.

Reaching into his pocket, Edwards broke his motionless pose by retrieving a radio. He spoke into it. "Do not go into the room. Repeat: do not go into the room. Report back immediately." Without breaking eye contact with Josh, he waited for a response.

"Bryant and Owens have already headed down there. We aren't able to make contact with them."

Thinking briefly, Edwards replied, "Stay there. I'm coming down."

"Copy."

To Lionel, Edwards said, "Wait there." To Josh, he said, "You, come with me."

"Josh…" Lionel said, as Josh followed Edwards into the site.

"I'll be fine," Josh said.

Lionel nodded, still affixed to the spot, as Josh entered the site. A police officer closed the gate behind them, and without a word, Edwards led Josh to the elevator. They boarded, and descended into the cavern. Josh decided to break the silence first.

"What are you going to do with the room?" he asked.

Edwards stiffened.

"You may as well talk to me. Surely you want to know what I know?"

"I have no guarantee that you know anything."

"Come on—you know I'm not making this up. That's impossible."

Edwards gave Josh a reproachful look as the elevator came to a halt. He slid the cage door open. "Maybe later," he said, then headed down the stairs. Josh followed.

Two agents waited for them down at the station. The train was gone, presumably deep into the tunnel with Bryant and Owens.

"Sir," one of the agents said, approaching Edwards, "we keep trying to get them on the radios, but there's no response."

"You need radios tuned in to our repeaters down here," Josh told them.

"Okay," Edwards said. "If we can't get in contact with them, how do we get to them?"

"There's usually a train, sir, but they've taken it."

Edwards addressed Josh. "Any other quick way in?"

Josh shook his head. "Only on foot. Takes about ten minutes."

"Then we go on foot."

"Yes, sir," the two other agents said at once.

There was no formality with hazmat suits this time; Edwards marched right on into that tunnel with purpose. If he didn't believe Josh now, he would soon. In a way, Josh admired the tenacity of the man, and the stubbornness with which he held his tongue. Surely he would have a thousand questions for Josh—but he didn't ask one. Not yet. He wasn't going to compromise his position that easily. There was a chance he wasn't going to compromise his position at all. He was a man who, by his own declaration, did not share what he did not need to share, and Josh wondered what else there was to find out. Whatever happened, Josh felt the need to keep his guard up. Edwards was not in this for Josh—he was in this for himself.

"How much further?" Edwards asked without looking back.

"About five more minutes," Josh replied.

What had Edwards given away so far? Not much. And that was what made Josh so wary. If Edwards had no ulterior motive, then why would he not be open with Josh, talk to him on a level and build the bigger picture together? After all, Josh knew more about this phenomenon than anyone, and still Edwards was being cagey about it. It didn't add up.

"There's the train," one of Edwards's agents said, pointing.

"Just a little further," Josh told him.

Edwards was hiding something. It was obvious. And he didn't seem to care that it was obvious. Alienating Josh was worth less than what he had to protect, and a man with something that big to protect would stop at nothing to do so. That man would be a dangerous man, not to be trifled with.

"Bryant!" Edwards shouted to a figure visible at the end of the tunnel. The figure, wearing a hazmat suit, turned and ran toward them.

"Sir!" he sputtered, voice muffled, then nearly tripped. He collected himself, carried on running, and arrived panting and ashen. He pulled off his facepiece, sweat glistening on his skin and soaking his hair.

"Where's Owens?"

"He—" Bryant panted. "He went in, sir."

"He went in? Why? I gave explicit orders to stay outside of the room—"

"I know, sir. I told him not to, but he wouldn't listen. He went in. Hasn't come out."

Edwards was silent for a moment. "Okay, Bryant. What can you tell me?"

Bryant, although calmer now, took a deep breath, uncertain about reliving the events preceding. "There's an energy in the tunnel up ahead. You can feel it. It gets stronger as you get closer to the room. The walls, they're like a crystalline metallic—"

"Yes, I know," Edwards interrupted hastily. "Tell me about Owens."

"He wanted to go in, sir, and I told him no. He said he'd be fine. Seemed entranced by the energy, wouldn't look away from the room.

As soon as he climbed down, there was this flash of light and I saw him go flying. He won't respond now, sir."

For the first time since the surface, Edwards looked directly at Josh. "You think *you* can go in there?"

Josh nodded. His chest was tight.

"Follow me," Edwards said, leading the way. The group followed, and Edwards stopped. "Just Mr. Reed. The rest of you, wait here."

Looking a little confused—except for Bryant, who was more relieved than anything else—the others did as they were told. Josh followed Edwards up to the drill and into the fresh tunnel, still round and intact.

Inside, the energy only became noticeable about halfway in. *It's still weak*, Josh thought. *Soon, its power will spread across the continent.* They could still get close without time being affected. In a few hours, things would be very different.

They stood together at the precipice. Darkness yawned around them. The air hummed with electricity. Then Edwards did something Josh hadn't expected. He smiled. It was involuntary, and Edwards seemed to have forgotten that he wasn't alone. There must have been a long road to this point for him, and now he'd made it. Then he snapped back to reality, addressing Josh.

"Prove it," was all he said. Josh knew full well what he meant, but nerves kept him frozen to the spot. Edwards folded his arms. "I'm waiting," he said.

There was no getting out of this if Josh wanted Edwards to believe him—he'd have to do as he was asked. The ladder was still propped up against the edge, and he made his way toward it.

"Slowly," Edwards instructed.

Josh stepped backward over the edge, feeling for a rung. Then he stepped down to another, and another, and another. Soon his head was below the edge, and then he was standing on the crystalline ground.

"I'm in," he called up.

Edwards didn't respond at first.

"Hello?"

"Okay, you can come back up," Edwards said at last.

Hurriedly, Josh clambered out. The Edwards he met when he was back in the tunnel was not the same as the one he'd left there. He was different: anxious perhaps? Uncertain? No—he was in awe.

"Do you know why you can do that?" he said.

Josh shrugged. "No."

The awe had a certain curiosity to it. Edwards circled Josh, who remained still, as if weighing up what he knew to be true against what he *hoped* to be true. "You say you've used... the portal?"

Nodding, Josh said, "Yeah."

Edwards had completed his circle, and by now the curiosity had flushed away any trace of reservation. "I believe you," he said. It seemed to be more of a big deal to Edwards than it did to Josh, like he was saying it for his own benefit. "I want you to tell me everything."

"Well," Josh began, but Edwards held up a hand.

"Not here."

"Where?"

"Langley."

"Why?"

"You'll see. There's a helicopter waiting. Let's go."

The CIA motorcade rumbled through the Manhattan streets, sirens yelping at anyone that dared get in their way. Josh clung on to his seatbelt as the driver hurled them around yet another corner without slowing down. They were heading for JFK—if they didn't roll over before then—but as they left Manhattan and entered Queens, Josh realized that they weren't going the usual way. They left the traffic behind, slowing to enter a gated area that spilled onto a long driveway. The gate rolled shut behind them and they sped down the drive, kicking up the loose stones that had accumulated since its last use.

The main airport was a few miles over to the left, big commercial airliners coming in low overhead and touching down a little way off from where they were headed. At the end of the driveway, the motorcade pulled up outside a row of small hangers, agents climbing out before the vehicles had come to a complete stop.

"Come on," Edwards said, disembarking. Josh followed, silenced by the whole situation. He jogged to catch up with Edwards, who was already marching across the concrete to one of the hangers, where a helicopter awaited them, blades already chopping at the air. Edwards ducked under them and Josh did too—he'd seen the movies—and they boarded the helicopter. Belt buckles barely fastened, they were in the air.

Edwards handed Josh a headset, and put on his own. "Thirty minutes," he told Josh, anticipating his first question. "Now—tell me everything you know."

Josh was uncertain: Edwards's sudden change of heart had thrown him, left him feeling vulnerable. "You tell me something first," he replied.

"In good time," Edwards said.

"How do I know I can trust you?"

Edwards laughed, but the humor in it seemed forced. "You came to me, remember?"

"I know what you're capable of."

Still smiling, Edwards said, "So it seems. Tell you what—how about I bring your family along with us, let you talk with them first, see what they think you should do?"

Josh didn't quite know how to react to that. Was it a threat, or a genuine reassurance?

"You'd like to see them, wouldn't you? I know how much they mean to you, Georgina and Joseph."

Swallowing, Josh said, "Yes." There was no malice in Edwards's tone that he could detect—but Edwards seemed like the kind of person who'd be good at hiding it if he wanted to. He was a professional manipulator.

"That's settled then. I'll have them brought to Langley immediately." He punched a message into his cell and pocketed it.

Just like that, Josh's family had been summoned. Clearly Edwards was keen to get the information he wanted. "So, Mr. Reed—you were saying?"

And Josh told him. He told him about drilling into the room, the material, the energy. The darkness. He told him about the headaches, the visit from the police, the CIA. Then he told Edwards about the visits, to him, to his colleagues, to his family. The picture frame. Edwards listened without a word. He seemed to be taking it in, but his expression was neutral. It stayed like that until Josh was talking about the portal, the trip to the future, the sun speeding up through the sky. Then Edwards's expression changed. It became more intense. He was hearing what he wanted to hear.

"Everything was in ruins, like it had been deserted for years," Josh explained. "It seemed like everyone had left in a panic. There were abandoned cars everywhere."

Edwards was giving his full attention. "Tell me more about what happened to the sun."

"It's—it's hard to remember, but the way it moved, it was like time was…"

"Accelerating?" Edwards suggested.

"Yeah—the further I got from the room, the faster time went. The sun moved through the sky quick enough to see. Days lasted minutes. Does that makes sense?"

"And then what?" Edwards asked, ignoring Josh's question. "You came back?"

"Everyone was gone. I had no choice but to come back again."

Edwards was silent for a moment, his face unreadable. Then he said, "The portal, what else do you know about it?"

"Well—as the energy in the room grows, its effects do, too. I don't know how to explain, but it's like a well that's getting deeper and deeper, and the longer we wait, the longer it takes to climb out. I think the room is supposed to contain it, but we—we drilled through it."

"Time is not on our side then."

"No," Josh said. "No, it's not. We've got half a day at best."

Edwards's expression seemed to suggest that what Josh was saying made sense, but Josh couldn't be sure. He wanted to ask, but he knew he wasn't getting any answers until they arrived at Langley. There was no escaping from Langley.

"So what do we do?" Josh asked.

Edwards broke from thought. "Don't worry about that. We'll take care of everything. All I need you to do is keep talking to me. I need every last detail."

Down below, the Potomac River could be seen winding its way across the horizon. The CIA headquarters, a blocky, symmetrical building surrounded by parking lots, and then trees, could be clearly seen in the crook of the river. It was a little underwhelming; Josh had expected something more… impressive. The housing developments dotted around the building and the highways beyond did not add to the sense of high security and global secrecy.

"There's not much else to tell," Josh said. "I've told you everything I know."

"As long as you're sure."

Josh wondered if Edwards was just bringing him to Langley to keep him secure, stop him from talking about what he knew to anyone else. The room, the portal, they were powerful pieces of technology, and of course Edwards wanted to keep them protected. He'd probably already had Josh's family flown in—the offer was simply a pleasantry. "I've told you what I know," Josh said. "Why can't you tell *me* anything?"

Edwards, looking out of the window, had a glint in his eye. He was close to something. The pieces were falling into place for him. What the outcome was to be, only he knew. "Because it would be better to show you."

Chapter 21

The helicopter set down just outside the building complex, where agents awaited them. They bustled Josh from the helicopter, leading him quickly to the main entrance. There were no pleasantries.

Under the glass arch they went, dappled by its green glow, and in through the sliding doors. It reminded Josh more of a mall than it did of an agency headquarters, despite the enormous CIA seal emblazoned on the lobby floor. Statues honoring the service of members gone by decorated the hall, stars and stripes adding color to the otherwise monotone marble décor. On the wall, a row of stars signified the sacrifices made for the agency. There were too many to count.

Twin reception desks bridged by a turnstile barred the way ahead. Edwards approached the receptionist.

"I have a guest pass waiting registered for a Mr. Josh Reed."

The receptionist tapped at the computer. "Is Mr. Reed here?"

"Yes—this is him."

"Mr. Reed," the receptionist said, "do you have any identification?"

"Uh, I have my driver's license?" he said, retrieving it from his pocket and showing her.

"That's fine. Please—" the receptionist directed Josh to an area marked on the floor—"stand here."

Josh did as he was told, realizing he was having his picture taken while Edwards and the other agents stood watch. It was incredibly surreal; after the noise and speed of the helicopter, waiting in line to have his picture taken gave Josh the feeling of being in a waking dream.

"And if you can place your hand on here," the receptionist asked, handing Josh a touch pad with a hand outline on it. He did so, waiting while the scanner did its job.

"I'm sorry, Mr. Reed," the receptionist said, tapping at the computer, "I'll need to do that again. The machine's a little temperamental."

"Oh, okay. Do I just keep my hand on the screen?"

"Yes please."

The second scan worked, and the receptionist printed a pass out for Josh. It expired in twenty-four hours, and was clearly marked in bright red letters that Josh was a guest of the facility under the invitation of Edwards.

They all trundled through the turnstile, then through a row of metal detectors. Josh had nothing metal on him beside his keys, and he passed through without problem, picking them up on the other side. Where he was and what he was doing there was only just starting to hit him, and it made his throat dry.

"When can I see my family?" he asked hoarsely.

"They are arriving shortly," Edwards said. "You'll see them very soon."

Their escort followed as they meandered through corridors of more black and white marble, and soon Edwards ushered them into a small room, where they waited in silence until Georgie and Joseph arrived. Edwards must have understood that Josh was going to be of no use until he'd got what he wanted.

"I'll give you all a few minutes," Edwards said, getting up to leave. "Then we must get to it." He shut the door behind him, leaving Josh alone with his family. Georgie looked scared.

"Daddy!" Joseph squealed.

Josh hugged them both. "It's okay…" he said into Georgie's hair. "I'm here."

Georgie looked up at him, eyes bright with fear. "What's going on, Josh?"

"I don't know yet," Josh said. "And I don't know how much I'm allowed to say. All I know is that I found something in the tunnels, Georgie, something big, and the CIA want to talk to me about it."

"What did you find?" Georgie whispered.

Josh looked around the room. Cameras, each corner. He noticed the table by the wall, bolted to the floor, thick metal eyelets on one side. This was an interrogation room. Secure. Definitely not private.

"I don't know if I can tell you. I probably shouldn't, not now at least. The main thing is you're safe. Did they treat you well?"

Georgie nodded.

"What did they tell you?"

"Just that they needed us to come with them right away, and that you were coming too, and that no one was in trouble—"

"No one is. We're safe."

"Safe from what?" Georgie said, voice cracking. "Safe from what, Josh?"

Joseph looked sad. "What's the matter, Mommy?"

"Mommy's okay, Joseph, don't worry," Georgie told him.

Josh said nothing. Her eyes searched his, and she knew he was holding back.

"If we're in danger, Josh, I need you to tell me…" she whispered. She clung to him with one hand, fingers digging in, and to Joseph with the other.

"We're not in any danger. We're safe. Please believe me."

Georgie's breathing was fast and shallow. She nodded. "Okay," she said.

"I promise," Josh added. She didn't trust him; he could feel it. He tried to catch her eye. "I found—I found a time portal," he whispered. "In a weird room deep below ground. That's what they want. That's why we're here."

Georgie sniffed, looking at Josh. Her expression was neutral, weighing up what Josh had said versus her ability to believe it.

"I swear to you."

Chewing her lip, Georgie nodded. "Okay, whatever you say."

"Please believe me. I'm here—we're here—so I can protect you." He tried to take her hand, and she pulled away.

"If you don't respect me enough to tell me the truth, then don't bother talking to me at all," she said.

Josh glanced at the cameras—he'd told Georgie more than he should have, he knew it, but he needed her to believe him. "Please, Georgie, I *am* telling you the truth…"

"How can I possibly believe you?" Georgie said, voice raised. "This is—this is bullshit, and you know it."

"Shhh!" Josh pleaded, looking anxiously to the door, but it was too late. The handle clicked down and the door swung open, and in breezed Edwards. He didn't look happy.

"I had to tell her," Josh said, stepping away from Georgie, hands held high. Edwards approached him, and Josh resolutely held his ground, albeit swaying backward slightly. Edwards stopped, then turned to Georgie.

"Mr. Reed is correct. He *has* found a time portal."

Georgie looked between them both, speechless, pale.

"Also, he specifically requested you be here for your own safety."

"It's *true*?" Georgie asked Josh. Josh nodded. Georgie looked down, blinking, struggling to take it all in.

"I can assure you," Edwards continued, "that what Mr. Reed says is entirely true. And now we must go. We have matters to attend to."

"I have to go," Josh told Georgie. She nodded slowly. "I'll see you very soon, okay? Bye-bye, Joseph."

Joseph waved goodbye. Georgie said nothing.

Edwards and Josh left the room, while two agents remained behind to guard it.

"Is that necessary?" Josh asked, watching them standing either side of the door as he and Edwards headed deeper into the building.

"Now they know," Edwards said simply.

Josh stopped. "What else was I supposed to do, huh? They get dragged from their home to the CIA headquarters and I can't tell them why? How do you think that feels for them, for me?"

Edwards, who'd also stopped, turned to Josh, standing nose to nose with him. "My family thinks I'm a quality assurance manager for a chain of shoe factories, Mr. Reed, have for nineteen years. They think I fly around the country inspecting shoe-making machines, doing health and safety drills. Do you know why?"

Josh kept quiet.

"I do it—we all do it—for *their* safety. The less they know, the better. You think about what you've discovered for a moment. Now imagine what would happen if word got out about this place. It would be chaos. People would be slitting each other's throats to find it. And that's just the normal people, our next-door neighbors who ask us how we are and tell us that the weather's going to be great this weekend. You want your family tied up in all of that? You want some stranger hacking down the front door to get to your family because they want what she knows?" Edwards backed away, wiping the spittle building at the corners of his mouth. Hands on hips, he continued. "The CIA exists to keep the people of America safe, and that means keeping secrets. If the people of the US knew about half the stuff we've kept under wraps—well, I dread to think what would happen."

Josh allowed himself a breath—he'd been holding it all this time. What Edwards said made sense, but he still couldn't help but feel angry about being put in that situation with Georgie. "So now what?" he asked.

"Now we have to keep you both under protection until we neutralize the situation."

"So my family will be kept safe?"

"Haven't you been listening?"

It was all getting too much for Josh. "Yes, sorry, I was. It's just—I'm tired, okay? It's been a long day."

"I understand," Edwards said, almost sympathetically. "But there's still more to come. Can you keep going for just a little longer?"

Josh nodded. "I suppose." Seeing Georgie and Joseph had really taken it out of him. Since discovering the room and the portal, he'd had an underlying feeling of helplessness, watching the same things happen over and over, memories of his repeated failures haunting his mind, but it nowhere near compared to the helplessness he had felt back there with Georgie. He knew she wouldn't believe him, but seeing her scared and angry and lonely and it all being his fault—he couldn't bear it. "How do you do it?" he asked Edwards.

"Do what?"

"Keep the secret? Keep them safe?"

"Years of practice," Edwards said solemnly. "It took a few marriages to get it right. Come on."

They resumed their walk through the halls of lies and secrets. The cold marble, the black and white, it was oppressive, disheartening. It was the perfect palette for a place that dealt solely in misery. Josh wanted out, but he knew he'd have to go deeper first.

The corridor opened up into a secondary atrium with elevators lining either side. Edwards swiped his card on the button panel and pressed down. Wherever they were going, it required even more clearance than where they were now. When the elevator arrived, they stood back to let two agents off.

"Sir," they said in unison, and Edwards nodded. He and Josh boarded, and Edwards pressed the lowest button.

"Just how high a rank are you?" Josh asked.

"Deputy Executive Director," Edwards said.

Jesus, Josh thought.

The elevator plunged downward, lights for the belowground levels flashing past in green on the display above the door. Then they changed to red, sinking two more floors before stopping. The doors did not immediately open, and Edwards had to scan his card once more and perform a retinal scan to get the elevator doors to part.

"Come on," he said, when the doors finally opened.

What was revealed on the other side was surprising to Josh; he'd expected tunnels of concrete and steel, steam squirting in jets from tubes running along the walls, but it was nothing like that. The walls were painted beige, the carpet was cheap, and the air was musty. There was no one to be seen. Edwards stepped off and Josh followed.

"Where are we going?" Josh asked, trying to keep up with Edwards's long strides.

"Somewhere no non-CIA operative has ever been before," Edwards said. "The archives."

They walked the rest of the corridor, until finally they reached a door at the end. After another keycard and retinal scan, it became immediately apparent why they needed to be so deep underground. The room on the other side was cavernous, stretching high above and far across. On the opposite side was a freight elevator, presumably where the stuff that filled the rows and rows of shelves had entered by. The shelves themselves towered overhead, laden with crates, nothing out on show.

"This way," Edwards said. Josh followed him through the maze of shelving, winding deeper into the shadows cast by these skinny metal valleys. "I said I wanted to show you something," Edwards continued, his pace slowing. "Now I can."

Chapter 22

In among the crates were two larger units, possibly the largest serviceable by the freight elevator. They were over twice the height of a person, and one had been lifted down from a shelf by a forklift truck already, as had a few other smaller crates. The crates themselves were metal, fastened with secure catches locked down by a card reader. The larger crates had ladders on one side, presumably to climb to the top with.

"I don't need to tell you that this goes no further than the walls of this room," Edwards said, swiping his card. "Although I can guarantee that no one will ever believe you."

The card reader beeped, flashed green, and the catches unlocked. A small puff of gas condensed in the air, swirling around the rim of the crate. What Josh had expected to see when he'd exited the elevator, he saw now.

"We found the first room," Edwards said as he began to release each catch one at a time, "during a mission to Cairo about twenty years ago. The local people had some crazy superstition about the spirits of dead kings guarding the pyramids, which of course we knew to be nonsense, however when an expedition team—who were using ground-penetrating radar to scan the hidden tunnels below the great pyramids—discovered an unrecognizable energy source that was distorting their readings, it was brought to our attention.

"We've seen this sort of thing before: superstitious populace kept away from an area with tales of otherworldly nightmares coupled with strange energy readings. Of course, we believed that the site was being used to covertly develop nuclear weaponry."

"In the pyramids?" Josh asked, bemused.

"Believe me, I've heard crazier. Seen crazier. In the interest of national security, we investigated, and I was heading up the team. I was a field agent back then, on the brink of landing a desk job, and it was going to be my last covert operation. I had a marriage to save, right? But guess what we found."

"A room, like in Manhattan?"

"Exactly. Our technology was far superior to the ground-penetrating radar used by the expedition responsible for the discovery, and we quickly learned that there was some kind of latent power, a dying light if you will, emanating from the scene. We tunneled from miles back to reach the room. We had to maintain secrecy. We still didn't know what we were dealing with.

"When we found it, it was partially collapsed. Forensic study showed that the room had decayed over an extremely long time. The energy readings, as faint as they were, gave us a date on its creation:

the Cretaceous-Paleogene period. Do you know how long ago that is?"

Josh shook his head. He was oblivious. Edwards had paused on releasing the catches—there were a lot of catches—and smiled.

"That's two hundred and fifty *million* years ago. So we then discovered that this room—or what was left of it—was made of an unknown material, and had been a container for some kind of energy source—one so powerful that we could still detect residual radiation, a kind we hadn't ever detected on Earth before. In fact, it was an energy we'd never detected at all, only in theory. Any ideas what that energy was?"

Again, Josh shook his head. All he wanted to know was what was in the crate.

"Hawking radiation. A theoretical type of energy released by black holes, formed from the quantum effects near an event horizon, where time is distorted to the point where it appears to stop, even theoretically reverse. We detected that energy, here, on Earth, a hundred feet below the pyramids. Can you believe that?"

Josh could not. Edwards continued, his face alive with excitement, talking at an increasing rate.

"So now we had not only an unknown material, we also had a reading of a previously theoretical energy from an event that occurred millions of years before humans even existed. We even detected an almost imperceptible level of time dilation—a shift in time like you experienced—around the source. But the main thing was—we had a lead.

"Searching for more traces of Hawking radiation led us to another site, this time in Albania. A similar story: local people afraid of an area, curious tales passed down through generations about disappearing people, etcetera, and best of all—readings of Hawking radiation. These readings were fainter, and the room we found there we placed back even further to the Permian-Triassic era."

Edwards paused, watching Josh. It seemed he was expecting Josh to say something. When he didn't, Edwards continued, with the story and with the unclipping of the crate.

"That room too was decrepit and lifeless," Edwards said, finishing the bottom row and working his way up the side, mounting the ladder to reach the higher ones. "Nothing left except for fragments of wall and a lingering radiation. We found five of those rooms in total, and then the trail went cold. The others we dated to the Triassic-Jurassic period, the Late Devonian period, and the Ordovician-Silurian period." With a distant expression he said, "We thought we'd hit a dead end."

"Until now?" Josh asked.

Edwards looped his arm around a rung and shook his head. "Not quite. We continued our research using the data we had. After all, we still had five fascinating discoveries to study. What could possibly have been so powerful that its ghost lingered on millions of years later in the form of Hawking radiation? There's only one thing it could have been: a rip so deep in space-time that it had the power to burrow into the past." Edwards climbed down from the ladder so he could approach Josh, his excitement elevating to almost madman levels of white-eyed fanaticism. "Those rooms were time portals too, Mr. Reed. Once."

"But how did they all get there?" Josh asked. "How did they form?"

"That was the big one," Edwards whispered solemnly. "There's no way these rooms could have been a natural occurrence, or even built by an extinct civilization. The materials, the energy—they must have been created by something else."

Josh swallowed, his stomach dropping. "But what…?"

"Hold that thought," Edwards said, returning to the crate to release the last row of catches, "until you've seen this." In silence he popped the catches along the top edge, then climbed down to pull the great door at the front. It swung open with a heave, and he walked it back to reveal what was inside.

At first, Josh wasn't sure what he was looking at. He recognized the crystalline material, but not the shape. A quadrupedal sculpture almost the height of the crate, layered with facets that shimmered in the light. He blinked. *Could it be…? No, surely not…*

"It's the creature that built the room, Mr. Reed," Edwards said, reading Josh's baffled expression.

Josh opened his mouth to speak, but no sound came out. The creature—if it really was a creature—looked almost like a crudely hewn elephant, minus the head and tail. It was like it had taken the rudimentary shape only temporarily.

"The trail had gone cold," Edwards said, walking slowly toward Josh but still looking up at the creature, "but only after we found one last source of Hawking radiation. In Canada, actually, close to the border. Buried just ten or so meters below the surface. We couldn't fathom what we'd found at first; all we knew was that it was made of the same material as the rooms. By this point, technology had improved enough for us to study it further, at the subatomic level, and we realized that the crystalline structure was not simply atoms hewn together with the same symmetry as diamond, or any other innate crystalline structure, no—this was bonded by something else: Hawking radiation. Space-time itself."

"I don't—I don't understand…" Josh mumbled.

Edwards looked fit to burst. He stopped next to Josh, admiring the creature alongside him. "These creatures *are* space-time, Mr. Reed."

"But… why do they come here?"

Edwards seemed unsure. "We *think* the creatures normally exist in a different dimension to us, that they come here in physical form every hundred million years or so. The portals are their doorway. Why they come here though—we don't know."

Josh had so many questions that he struggled to think of a single one clearly. "The room," he said, his throat tight. "It's protected. They protect the portal."

"That seems to be correct."

"Then why can I go in there? Why does it take me back in time?"

Edwards folded his arms. "I'm afraid you've caught up to speed now. This is as much as we know. These creatures seem to exit our world and enter theirs via these portals, but why you have been given access, I don't know. As to why you're brought back in time, I can only imagine that your physical being is unable to enter their dimension, and so you are simply deposited back where you first started.

"As for the creature, clearly something happened to destroy it before it could return—it must have created the portal in Manhattan but never been able to enter it. Why you can is a mystery—but a fascinating one, and one that will hopefully open new doors in this investigation." Excited, Edwards grappled one of the smaller crates and wheeled it over to Josh. He swiped his card and opened the lid. Inside was a sphere, just like the one inside the room, only smaller—much smaller. About the size of an apple. "Pick it up," he said to Josh.

Josh hesitated, then picked it up. It was heavier than he expected. He turned it over in his hands, staring at it. It was warm, buzzing with latent energy. The swirling reflection seemed to swirl faster the longer he held it. "What is it?"

"We found it dropped near the creature," Edwards explained. "We think it's the key to opening these portals. We call it a seed."

Josh stared into the swirling chrome of the seed. It was hypnotic, calming to look at. It absorbed his thought, drew it in, emptying his mind. In its place came a thread, weaving from the seed, filling his mind with new images, new thoughts.

The seed, it was the answer. This realization came like a whisper heard, not an idea imagined. It willed him to return it to the portal. The comfort he felt in that room, the familiarity, it was washing over him. He wanted to be back there, this time with the seed. It felt right.

"Mr. Reed?"

Josh looked at Edwards, then back at the seed. It was inert. "Yes?"

"Are you okay? You don't appear to be listening."

Josh put the seed back down. "Yes, I'm fine. Just… just thinking."

"Well, okay, but I need you to pay attention. This is very important."

Josh nodded. "Okay, sorry. I'm listening."

Edwards continued to talk about his theories as to how the portal worked and how the seed held the Hawking radiation needed to create one. He was obviously enamored with this technology, in his element talking about it, despite knowing so little of its origin. This was his muse—this was what he would stop at nothing to protect. Twenty years, he'd said, dedicated to finding this answer, and here it was, tantalizingly close.

Yet Josh couldn't help but cling onto the decaying warmth the seed had given him. He'd been chosen. Why, he did not know, but he had. The creature, lifeless, never fulfilled its charge, never returned back to the portal, and it was never closed. The other rooms, the other portals, they had all been closed, leaving nothing but residue. The room below Manhattan, it was a danger, and he'd seen it. The seed was the answer. It had to be returned to the portal. He had to close it down.

"I've got something else I'd like to show you," Edwards said, grabbing Josh's attention again. "Follow me." He headed away, toward the service elevator, without looking back. Josh stayed planted for a moment, processing everything he'd just taken in. He realized why he couldn't trust Edwards: putting this mission before three marriages left him with nothing else to fall back to. It was his everything. Whatever decisions he'd make, he'd make for himself, and for no one else. To him, there *was* no one else.

Josh took a breath. "Wait up," he called out after Edwards, jogging to catch up with him.

Chapter 23

Toward the back of the large storage room—where the freight elevator was—another smaller elevator awaited. They boarded. This elevator only had one other stop: down. The carpet pile and shiny buttons still looked like new; this elevator rarely got used. The doors closed and they descended.

"Few people have ever been to this place, seen what you've seen," Edwards said. "And even fewer have been where we're going next."

Josh could still feel the weight of the seed in his hand. It had been alive, like the sphere in the room was, and it had spoken to him. Should he tell Edwards? He wasn't sure. He would wait until he'd seen whatever else it was that Edwards wanted to show him. He was only now starting to come to terms with the fact that what he'd just seen, by all definitions, was an alien. Its crystalline, simplistic form, its great, lumbering shape—it wasn't what he would have expected, had he been asked to guess. He wasn't entirely sure he believed it at all, despite everything that had happened to him. Looking at Edwards, he asked, "Why are you showing all of this to me?"

"When you entered that room, Josh, you did more than discover the next step in a journey to finding out how these portals work—you became the next step. You *are* the next step."

At this, Josh frowned. The next step? It sounded like Edwards had something specifically in mind for him. Before he had a chance to say anything, the elevator came to a stop, and after more card swiping and retinal scanning, the doors opened.

"Follow me," Edwards said, leading the way. The corridor was short, clean and white, filtering them through an airlock where they walked over a sticky pad and were blasted with gas.

"What is this place?" Josh asked as they entered a larger white room filled with three rows of unattended desks, covered in scientific equipment.

"This is our lab," Edwards said, "where we tested all of our theories. The group was small, as you can imagine, but we learned a hell of a lot even from a few samples."

"Where is everybody?"

"You'll soon see, Mr. Reed. But for now, let me show you something."

The room put Josh in mind of his school science labs, but more intense and better equipped. The equipment he did recognize—microscopes, test tubes, computers—was dwarfed by that which he did not, mainly large, creamy white boxes with lights and switches that were, at present, all off. This room seemed like it had been untouched for years, presumably after every avenue of research had been exhausted.

Edwards stopped in front of a small white refrigerator. He opened it and pulled out a tray. "This is where we learned how to make it."

"Make what?" Josh said, trying to get a look.

Edwards placed the tray down on a desk and lifted off the thin cover hiding its contents. "The crystalline material. We call it Hawkene."

There it was, just as Josh remembered it, shimmering and uneven. It was laid out in shards, spaced equally apart. Under the bright lights of the lab it had a translucent quality, an iridescence glowing beneath the surface.

"Touch it," Edwards said, gesturing to Josh. Josh hesitated, wondering why Edwards had such an interest in him holding and touching everything. Edwards, having picked up on Josh's mistrust, put a finger on a shard himself. "See?" he said, the material beneath his finger remaining as it was. "Nothing."

Still hesitant, Josh reached out to touch the material. Fingertips tingling with apprehension, he stroked the surface lightly. To his surprise, the iridescence glowed, then faded, tracing the path he had laid out with his fingers. He pulled away, withdrawing his hand to his chest as though he'd been shocked, even though he had felt none of it.

"Interesting…" Edwards said, watching the iridescence fade.

"What just happened?" Josh asked. For the first time, he felt vulnerable, properly vulnerable, as though Edwards was steering him through a prescribed journey to a destination unknown.

"Relax," Edwards said. "Everything's fine. I've seen this before."

Josh wasn't reassured. Then Edwards pushed two of the shards together.

"Touch them both."

Again hesitant, Josh reached out and put a finger on each shard. They both glowed, and he kept his nerve, watching as the glow increased. Edwards was fascinated.

"Keep still for a moment," he said, watching the shards shimmer. The two pieces, almost imperceptibly at first, began to knit together, binding the surfaces into one.

Josh, heart thumping, pulled away, and the glow receded. "What happened?" he said, breath short.

"The material is intelligent," Edwards said. "It recognizes you. It knows you." Evidently, he was very pleased with this. Before Josh could ask any more questions, Edwards pulled out his cell, dialed and held it to his ear. "Is everything ready? Good. We'll be there soon." He hung up.

"What's ready?" Josh asked.

"You see," he said, putting the tray of Hawkene back in the refrigerator and shutting the door, "we haven't only been relying on what we've found—we've been trying to take steps forward with the technology ourselves. Time, Mr. Reed—time. Imagine having the ability to control it, bend it to your will. That's a power with endless, unimaginable possibilities. Stopping wars, genocide, disasters—all suffering could be a thing of the past—quite literally."

"What have you done?" Josh asked uneasily.

"We've made our own room, Mr. Reed, with the Hawkene. The seed, we know it creates a portal, but we don't know how. We've tried, but with no success. It has a protective energy, like the room—"

"What do you mean? You let me touch one! I could have died!"

Edwards grabbed Josh by the shoulders, his excitement taking over. "And you were fine! Like the room, Mr. Reed, you were fine. That's how I knew. When you went in that room, I knew. Somehow, you've been allowed access, and I think that means you'll be able to go into our new room and create a new portal…!"

Josh pulled away, stunned. "But—but we don't have time… we need to close the portal in Manhattan, before—"

"Josh," Edwards interrupted. "Josh. Please. Don't you see? This is the discovery not just of a lifetime, but of *humanity*. If we close that portal, then what? We could be throwing away everything, shutting it all down. The rooms—they'll end up like the ones we found in Egypt, in Albania—dead. I can't let that happen. I *won't* let that happen."

In Edwards's eyes, Josh could see that obsession, that same look his wives had probably seen and been driven away by. He'd seemed human before, but when he was like this, he was more animal.

"People die," Josh said quietly. "Manhattan becomes a wasteland. Who knows how far it goes." He paused, wondering if he should say what he was going to say next. "The seed, it—it spoke to me. I need to take it to the portal, close it down. That's why I've been chosen.

The portal shouldn't be open, not anymore. It's not safe for us, or for them. They want me to close it." The realization came as he spoke it.

Edwards, eyes still wide, looked disappointed. "I see. Well—that makes sense." He sighed, looking at his feet, then back at Josh, eyes searching. "But please be reasonable. There's so much to learn here, so much good we can do. It won't take long, I promise. Our room, it's safe. We can seal it up. All we need is for you to take the seed in, and then we can go to Manhattan, close the portal. Then everything will be safe. But we can't do that first, we *can't*. All this—it would have been for nothing."

"Can't you seal the room in Manhattan?"

Edwards shook his head. "Hawkene takes too long to make. We don't have enough time."

Josh was stuck. The wilderness of Manhattan played behind his eyes, the hollow shell of a city that had been home to millions of lives. Where had they gone? Where were Georgie and Joseph? Had they even survived? Yet he could sympathize with Edwards's position, twenty years of work and research that built to this final moment. The power of time travel. The future of humanity. Josh held it in his hands. "How long will it take?"

"We can be there in thirty minutes. We'll be back in Manhattan in ninety at the most."

That should be enough time. "Okay," Josh said warily. "I'll do it."

"Excellent. Then we must leave immediately."

"I want to speak to Georgie first."

Edwards sighed, thinking. "Fine. But you must be quick."

"I will. And I want you to promise me that whatever happens, she and Joseph will be kept safe."

"So long as we reach a mutual satisfaction, you have my word."

Josh hesitated. It was the best offer he was going to get. Begrudgingly, he agreed. "Okay then."

They retraced their steps back into the upper portion of the building, mingling once again with agents working their day-to-day jobs, all of them most likely unaware of the significance of what had been going on below for the past twenty years. If Josh were to blurt it out now, would any of them believe him? He still didn't quite believe it himself. A word he didn't want to think of—because of the absurdity of it—jumped into his head: *aliens*. Was that hulking obelisk really an... an alien? A life force from a layer of the universe they could neither see nor occupy themselves? It was an elaborate story, outrageous in fact, but somehow Josh had a sense that it was all true, all real.

And if it *was* all real, then so was the portal, and the seed. And the seed had told him that he needed to go back into that room and shut everything down. But if he did, what would happen to him? Would it be like nothing had ever happened? Or would he emerge decades into the future, into a world he didn't recognize?

"You've got five minutes," Edwards said, parting the guards outside the room. "Then we have to go."

"Okay, five minutes," Josh said, walking through the open door and stepping in. The door was closed behind him, leaving him alone with Georgie, who was waking up, and Joseph, who was still asleep.

"Is everything okay?" Georgie slurred, still half-asleep.

Josh didn't answer immediately. He wasn't sure how. "Fine," he said eventually. "Listen, I've got to go now—"

"Go where?" Georgie said, fully awake in an instant.

"I don't know. They haven't told me. But they need my help."

"I thought they needed your help here?"

Josh sat down next to her and held her hand. "They had to show me some things here first, so I knew what I needed to do."

"Show you? What did they show you?"

"I can't say."

Georgie looked him deep in the eyes. "Is everything okay?"

"We'll be fine. I've made them promise to look after you."

"And what about you? What's going to happen to you?"

Josh stiffened. He had to look away. "I—I don't know exactly just yet." Heat was building up behind his eyes. "I'm sure I'll be fine."

"You promise?"

Josh could feel Georgie looking at him, but he couldn't turn to face her. "I'll do my best."

"And I'll be waiting for you, you understand? You need to come back, for me and for Joseph."

Josh's eyes began to blur. He blinked them clear, sniffing, trying not to think about when—or if—he'd see them again. "Okay," he said. "I will." He squeezed her hand and then stood. "I have to go now," he said, taking a last look at them both. "They may need to take you somewhere safe, so go with them, okay?"

"And you'll meet us there?" Georgie asked, trying to sound optimistic.

"I'll meet you there," Josh whispered through a tightening throat. He went to leave, then stopped. "I'm sorry," he said.

Georgie, smiling weakly, shook her head. "It's okay. You've got to help them. I understand."

"No, not that. I've been a bad husband, a bad father, and I'm sorry. I'm sorry I left you in Niagara, I'm sorry I left you for my job, I'm sorry—"

"It's okay," Georgie said. She was crying now, her smile completely broken. "We can only change what's in front of us."

"And I want to," Josh said.

"Then I'll be waiting."

The door opened, and the guard beckoned Josh to leave. He looked at Georgie and Joseph one last time before he left. "Goodbye," he said.

"Goodbye," Georgie replied.

Chapter 24

Josh, Edwards and the two agents left the building in a rush, bundling through the security checks with little more than a wave. The metal detector went off as Josh went through it, but Edwards just kept going, shouting at the guard there to shut the sound off. Josh followed on without a word. He had made it out of the building, and the cool early evening air under a slowly purpling sky was as soothing as it was going to get.

"Over here, sir," an agent they met outside directed them.

"Is the seed on board?" Edwards asked him.

"Yes, sir."

Edwards nodded, pleased. They followed the agent on to the helipad and boarded the helicopter. Their agent escort left them there, leaning into the gust blowing down from the idling blades. Within the helicopter, they took a seat on the rear bench and donned their headsets.

The lights switched off and the cabin went dark, before a red light flicked on overhead. Shadows jumped and loomed, stretching into a distorted reality of the interior. The slapping of the blades built to a solid thump, the helicopter shaking then leaning forward as it pulled them into the air. Once they'd gained altitude, the thumping receded enough for Edwards to talk.

"When we arrive it'll be dark," he said. "We'll be landing on-site and going straight down. Everything is set up as it needs to be for you to proceed."

"So what do I need to do?" Josh asked.

"We simply need you to take the seed into the room. That's it."

"And then what?"

"We'll find out."

The helicopter bumped along through the air. They were flying low, and fast. The air was close, and Josh was starting to feel a little sick. He needed to distract himself. "How did you work out how to make Hawkene?"

At first, it didn't seem like Edwards was going to tell him. Then he said, "It wasn't easy, but our studies showed us that what we thought was impossible was in fact possible. We have the best minds in the world, Mr. Reed, and they worked non-stop until they cracked it."

"How did they do it?"

"Trial and error. We were working in the dark, beyond our understanding. It was more a case of reverse engineering the problem than simply starting from nothing. Having the material to study made it a lot easier, but it didn't make it easy, not at all. But even the Hawkene has huge technological potential. It's strong, it's light, it has electromagnetic capabilities—it could well be the next wonder material."

Edwards seemed to be skirting the question. Why, Josh didn't know, but he knew enough to understand that when Edwards avoided revealing something, it was deliberate. The only difference was that he was pretending to answer rather than flat out refusing—perhaps to appease? Josh changed the subject. "What's going to happen if you make a portal?"

"Research, and lots of it. There's much to learn, much to understand. What you're doing, it buys us time. You have a gift, Mr. Reed, and we need to make the most of it. Not just for us, but for humanity."

"And if it doesn't work?"

Edwards didn't say anything or look at Josh for a moment. "Then we start over."

The helicopter buffeted violently for a minute, banking sharply then straightening up. Josh felt a warm unease creeping up his collar, and it wasn't the motion sickness. It was the feeling of regret, of not spending the time he should have with the people he loved. Faced with the possibility of not seeing them again for a very long time, he realized he'd been stupid in passing up the opportunities he'd already had. It shouldn't have taken all of this to make him understand.

"You're doing the right thing," Edwards said. Josh's thoughts must have been etched on his face more clearly than he realized.

"It's not just that," Josh said. "I—I should have been there for them."

"Your family?"

Josh nodded.

Edwards checked his watch, then looked to Josh. "When I told you it'd taken me several goes to make marriage work, well—that isn't quite the truth." Edwards's tone had taken an unusual softness, a calm that Josh hadn't seen before. "I haven't made any marriage work. They've all failed. My dedication to this mystery has been and will be the only thing in my life. Sometimes that's just the way it's got to be."

In a way, Edwards was right. Josh had decided to make his job the priority in *his* life, and there probably wasn't any other way it could have been. It was demanding and antisocial, with no flexibility and no time to spare. But he had known that all along. He had used it as an excuse, a responsibility to avoid the one he really needed to commit to. His fear had stood in his way. "Is it ever too late to let go?"

"You're asking the wrong man," Edwards said somberly. He checked his watch again. "Right, we're almost there. Are you ready to make history?"

Josh said nothing. The helicopter's rotors spun up—and so did Josh's stomach—as the craft slowed and descended, making contact with the ground with quite a thump. An agent outside pulled the door open for them, and they disembarked. It was night by now, yet Josh had to shield his eyes from the blinding spotlights blazing down. He barely had any time to even catch his breath before some awaiting agents unloaded the seed in its container and then ushered them toward a small building in the middle of the grassy site. The helicopter blasted wind and noise onto them as they made their way toward it.

"Please," Edwards shouted over the mechanical gust, gesturing for Josh to board the elevator nestling within the small building. Josh boarded; so did Edwards, as well as the agent carrying the container. Edwards closed the cage and pressed a button, and they plummeted deep into the ground.

"When we get down there," Edwards said, talking above the rushing wind blowing up through the elevator shaft as they descended, "I'll show you to the room. We have the seed, and there's a section of Hawkene ready to seal the entrance when you're done."

Josh nodded. "Okay. Is there anything else you need me to do?"

"That's it."

"And then we go to Manhattan?"

"Exactly."

Josh couldn't help but feel that there was more to it. It seemed too simple, too easy, but there wasn't a whole lot he could do about it.

The elevator opened up below into a small chamber, where thick tubes ran along the ground, bypassing complex equipment covered in glowing lights and swathes of buttons.

"This is where our team has been working since moving from the lab," Edwards explained.

"Where are they now?"

"Reassigned. No one's been down here in a while."

They came to a stop and Edwards pulled the cage open.

"Follow me," he said, walking in the direction of one of two smaller tunnels leading from the chamber. Josh jogged to catch up, with the agent following carrying the container. They entered the tunnel, which quickly narrowed, the thick tubes following alongside. As they got toward the end, Josh had to duck a little.

"And here it is," Edwards said. A small hole greeted them, lined with Hawkene. A machine, grasping a piece the same size as the hole, waited, the thick hoses that had trailed the tunnel with them buried into its base. "I'll be waiting topside for you while you take the seed in. Once you're done, exit the room and we will remotely seal it behind you with this."

"And where will I go?"

"Come back to the elevator and return to the surface. You'll be picked up there."

Josh looked into the hole. It was jet black. It wasn't cold in the tunnels, but he felt cold.

"Here," Edwards said, passing him a flashlight. "You'll need this."

Josh took it. Then Edwards directed the agent to set the container down, dismissing him afterward. Edwards swiped his card in the lock as the agent returned to the elevator, and the container opened. Inside was the seed.

"This is what you'll be taking in with you."

"How will I know if it's worked?"

"You'll know."

Josh went to reach for it, but Edwards stopped him. "Not just yet. We'll give you the signal over the PA when we want you to begin."

With his hand still frozen in mid-grab, Josh took that thought in. Edwards wasn't taking any chances. He clearly didn't know what was going to happen, but there was no point arguing; the only way Josh was going to get to Manhattan was to do as he was told.

"Is there anything you're not sure about before I go?" Edwards asked. He seemed nervous—excited nervous.

"I think I've got it. Wait for the signal, take the seed into the room, see what happens, come back out, go to the surface."

"That's it. Okay, well—I'll be going now." Edwards gave Josh a cursory glance before turning on his heel and walking quickly out. Josh watched him for a moment before directing his attention back to the room. It was still dark—as if it were going to be anything else—and it was most certainly foreboding. The room in Manhattan, it was welcoming, inviting, familiar. This was none of those things. It was empty, lifeless.

He looked at the seed. It swirled silvery, small, yet so powerful. Could this thing really contain enough energy to send the world into chaos? It certainly seemed that way. Josh couldn't help but think that Edwards was playing with fire. His fingers tingled with anticipation as he waited for the call. The tunnel was quiet, save for the beating of his heart in his ears. Ahead, the hole loomed. He would have to duck to enter it. It was so dark. So ominous.

"Mr. Reed?"

The voice over the speaker made Josh jump. He clutched his chest, blinking to slow his heart.

"You may begin."

After a few calming breaths, Josh picked up the seed. Again it swirled harder, that energy and warmth flowing into him. Suddenly, a pain shot up his arm, and he dropped it back into the container again.

"Mr. Reed, please continue."

Josh looked up, massaging his arm. The pain had been like a shock, a mild one, and his bones still tingled. Up by the speaker he saw a camera; Edwards was watching. He swallowed, fixing upon the seed again. Why had it hurt him? It was like a warning. If it had wanted to kill him, it surely would, but it didn't. The jolt was a message, not a punishment.

"Please, Mr. Reed, we are short on time."

Edwards was right. He was holding Josh to ransom here. If Josh wanted to get back to Manhattan, he had to do this first. He held his breath as he reached for the seed, anticipating another shock. His fingers grasped and he lifted the seed up—and this time it was fine. The warmth and energy flowed through him, with no sudden bursts of pain.

"Okay, good," Edwards said. "Now, carefully, take it into the room."

Holding the seed with a delicate touch, Josh crept toward the black hole. His muscles were tense with apprehension, his mind racing with the possibilities of why it had shocked him. Ducking into the blackness, he let the weight of the seed rest in one palm while he used his other hand to retrieve the flashlight. Flicking it on and pointing it down, he saw a ramp into the room, like they'd had in Manhattan.

"Good," Edwards's voice was saying back in the tunnel. "Keep going."

One step at a time, Josh edged down the ramp. The seed was heavy, and seemed to be getting heavier. And warmer. From the wash of the flashlight, the swirling was also speeding up, emitting a glow of its own.

He was at the bottom of the ramp. How far in did he need to go? The seed was almost unbearably hot, and he didn't know how much longer he'd be able to hold it for. Walking further in, the flashlight glimmering off the Hawkene, he winced as tingling heat seared his palm.

Then a sudden agony filled him—but it wasn't his agony. It was a *sense* of agony, from something else. A warning. He dropped the flashlight to the ground, where it bounced and rolled away, tossing the seed to his cooler hand to ease the pain. Yet still that sense enveloped him. Something was wrong. Not here, in this room, but nearby. The seed, it was crying out to him, calling for his help.

He had to go. Now. Wrapping the seed up in the front of his sweater to make it easier to hold, he ran back to the ramp, the flashlight forgotten. He followed the glowing hole in the wall and soon he was ducking out to exit into the tunnel.

The PA crackled. "What are you doing, Mr. Reed? Go back into the room, please."

Josh ignored Edwards, and as he cleared the tunnel and headed into the deserted chamber, he could feel the heat of the seed warming through his sweater.

"Mr. Reed? Stop where you are, Mr. Reed, immediately!"

Again, Josh ignored him, running past the elevator shaft and toward the other tunnel, following the tubes. That was where he needed to go. That was where the cries were coming from.

"Mr. Reed," Edwards said, without emotion, "whatever you think you're doing, I suggest you stop. Please return to the elevator shaft. I will meet you there."

Josh could see that the tunnel ran down deeper underground. As he entered it and sprinted along it, he could see that it curved ahead, the pipe following into it. Josh sprinted even harder, lungs screaming agony and razors slicing his throat. He could smell burning material, just his fingertips supporting the seed to avoid them getting fried.

"Reconsider what you're doing, Mr. Reed. We don't have time for this. Let's go to Manhattan now. We need to go to Manhattan. Come to the elevator, Mr. Reed, so we can go."

The tunnel straightened, then dived down deep. The seed was too hot to hold now, and Josh wrangled his sweater off as he ran, trying to carry the seed without touching it at all. He stumbled, sweater halfway around his neck, and had to slow to get it off.

"Come back, Mr. Reed. Come back and do what you know is right."

With the seed now tightly wrapped in his sweater, Josh sprinted on. The pipes followed down the slope, and Josh ran as fast as the agony flaring in his side would let him. As the tunnel flattened out, it opened up into a cavern filled with equipment that reached up high toward the ceiling, like skyscrapers. The pipes wound deep into the equipment, and slowing, he followed them in.

The room was empty and quiet, and he moved as quickly as he dared between the towering machinery. It all appeared to be off, or at least standing by, covered in settled dust that hadn't been cleared off in a long time. The equipment also looked old, dated, like it had been installed over a decade ago.

This room had been here even longer than Josh had imagined. It had probably once been a hive of activity, but it was deserted now. The project wasn't simply on hiatus; it had been shut down, had been for years. Josh began to understand more clearly Edwards's obsession with the place: he'd thrown everything away to pursue it, and it had led him nowhere. Now he'd had another taste of the success he'd hoped to achieve before, and he wasn't going to let that slip. The PA had been quiet for a minute or two now, and that could only mean one thing—Edwards was coming down to get him.

So all Josh could do was move onward. He sensed he was near where he needed to be, where the seed wanted him to be. Thin wisps of smoke were rising from his sweater, and he could feel that heat radiating from it. It wouldn't last much longer.

A deep rumble threw Josh from his thoughts and spiked his heart rate.

What was that?

It sounded like it had come from within the walls of equipment. He continued through, holding his breath, each step careful. He walked and he listened. The sweater was beginning to hiss, growing louder with each step.

The rumble came again, and Josh stopped. It had come from the center of the room, from among the most concentrated area of machinery. Edging his way between the towering devices, he came across a clearing in the middle of the room. There was pit dug there, deep and wide. He leaned over the edge to see below, and what he saw nearly made him fall in.

Chapter 25

The first creature had been hewn from crystal, an almost amorphous shape with a vague hint of biological design, but this was different. The facets of crystal writhed in among themselves, swirling as the portal swirled, glinting with life and energy. Almost… almost as though it were breathing.

The pipe, the one that had run all the way down the tunnel, fed into the pit, down under the creature. Was this how they were making the Hawkene? This creature, clearly weakened, must have been just about able to produce the crystal, which Edwards then used to build the new room. It was being held prisoner, exploited for its abilities. It was writhing gently, groaning, calling out to him. It was in distress, held against its will.

Josh looked on, rooted to the spot. Edwards had held this back from him. He'd known that Josh would have been appalled. What else had Edwards held back? His determination to see his life's work come to fruition had turned him into a ruthless machine. What would he do to Josh if he caught him now? Josh couldn't be sure. Better just to get out of there, and fast.

Looking about, he saw a smaller exit at the other side of the room with what looked like another elevator cage in it, but before he could move, a voice echoed across the cavern.

"Mr. Reed, I know you're in here!"

It was Edwards. Without thinking, Josh took off toward the rear exit, jumping over the pipe that fed into the pit. As he jumped, the seed went heavy against his sweater, sizzling through the material. It thumped onto the ground and rolled into the pit.

"No!" Josh cried out, but it was too late. Many pairs of running footsteps were heading his way, and he had to go. Leaving the seed behind, he ran, jumping over equipment and cables as fast as his legs would take him. But even as he ran, he could see that the elevator cage was not there. He could press the button to call it—it was lit— but he'd have to wait. Crashing into the far wall, Josh repeatedly bashed the button, but his fears were confirmed: the elevator was a long way off. He could hear it trundling down, but it wasn't going to get there fast enough, nowhere near. The deep groan from the pit sounded again.

"Get someone covering the exit!" Josh heard Edwards yell, and through the equipment he saw one of the agents sprint back up the slope and out of sight. The remaining agents, however many there were, continued their pursuit, appearing one by one, weapons raised.

"We have him, sir!" one of them shouted.

Edwards appeared last, a sheen of sweat clearly glistening on his brow. He had run—they had all run—to stop Josh. This was a definitive blow for Edwards, as Josh realized that none of this was orchestrated to his plan any more. It was all improvised from now on. Josh needed to be extra careful. He'd seen Edwards's wild side in passing before, and he knew it was dangerously unpredictable.

"Mr. Reed," Edwards said, arms outstretched in a display of welcome. "It seems things have got a little out of hand, don't you think?"

"Why?" Josh shouted back, pressed against the wall, listening for the elevator as it slowly wound its way down the shaft. "Why didn't you tell me?"

"Haven't you figured it out already?" Edwards said, touching his fingertips together. "You're a clever man."

As ever, Josh felt like he was being wound into a trap. Chest rising and falling, he thought carefully before he spoke, while the creature groaned again. "I want to hear *you* say it."

Edwards shrugged. "And why would I do that?"

Think, Josh, think. "Because… because I still have the seed," he lied. "And if you come near me—well, you know I'm the only one who can touch it." Judging by the slip in Edwards's grin and the way the agents all shuffled back a half-pace meant that they all understood the threat, and still believed that Josh did indeed have the seed. Josh went with it. "And you can't kill me, because I'm the only clue you have left."

Edwards's grin returned, unmatched by his eyes. "You're cleverer than I thought," he said, voice perhaps wavering a little. "This is why we must work together."

"The portal is dangerous," Josh said. "Why can't you understand that? It needs to be destroyed."

"I'm afraid I can't let you do that," Edwards said. "I can't let you destroy the most important technological advancement mankind has ever discovered."

"But don't you see?" Josh bellowed at him. "There won't *be* a mankind if you don't shut it down! I've seen it! I know what happens!"

By his body language, Edwards looked like he wanted to explode, but he held his station. "How do you know that your plan will even work?" he said calmly. It was a good point. Josh had put blind faith in the guidance of these—these beings—to tell him what he needed to do. Could he trust them? He had no other choice.

"You know it will, Edwards."

Edwards ruffled at having his name used.

"You know it'll work, because you won't let me do it."

"Merely a precaution."

A clank from the elevator shaft told Josh that it was nearly there. Why was it taking so long? It felt like hours had passed, although it had only been seconds. "No, it's not," Josh said. If Edwards really believed the seed would not close down the portal in Manhattan, then why was he so vehemently against it?

A realization dawned on Josh. "Oh God…" he whispered. "When I touched the Hawkene shards and you told me you'd seen them glow like that before—that was because it's happened to you too, isn't it?"

Edwards was making no effort to hide his anger by this point, but he was silent. Josh continued.

"When you first found them, the creatures, you were given the same power I have, the same authority, weren't you? But you didn't use it to help them, you used it to capture them, exploit them. And one of them died, and your power was revoked. You know the seed will shut the portal, because you feel it too."

It was a stalemate: until the elevator finally arrived, neither party could make a move. The next words Edwards spoke would be the decider. "Show me the seed," he said. Josh's stomach dropped.

"What?" he asked.

"Show me the seed."

"I—I don't need to. You know I have it."

The grin reappeared. "He doesn't have the seed," he said to his fellow agents.

"Yes I do!" Josh yelled. "Stay away!" He looked up over his shoulder; another few seconds and the elevator would be there. The agents still couldn't shoot him, but they could most certainly grab him and restrain him.

"Take him down," Edwards commanded.

The agents sprinted toward Josh, running either side of the pit while Edwards stayed rooted at the head of it. The ground rumbled as the agents sprinted, and Josh prepared himself for the impact. Then the whole room shook, and a wailing sound of tortured metal followed. The agents stopped in their tracks to look back at the pit. Edwards stepped backward, thumping up against a wall of equipment.

From the pit, the creature rose, its shimmering, amorphous form climbing out in great, staggering motions. As it emerged, Josh could see the seed embedded in its side, pulsing gently. The agents aimed their weapons, but Edwards held up a hand.

"Don't shoot it!" he cried out.

The creature emitted another deep rumble, and then a high-pitched scream that had all of them clutching at their ears. It stood tall over Edwards, looking down on him, its crystalline form shifting and writhing. Then it began to collapse in on itself, folding layer over layer, disappearing within its own folds as it shrank toward the ground. The agents tracked the creature with their weapons as it grew smaller, its quadrupedal state blurring into one twisting pillar of swirling crystal.

It shrank until it was no taller than Edwards himself. Josh stared on, rooted to the spot. Then a crack, as the pillar began to split. Starting from the bottom, it tore in two, separating into halves right up to its middle. Tendrils also emerged from the top, curling down its sides.

Josh realized what was happening, and he could see that Edwards had realized too: it was taking Edwards's form, albeit crudely, and when it was done, it stood before him, a mannequin of crystal. The elevator arrived, but Josh did not move—he watched.

The creature took a step toward Edwards, a shaky, cumbersome step. It staggered, catching itself with slow corrections, almost like a robot learning its first steps. Edwards had gone pale, hand still raised from his command to hold fire. The creature, a pace or two away from Edwards, seemed to be studying him. Its crystalline shape, seed still embedded in its back, pulsed as the Hawkene had done when Josh had touched it.

Then, in an instant, the creature slammed Edwards back into a metal panel, sending him tumbling to the ground. Dazed, Edwards crawled away from the creature as the other agents opened fire on it, bullets splintering chunks of crystal from its body that were exhausted of color before they even hit the ground.

"No!" Edwards shrieked, still on the ground, holding his head. "Stop!"

The creature howled the high-pitched scream again, then tumbled onto all fours and galloped out toward the exit.

"Don't let it get away!" Edwards screamed, waving frantically at the other agents. Josh took this as his opportunity to leave, pulling the elevator cage open and jumping aboard. Button punched, the cage began its journey upward, leaving the echoing shouts of Edwards behind.

As the elevator trundled up, it gave Josh a chance to catch his breath and think. What now? He didn't have the seed anymore. There was only one thing for it: he'd have to go back to the portal and start all over again.

He checked his cell: no signal. When he reached the surface, he would check again, call Lionel. If he wasn't already in CIA custody, he'd know what to do. The East Side Access tunnels would most certainly be guarded by now, but Lionel would know of another way in, surely? If anyone knew, it would be Lionel.

When the elevator finally reached the end of its slow journey, Josh retracted the cage and cautiously stepped out into the cold night. He was in a forest somewhere, the entrance shrouded in undergrowth to keep it hidden. The view was thick with trees and he could see no further than ten or so meters. Even the night sky was blocked by the canopy, only a few moon rays making it through for him to see by.

Checking his cell, he saw he still had no signal. Fortunately it seemed like the agents sent to capture him hadn't arrived in time. *Better make myself scarce*, Josh thought. He headed away from the hidden entrance, walking in as straight a line as he could.

Soon, he came to a clearing which surrounded a hill tall enough from which to see above the trees. The sky was clear, and the crescent moon was bright, so he climbed the hill to survey the view.

In almost every direction, all he could see were trees. There appeared to be a road cutting through about a mile away, and another few miles further he could see the glow of a small town. It would take at least an hour to walk there. He checked his cell again, and up there he had just enough signal to make a call. Dialing Lionel's number, he waited and listened. It rang, then clicked.

"Josh, is that you?"

Relief flooded through him. "Yeah, it's me."

"Are you still with the CIA?"

"No, are you?"

"No. I went home after you went below ground. They tried to pick me up later though—I was out shopping and when I came back, my place was broken into."

"Where are you now? Actually, don't answer that."

Lionel laughed a single laugh. "No shit. I'm safe though. What's happening to you?"

"Can't say just now, mainly because I don't know where I am. Listen though—can you do me a favor?"

"Sure, what do you need?"

"You remember Mr. Miller, don't you?"

A pause. "The executive? Yeah…?"

"Remember the day we met him?"

"How can I forget?"

"Do you remember where that was?"

"What do you—oh, right, I see. Yes, I remember."

"Well, I need in. Covertly."

Lionel didn't answer.

"Lionel, are you there?"

"I'm here."

"What do you think?"

"I think it's a bad idea."

Josh hugged himself. He was getting cold. "But is it possible?"

"Hang on a minute."

A minute passed. "Well?"

"I'm checking."

"Check quicker."

More silence. Then Lionel spoke again. "It's possible. It won't be easy though."

"Great. I'll call you again when I know where I am."

"Okay. Speak soon."

Josh looked around at the endless scenery once more and sighed. "I sure hope so."

"Speak then. Bye."

"Bye." Josh hung up. That was one problem solved: Lionel would be able to get him into the tunnels. But he had another problem—how to get there in the first place. He had two choices: he could head for the road, which was closer, in the hopes someone would pick him up—although he hadn't seen any lights traveling along it—or he could head straight for the town and pray he got there before anything irreversible happened.

There was a small glimmer of hope among all of this: so long as he headed *toward* Manhattan, time should be on his side. He wondered how much of a temporal effect the portal was having by now, but the thought trailed off when he heard a distant noise.

Looking along the road, he scanned it for lights, but couldn't see any. He kept turning slowly, shielding his eyes from the bright moonlight, listening to the slowly increasing volume of whatever it was he could hear. It was deep and droning, and it was only when he'd turned fully around that he could see what it was.

A searchlight, scanning the trees, hung way above, slowly marching toward him as the drone got louder. The drone became a thump, blades speeding around and around to keep the spotlight airborne, as the CIA helicopter scoured the forest for… for him.

Chapter 26

The helicopter was moving quickly, hunting for its prey. Josh wasted no time, stumbling back down the hill, heading, he decided in a flash moment, for the road. There was no chance of making it to the town before he was spotted, especially if they had some kind of infrared camera on that helicopter. He was the only living thing about, the growing thud of the helicopter's blades likely scaring everything else deeper into the forest.

He ran as fast and as hard as he could, heading in what he hoped was the most direct route to the road. What he'd do once he got there, he didn't know, but for now he kept that at the back of his mind, concentrating on not slipping over or tripping up. Trees and bushes whipped past, branches licking him with stinging glances, but there was no time to stop and staunch the pain. Gritting his teeth, he ran, while the thump got louder and the lights got brighter.

As air ripped his lungs raw, he began to worry he was heading in the wrong direction. A creeping thought distracted him: didn't people always travel in big circles when they were lost? How big? Enough for him to loop back around before he reached the road? He hoped not, and dug his heels in deeper and pushed on. The canopy overhead danced with the buffeting wind of the helicopter as it soared close by, dipping and dancing in a zigzag motion to cover ground fast. Comforted by the fact it hadn't seemed to have locked on to him, he focused on what appeared to be a clearing up ahead and sprinted into overdrive.

Bursting through the leaves, Josh found himself on the open road. Relief nearly made his legs buckle, but it was short-lived. The road, as he'd suspected, was deserted. There would still be at least a couple of miles to go before he reached the town. Looking up and down the road, a soft glow of light staining the night sky indicated the direction he needed to go, and he began to jog toward it. Although his heart was pumping and his adrenal gland was firing at full capacity, he could not muster any more speed. His stomach rolled and his head swam, the flight from the forest the most energetic thing he'd put himself through in decades. The helicopter was scouring a different patch now, so he had some space to breathe.

Legs heavy, throat stinging, he trudged on, the glow ahead seeming to get no brighter, nor closer. If he could have collapsed onto the ground and slept there, he would, but there was no time. Every wasted second was another where Edwards was predicting his next move, figuring him out, and Josh knew it wouldn't take long for him to guess what he'd do next. Josh prayed that he'd be able to get to Lionel first.

It was only when Josh snapped from that semi-conscious line of thought that he realized the helicopter had gone completely. He felt like he should be happy about it, but he knew he couldn't. If anything, it was worrying. Edwards had not been a man to give up, and so this terminated search had to be the result of a proactive decision to do something else, rather than the abandonment of his only lead. He knew. He knew where Josh was going next. It was the only choice Josh had left.

A street sign proclaimed the border to the town—Monroe—one mile away, so Josh kicked down a gear and forced himself to pick up his pace. Ten or so minutes and he'd be there—then he could find out where in the hell Monroe was and get back to Manhattan.

That last mile was torture. The road bent slowly uphill, unnoticeably at first, but soon the doubled weight of his leaden limbs and the increasing ascent sent screaming messages from every corner of his body direct to his brain, all telling him, for the love of God, to stop. But he didn't stop. He couldn't stop. This small town in this forest was his only lifeline, and he would get there or die. When the first streetlight rolled overhead and the first house came into view, he let out a wheezy yelp of triumph, feebly punching the air to celebrate to a crowd of no one. Midnight had to be closing in fast, and soon the effects of the time well would be noticeable, but for now everyone was asleep.

A sign overhead directed him to not just a welding supply and post office, but also a mini mart. It was just around the corner, and he slowed his pace to a walk while he tried to catch his breath. To his relief, the mini mart was still open, and there were payphones outside. Better to use one of those than his cell again. He needed to break a ten dollar bill for change, so he stepped inside and grabbed a drink and candy bar and took them to the cash register, which was shrouded with thick, bulletproof glass.

The old man behind the glass was snoozing, a newspaper draped over him like a blanket. Josh tapped on the glass and the man snorted awake, blinking to bring himself back to the present. He looked over at Josh a little hazily, then creaked onto his feet and hobbled over.

"A little late to be buying candy," he said, sounding disgruntled. He took the items and punched them in, the price appearing on the screen. "Bag?"

"No thanks," Josh replied.

"First that darned helicopter, then you," the man continued. He seemed to be talking more for his own benefit than for Josh's. "An old man just wants his rest."

"I understand."

"That'll be three dollars and forty-nine cents, please."

Three dollars? Josh thought. Even the New York Ritz-Carlton wouldn't have charged that much. He said nothing however, and handed over the money. The old man took it, getting a glance at him.

"You seem awfully flustered for a man buying candy in the middle of the night," he said. Josh was starting to get annoyed with him, but bit his tongue to try and maintain his anonymity. He wanted to slip in and slip out, and not cause a fuss.

"Just out for a run before the night shift," he lied.

"Night shift? Where'd you work, then? I've not seen you before, and I've seen everyone in Monroe."

"The, uhm…" *Think, Josh.* "The post office. Starting tonight. Covering a shift for a week while some guy's off sick." *Too much detail, too much detail…*

The old man eyed him, passing his goods and change back through the slot. "You mean Tom?"

"Yeah, sure—Tom."

"There isn't any Tom at the post office. You're lying."

Josh sighed. His head was thumping and he felt both hungry and sick. All he wanted was to go to bed, but he knew that wasn't going to happen any time soon, certainly not with this prying old fool getting in the way. "I don't know, that sounded right. Look, I'm going to go now, okay? You have a nice night."

As he took his change and his food and left the mini mart, Josh kept his eyes down. He could feel the old man's glare follow him through the store, and the relief of the door clanking shut behind him and the cool night air on his face was stronger than it really ought to have been.

Wiping his brow with his sleeve, he opened his drink and took a swig, the lukewarm liquid soothing his throat and easing his thumping head. The candy bar went down in just a few bites, the instant sugar rush lifting him slightly from his dizziness. He could go on for a few hours more at least. Now to call Lionel.

He fed some coins into one of the payphones and dialed Lionel's number. It rang for a while, and Josh began to worry that Lionel wasn't going to answer, but eventually he did.

"Who is this?" was Lionel's greeting.

"It's me."

"Jesus—you had me worried there. I thought it was the—I thought someone else was phoning."

"Sorry. Wanted to keep things off the grid I guess. Do you have a payphone nearby?"

"Sure."

"Ring me on this number from it, and quickly. I'm sure it won't take long for them to figure out what's going on."

"Will do," Lionel said, then hung up. Josh waited a few minutes for Lionel to call back, falling into a daydream while he leaned against the wall next to the payphone. When the phone finally rang, he jumped out of his skin. He grabbed the receiver and put it to his ear.

"Hello?"

"I'm outside."

"Did you understand my message earlier?"

"I think so," Lionel said, sounding unsure. "You want another way into the East Side Access tunnels, right?"

"Yeah."

"I think we can do that."

"Great. I don't want to say anything more about it on the phone. Where can we meet?"

"Where are you now?"

Josh checked around him to see if he could find out any more clues as to where he was. "Don't know. Some town called Monroe, in the middle of nowhere."

"Monroe? Isn't that in Pennsylvania?"

"I've got no idea."

"Hang on a sec."

"Lionel, what are you—"

"I said hang on a sec!"

Josh waited. "Well?"

"As I thought—you're in Pennsylvania."

"Shit. How long will it take to get to Manhattan?"

"About three and a half hours by bus."

"Well, I guess that's how long it'll take, then. I'll meet you outside the usual."

"The usual?"

"Yeah, the usual. You know…?"

"Oh right, I got it. See you then."

"Before you go," Josh added, checking his watch. "I need you to know that some weird stuff could start happening soon, so you need to go there now and stay there until I arrive."

"Weird stuff? What weird stuff?"

"It's hard to explain. I just need you to wait for me, and not worry about anything. I'll be as quick as I can. I'll explain everything when I meet you."

"Okay…" Lionel said, sounding uncertain. "I'll see you when I see you."

"Thanks. I appreciate it."

"Any time."

Josh hung up the phone. He didn't have a lot of time to think about his next move, however, because the flashing blue and red lights of a police car pulling up beside him took up all of his attention.

"Shit…" he muttered to himself. This was the last thing he needed. He looked through the glass into the mini mart to see the old man glaring at him from behind the counter. *Crazy idiot*, Josh thought. He had to get out of this, and quickly. Time was not on his side—at least, not until he got back to the portal.

Two officers stepped out of the car. The first—and the taller of the two—approached Josh with a slow, wary gait, while the other stayed back. They were both pointing their flashlights at him. Josh shielded his eyes, trying to stem the rising thump behind them.

"Good evening, sir," the taller of the two men greeted him. "Can I ask what you're doing up at this time of night?"

"I'm just out for a run," Josh said.

"It's a little late for that, don't you think?"

"So I've been told," Josh replied. "Have I done something wrong, officer?"

The officer continued to approach, until he was within reaching distance of Josh. "Well, that's what we're here to find out," he said, shining the light from one of Josh's eyes to the other. "Can I ask your name, sir?"

Josh hesitated. "John. John… Edwards."

"Well, Mr. Edwards," the officer said, "have you been taking any drugs this evening?"

"No, no, of course not—"

"Are you sure?" the officer asked, peering at Josh. Josh suspected his probably bloodshot eyes and pouring sweat gave him the appearance of someone whose veins ran thick with opiates, likely the reason the old man in the mini mart had reported him in the first place.

"I'm sure."

"Okay," the officer said. "Well, I'm going to need to see some ID, please."

Double shit. "I don't have any on me."

"Well then, I'm afraid we're going to have to take you down to the station," the officer said, reaching behind him for his cuffs.

"Wait!" Josh said, holding up his hands to stop the officer. "Wait. I have ID."

"But you just told me you didn't."

"I do. I lied. I'm sorry. I'm—I'm a celebrity, and I just wanted some privacy, that's all." Josh reached into his pocket and retrieved his driver's license, handing it to the officer. The shorter officer approached and took the license from his colleague, taking it back to the car to run a check.

"A celebrity, huh? I've never heard of you," the taller officer continued.

"It's a reality TV show on—"

"Sir, I'm going to ask you to keep quiet from now on. I think you've said enough."

"Yes, of course."

The officer folded his arms. "You celebrities think you can just do what you want, don't you?"

"No, sir."

"Shut up! I told you to keep quiet!"

The shorter officer emerged from the vehicle and called over to his colleague. "Hey, Sergeant," he said. "You'd better check this out."

"You wait right there," the taller officer told Josh. "Make one move and you're done." He returned to the car to talk with the shorter officer, and then they both looked at him together, speechless. They talked again, and drew their weapons.

"Okay, sir," the taller officer said, pointing his pistol square at Josh's chest, "I want you to put your hands behind your head and turn around, okay?"

It was all going wrong. Josh couldn't believe it. With no other options left, he put his hands behind his head and turned around, just like he'd been asked. He could hear the officers approaching.

"I want you to kneel down, okay? Slowly, to the ground. Now. Do it."

Josh detected a hint of fear in the taller man's voice. This quiet town was probably unlikely to house many criminals, and if Josh's suspicions were right, the flag against his name that had startled the pair probably listed him as one of America's most wanted. These officers were nervous, and likely inexperienced. They were doubtless just as scared as Josh was.

"I'm going to cuff you, okay?" the taller officer said from right behind him. "Don't move."

There was only one chance to get out of this. If Josh didn't take it, he'd be done.

He took a breath, and made up his mind.

Chapter 27

As Josh felt the taller officer take hold of one of his wrists, he exploded backward, tumbling into him and sending them both to the ground. They each scrabbled to right themselves, but Josh was quicker, climbing on top of the officer and wrestling for his pistol.

"Don't move!" the shorter officer yelled. Josh had no time to look, but he knew the second pistol was firmly pointed at him. The whole while there was no clear shot, he'd be okay, but the minute there was… he didn't want to think.

The taller officer took a swing at Josh that landed in his ribs, winding him, and he collapsed onto the officer's writhing mass. The pistol was beneath him, he could feel it, and as he wheezed air back into his lungs, he clawed it from its holster. Knowing what he was trying to do, the officer was flailing to knee Josh in the chest and push him off by the shoulders, but it was too late—Josh had the gun. He rolled back, holding it with both hands as he stood up slowly.

"Easy…" the taller officer said, holding up his hands. He was still now, chest pumping, eyes wide and unblinking.

"Drop the weapon!" the shorter officer yelled, pistol still raised, panic written all over his face.

Josh's hands were shaking, the snub-nosed pistol, now slippery with sweat, bobbing up and down. The cold realization of what he'd just done and was still doing turned his stomach. For a moment he considered giving it all up and turning himself in, but no matter how much he wanted it to be, that was never going to be an option. He gripped the pistol tighter, and licked his lips. "I'm going now," he said, trying to firm the waver in his voice. "Don't try to follow me. I don't want to hurt anyone. I'm not a bad person."

Neither officer had anything to say to that. The stalemate lingered, and Josh knew the only way out was by his command.

"Both of you, stay where you are. You, put your gun down."

The shorter officer shifted from foot to foot. "I'm afraid I can't do that."

Josh checked back inside the mini mart quickly. The old man was gone. Probably calling back to the station to get whoever else was there down on the scene. He didn't have long. Sidestepping around the grounded officer and keeping the pistol trained squarely at him, Josh moved toward the police car, his actions slow and his eyes keen. The shorter officer followed him with his own pistol, still rooted to the spot. As Josh got closer to him, he switched his own aim to point at the shorter officer instead, making him twitch.

"Easy…" Josh muttered. "Easy." He checked the officer on the ground quickly; he hadn't moved. A few more steps and he'd be close enough to touch the shorter officer.

"That's close enough," the officer said, taking a pace back and firming up his grip on his pistol.

"Give me the gun," Josh said, trying not to sound like he was begging—although he was.

"Not going to happen. Stay where you are or I *will* open fire."

"You don't want to do that," Josh said, trying to sound commanding. "If you shoot me, I'll shoot back. I might miss, but do you want to take that chance?" He took another step closer, and the officer stepped one back.

"Don't test me," the officer said.

"Give me the gun."

In a split second, the officer on the ground rolled over to his knees and was halfway up when Josh switched the gun back to him. "Stay down!" Josh yelled, making the officer freeze. Sliding the gun from one to the other, he tried to catch his breath, his heart beating so hard it felt like he was going into cardiac arrest. "I told you I don't want to hurt anyone, but if you try to stop me I swear to God I will shoot you both! Now get out of my way!"

The two officers shared a look. Josh knew as much as they did that no one here wanted to get shot, let alone die, and he watched the wordless conversation between the two officers as they decided what they were going to do next. Almost imperceptibly, the officer now squatting on the ground nodded.

"Good," Josh said. "Step aside."

The shorter officer blocking his way hesitated, then lowered his gun and did as he was told. Making sure he kept facing them both,

Josh continued to make his way around to the car, backing up toward it once he was between it and them.

"I'm sorry," he said, slipping in through the open door, gun still raised. "I hope you don't get into any trouble because of this."

The engine was still running, and Josh pulled the door closed, slipping the car into drive. He pulled away slowly, one eye on the road, one eye on the officers, barrel unwavering. Once the officers and the mini mart were out of sight, he put the pistol down on the passenger seat and collapsed back into his own. "Holy shit…" he muttered to himself. Running his shaking fingers through his hair, he briefly relived the moment. It had only happened minutes—if not seconds—ago, yet it didn't feel real, like he was experiencing someone else's memories. "Holy shit…" he said again.

But there was no opportunity to linger on the past for long. His whereabouts would be all over the radio very soon, and the car he was in would be a prime target. He needed to ditch it quick. Steering the car out of Monroe, he trundled along the tree-lined road between it and the next town over—Towanda—pulling over a half-mile out. Rolling the car gently into the forest, he went in far enough for it to be obscured from the road. He killed the ignition and looked over at the passenger seat, where the gun was still sitting.

It gave him the chills to look at it. He'd very nearly been shot, could've died. And then he realized something: if he *had* died, he'd have started over, back in the room, just like he wanted. It was a horrible thought, but not as horrible as the one that came next: *death was still an option.*

Carefully, as though it might blow up in his hand, he picked up the weapon. While he'd been high on adrenaline, the gun had felt natural in his grasp, and he'd barely noticed even holding it, but now, in the coldness and quietness of night, it felt different. Immediate. Definite. Turning it over in his hand, he watched the moonlight glint off its scratched surface. It was a simple device: cock the hammer, release the safety, aim and pull. That was it. He cocked the hammer, released the safety. The gun was live.

A metallic taste preempted the arrival of the barrel, which he bit down on gently. A whiff of gun oil spilled up the back of his nose, making him cough. His heart dipped into spasms. He knew what he had to do, knew what the outcome was, yet time had somehow frozen. His hand, it wouldn't respond. Signals from his brain were sent, but all his hand could do was shake. Does not compute. File not found.

Taking the barrel out of his mouth, he wiped the sweat from his face with his sleeve and tried again. A reset. This time he could do it. Bite down on the barrel and squeeze. Bite down on the barrel and squeeze. *Bite down on the barrel, and squeeze…*

It was no use. He couldn't. He was too scared. He realized he was shaking, the barrel rattling against his teeth. Inside, he wanted to explode, let the shame out with a burst of anger to reassure himself that he was still strong, but all he could do was put the gun back down on the passenger seat and climb out of the car. After taking a moment to recompose himself, he abandoned the vehicle, traveling the remainder of the way to Towanda on foot.

Towanda was just as quiet as Monroe—albeit bigger—and he wandered around until he found a bus stop. The nearest large town was Wilkes-Barre; he'd be able to get a bus direct to Manhattan from there.

There wasn't another bus to Wilkes-Barre for twenty-seven minutes, so Josh took a seat on the nearest bench and waited. Sleep began to weigh his eyelids heavy, and by the time the bus arrived, it jerked him awake. Nauseated and lethargic, and with the taste of metal still in his mouth, he boarded the bus and paid the fare, then chose his seat from all but one.

Route 6 was quiet, winding through the forest past Wyalusing, Laceyville and Meshoppen. Everyone was asleep, and nothing stirred. The only other person he saw—besides the bus driver and the man sleeping at the back of the bus—was a motel worker emptying a black sack into the trash as they wound through Laceyville. Other than that, it was all quiet. Josh was glad for the peace.

"Wilkes-Barre!" the driver yelled out, making Josh jump. He'd been dozing again. The man at the back was already gone. "Last stop!" the driver added. Josh stood, stretched and yawned, making his way to the front as the driver pulled up in the bus terminal. The brakes hissed as they came to a stop, and Josh disembarked, his lungs filling with diesel fumes. The terminal wasn't empty, but it wasn't busy either, and the concrete walls echoed with the sound of rumbling tires and engines.

Josh found a timetable and located the correct stop for the bus to Manhattan. Two and a half more hours along I-80 and he'd be there, if he didn't die of exhaustion first. He had thirty minutes to wait before the bus arrived, and there was a fast food restaurant just across the way, so he headed in that direction to get some coffee and something more substantial to eat, the candy bar long since past its usefulness.

The restaurant was busier than he'd expected, but nice and quiet, and clean enough. He ordered and sat down, sipping hot coffee through a plastic lid between nibbling at an overcooked and lava-hot hash brown.

"Mind if I sit with you?"

Josh looked up to see an expectant-looking man, youngish, in a suit and rain coat, holding a tray of fast food. "Sure." The company might help keep him awake.

"Thanks," the man said, setting his tray down and taking off his coat, hanging it on the back of his chair. Before he took a seat, he held out his hand. "Michael," he said. Josh shook it. Should he give a fake name? Was there any point?

"Josh. Pleased to meet you, Michael."

"Likewise," Michael said, seating himself and taking a bite of his breakfast burger. Grease ran down his chin, and he caught it with a napkin. "What business are you in, Josh?"

Josh took another gulp of coffee. By now it was cool enough for him to realize how bad it tasted. "Tunneling."

"Tunneling? How interesting! What kind of tunnels do you... tunnel?"

Michael's enthusiasm was almost fascinating. At these small hours of the morning, here he was, fired up enough to talk to a stranger about holes. "This and that. Mainly infrastructure."

"Any projects I might know?"

Josh almost told him about the East Side Access, then thought better of it. "Probably not. Mainly sewer upgrades in old towns. Nothing exciting."

"Is that why you're out here?"

"Yeah."

Michael snorted. "The sewers around here could do with fixing. They flood every time someone spills a drink."

Josh couldn't help but smile. That was pretty funny. "So what's your game, then? Sales, I'm guessing?"

Michael rolled his eyes. "Is it that obvious?"

"The only men I know as cheerful as you are the ones trying to sell me something."

"That's very cynical," Michael said with a brazen grin. "But yes, I'm in sales."

"What're you selling?"

Holding up a hand, Michael said, "Don't worry, I'm not going to try and sell you anything. Just wanted to liven up a long wait for a bus with a little chat. And I broker vacation deals, by the way."

"Vacation deals, huh?"

"Yes—the client gets in touch with me, tells me where and when they want to go, and I call around to put a package together for them as cheap as I can."

"And that works out cheaper than those vacation packages you get online?"

"It sure does," Michael said, grinning proudly.

Josh nodded. "Fair enough." His chest went light for a second as he thought about Georgie and Joseph. He wondered where they were, what they were doing. If they were thinking about him. "How much is a vacation to Niagara Falls right about now?"

At first Michael wasn't sure if Josh was messing him around, but it didn't take him more than a second to whip out a tablet and start tapping away. "When are you thinking of going?"

"Tomorrow."

Michael paused, his grin slipping a little, then resumed tapping at his tablet. "Well, the cheapest flight is just under two hundred dollars round-trip, and I'm sure I could get another ten percent off that if I call around. Where would you like to stay?"

"Somewhere nice."

"Okay," Michael said. "Star rating? Facilities? I can find you something that way."

Josh looked at his watch; his bus would arrive in just a few minutes. He drained the last of his coffee—which was already kicking in, he was relieved to find—and stood up. "My bus is going to be here soon. I've got to go. Sorry."

"Yes, of course," Michael said, standing. He reached into his jacket pocket and fished out a business card. "Take this, and give me a call when you want to finalize the details."

Josh pocketed the card. "Thanks. You take it easy," he said as he left the table, heading for the exit.

"You too," Michael called out from behind.

Stepping back out into the noise and the diesel, Josh rubbed his hands together. As the last dregs of adrenaline in his system finally wore off, the cold began seeping in. It was a chill night, one that seemed to keep going and going and going.

His bus was pulling in, and he made his way over to it, one of four people waiting in line. They all boarded, trading the sound of engines for the vibration of loose panels, and the stench of diesel for the thick fug of years-old dust. He took a seat, and then a breath. It was strange, sitting here, the bus in no rush, the people on board immune to his thoughts. They were all carrying on like nothing was going to happen, and little did they know that in just a few hours, chaos would rain down. The calm before the storm. He'd never really understood that before, but now he did.

The doors hissed shut and the bus revved and pulled away. Josh watched through the window, trying to pick out Michael in the restaurant, but he was gone. Another soul, another life, just like his, another journey that had touched his own for just a fraction of a second. Josh wondered what kind of secrets Michael had, if they were as big as his own. To him, they probably were.

I-80 was all trees and towns for at least two hours, and Josh managed to zone out for the most of it. The hot blower down by the seat and the humid air stopped him from falling asleep completely, and his brain swam in a semi-conscious dreamlike state where he was running from a CIA agent who wanted him to destroy the world with an alien time portal device. It was only when the bus driver called out for Parsippany-Troy Hills, the last major town before they entered the metropolis, that he realized the dream was real.

Chapter 28

There hadn't been many moments in Josh's life where he'd wished that everything could change. There had been a time, back when he was a kid, when he'd stolen ten dollars from his mother's bag and got caught a week later. The lurching reality of what he'd done had come crashing down on his juvenile mind and made him want to die.

Equally when he'd taken the overtime, flown back from Niagara. The whole plane journey to JFK, he'd felt sick. He'd wanted to vomit, but he couldn't. His body held it in, as if to punish him.

And now here he was again. For a sensation spread by decades between instances, it felt so uncomfortably familiar that he—like he had the other two times—didn't see how it could ever pass. He tried to blame it on the hot, dusty air of the bus, but there was an unshakable truth in his gut that told him he was heading toward almost certain failure. How was he supposed to do what he needed to do? How many times did he have to try? One man against the might and minds of the country's prime intelligence agency? Against a man whose dedication and tolerance for sabotage were immeasurable on any kind of human scale?

Josh was done for. And not in the sense that he was going to die, no; Edwards had more sense than that. To kill Josh would be to send him back around, to give him another chance. What Edwards had in mind for him would be far more permanent than death. He shuddered.

As the bus wound its way through Newark and into Jersey City, the nausea really started to hit. He needed a plan this time, something that would take him through to completion, to destroy the portal. Josh knew that with Edwards opposing him, nothing would be easy.

But what if, after he'd gone back in time, he just… surrendered? Left the room, spoke to Edwards like he knew nothing, then went straight home? Sure, Edwards's men would be along to pick him up, but he'd be okay with it. He'd get them to pick up Georgie and Joseph, too. Then whatever was going to happen… could happen. Maybe they'd live in a bunker until a ripe old age together and see Joseph grow up in whatever way was possible…

The mere thought turned Josh's stomach even harder than it already was. He knew what he had to do. The responsibility bestowed upon him was too great. It was *his* fault the room had been breached, *his* fault that Edwards had found it. Who knows—if the room hadn't come up on his radar, Edwards's whole team could have been disbanded. Dead end. Cold trail. File it away under *things that could have been.*

But no amount of wishing otherwise made the truth change. He'd spent too long shirking his responsibility as a husband and a father, and that attitude needed to stop. No more excuses. No more distractions. No more lies.

"Midtown," the driver called out, as the bus came to a stop on West 42nd.

Josh licked his dry lips, considering staying where he sat. The doors would close, the bus would drive on and Josh could get away, far, far away.

A hiss signaled the changing of destiny as the exit sealed itself.

"Wait!" Josh shouted, scrambling up out of his seat, so fast the blood rushed from his head. He teetered, dizzy, along the aisle, jogging to the front of the bus. "I need to get off here!"

The driver tutted, and opened the doors. "Goddamn drunks," he muttered to himself as Josh tumbled off the bus.

The cold air hit Josh hard after the stifled confines of public transit, and he took deep breaths to calm his thumping chest. Midtown was quiet—there was no reason for anyone to be up this early in the morning—with only the odd car and cab prowling the moon and lamp-lit streets. It was a forty-minute walk to the deli on 62nd and 1st, the usual place he and Lionel frequented for lunch and their meeting place tonight. He immediately got off of 42nd, winding back and forth block by block toward his destination, taking care to keep a comfortable perimeter around the site and around Central Park.

Walking briskly, he soon worked up a healthy sweat, gulping lungfuls of air as he tried to keep his mind clear and his senses alert. As he marched down 54th, his ears pricked. Something had changed. He listened hard, to the hiss of cars passing, to the gurgle of the drains beneath his feet, to the burble of exhausts trailing away from him.

That's what was wrong: no cars were passing him. A car, lingering behind, idled as it trundled at his speed, closing slowly, keeping back. How long had it been following him? It could have been seconds, it could have been minutes. Josh had been so locked down in his own head that he couldn't be sure. Taking deep breaths he pushed on, building his speed, turning onto 3rd Avenue.

The street was wider here, with more people on the sidewalk and more cars on the road. Josh listened as the quiet creak of tires pushed straight on… then turned to follow him. Should he run? Where would he run to? Perhaps he could double back on himself, make it hard for the car to turn around and follow him?

No, that wouldn't work. 3rd was wide enough for it to swing back, and then it would all be over. Josh stopped, looking over his shoulder to see the car that had indeed been following him pull over. It was a black sedan, gleaming, and Josh watched as the driver rolled down the window.

"What do you want?" Josh asked. He tried to sound firm, but the strain in his voice let him down.

"You've been walking a while," the man said. He was older, scruffily dressed. Needed a shave. "Why don't you get in?"

Josh's heart sunk. He'd tried to be careful, but his exhausted brain had let him down. He approached the car. "Edwards not got the decency to pick me up himself?"

The driver frowned. "Whatever you say." He nodded to the back door, an indication for Josh to board. With a sigh partially of defeat and partially of relief, Josh pulled the rear open. The smell of alcohol and stale vomit wafted from within.

Hesitating, Josh asked, "Where'd you say you were from?"

"I'm not from no one," the driver said. "Do you want a ride or not?"

Josh blinked. He'd been an idiot. This man wasn't a CIA aide, sent to collect him; he was an unlicensed cab driver. Josh shut the door, stomach fluttering with relief. "No, that's okay," he said. "I think I'll keep on walking."

"Suit yourself, asshole," the driver said, pulling away with a chirp of his back tires. Josh, barely given the chance to stand back, watched in stunned silence as the black sedan rejoined traffic, winding left onto 55th, presumably to seek out more unsuspecting walkers. He wiped his brow, surprised to find so much sweat beading there. Looking at his damp palm, he laughed out loud to himself. "Well, shit," he said. A man walking by the other way gave him an odd look.

There was still hope, Josh realized. He could still make it. He hoped Lionel had been able to make it, too. Reenergized by his near miss, Josh broke into a light jog as he navigated the last four blocks of his journey. As he threaded his way onto the quiet 62nd and 1st, he scanned the shadows outside the deli ahead for any sign of his friend. From there he could see no one.

His heart sank as he reached the deli, shutters down, the tables and chairs that normally littered the sidewalk presumably stacked up inside, and he stared at the shop front a while before admitting to himself that Lionel really hadn't made it.

What could have happened? Had Lionel come and gone, tired of waiting for Josh to travel across the state? Perhaps he'd not made it here at all, either having been intercepted by Edwards, or just deciding not to come? Maybe he'd contacted the CIA, told Edwards about the meeting, and Josh was about to get intercepted himself?

A hand touched his shoulder, making him jerk with fright. He whipped around, fists ready, to see Lionel stepping back, hands raised.

"Whoa…" Lionel said. "Easy there…"

Josh's chest felt like it was going to tear in two right down the middle. He clutched it with one hand, leaning against Lionel with the other. "Jesus…" he wheezed. "You nearly made me shit myself…"

The two of them, alone on the silent street, laughed. Josh shook his head, unable to quite believe or comprehend the situation.

"I hope I wasn't too long," Josh said once he was able to support himself again.

"No," Lionel replied, looking at his watch. "So are you going to tell me what's going on?"

The last remaining trickles of humor in Josh ran dry. "Yes, of course."

"Does this—" Lionel started, looking concerned, "—does this have anything to do with—with you going back in time?" The way he spoke made it sound like he still had trouble believing it, and Josh didn't blame him. He nodded.

"Yes. When we drilled through the wall of that room, I found a time portal—"

"Wait," Lionel interrupted. "You're saying that not only have you been back in time, but the portal is in a room below Central Park?"

Josh nodded. "Yes," he said simply. Reacting to Lionel's expression, Josh added, "That's the honest truth, and it needs to be shut down."

Lionel, mouth open from the question he'd just had answered, shut it again and nodded. His eyes glazed as he processed the information, refocusing when he went to speak again. "Shut down?"

"It's a long story. If I don't, then the temporal effects will start to hit Manhattan, then America, then... who knows how far it will go."

Lionel swallowed. His eyes were big and white. "What do you mean by temporal effects? Is that what you were talking about when you called earlier?"

"Yes. I mean chaos. Mass exodus. I've seen it."

Nodding slowly, Lionel said, "And you need to get back into the room to stop all that... all that from happening."

"That's right. A back way, so the CIA don't know."

"Jesus..." Lionel said, looking up and down the street. "Why aren't you helping them? I thought you wanted to help them?"

"Edwards, it turns out he—he can't be trusted," Josh said. "But I need *you* to trust *me*. He's willing to make some pretty big sacrifices to get what he wants, and I've got to go back in time again and stop him. It's the only way."

Josh could see that Lionel would rather have been anywhere but there, but he could also see a glint of resolve in him, too. He watched as Lionel chewed his lip, hands on hips, eyes locked on Josh's own.

"All right," he said at last. Josh exhaled; he'd been holding his breath, waiting. "I believe you."

"So you can help, right?"

"Yeah, I can help."

"So how do I get in? Is it easy?"

Lionel's silence gave him all the response he needed. "Steam drains," he said simply. "That's the only other way in."

Josh's blood ran cold. He'd seen the steam drain plans in passing and knew he was in for a rough time. "How long?"

"About half a mile. Runs into the 65th Street sewer."

Nodding, Josh said, "Okay, I can work with that. Tight? Where does it come out?"

"You'll be on your hands and knees for the worst of it. It'll feed you out at an inspection chamber halfway between the staging area and the station at the end of the tunnel."

It could be worse, Josh told himself. Why he told himself that, he didn't know. It was like some kind of gut reaction to gloss over just how bad the prospect of crawling through half a mile of pipe was. "I guess I've got no other choice."

"I guess not."

Josh took a deep breath and let it out again slowly, then patted Lionel on the arm. "Thanks for your help, man."

"No problem. Any time."

"Wish me luck."

Lionel laughed. "You don't need it. You're the luckiest son-of-a-bitch I ever met."

Josh smiled. He knew Lionel was talking about Georgie and Joseph, and even if he wasn't, it was the first place Josh's mind went. "Thanks. I suppose I'd better be getting on with it then. Where's the best place to get into the 65th Street sewer? 65th Street I'm guessing?"

"Yeah." Lionel seemed suddenly distracted. "Hey, Josh—what's going to happen to me when you go back in time?"

The thought hadn't occurred to Josh before. Would this version of events continue as it was without him, or would it vanish into nothing? Had his previous timelines continued on as well? He had no way of knowing. "I—I have no idea."

Lionel grimaced. "Okay, that's okay," he said. "I'm sure it'll all be fine."

"I'm sorry," Josh said. He'd given no thought to his friend, and he was repaid with guilt because of it.

"You've got to do what you've got to do."

"I do."

"Well then, let's not waste a moment longer." Checking the street was still clear, Lionel led Josh down to 65th Street. They walked in silence.

"Help me lift this," Lionel said once they were there, squeezing the tips of his fingers around the edge of a drain cover. Josh helped him, and together they heaved the dead weight up and away from the hole beneath. It was dark, and it smelled bad. Really bad.

"Aw, man…" Josh said, peering in.

Patting Josh on the back, Lionel said, "Time to go save the world, huh? There'll be traffic along any moment now, so better get in there quick."

Although he agreed, Josh struggled to move. "It smells like something died down there…"

"Something probably did," Lionel said, nodding agreement.

Fruitlessly taking a deep breath, Josh turned around and backed down onto the ladder fixed to the inside of the drain. Rung by rung he fed himself in, until he was almost completely beneath the level of the road. "Where am I going, by the way?"

"Oh!" Lionel said, startled by his own forgetfulness. "Of course. How stupid. Go down to the left and keep going until you see the new jointing. That's the pipe you need. Head down that and the first joint you can fit in is the one you'll be taking to get to the room."

"Right, okay. That way?" Josh said, pointing.

"Yeah, that way."

"Great. Thanks again." Josh held out a hand. Lionel shook it.

"No problem. I guess I'll be seeing you yesterday."

For a brief second, Josh didn't understand. "Oh, right," he said, chuckling weakly. "I guess you will. See you yesterday, then."

And down he went. He could hear Lionel grunting as he shifted the cover back into place, throwing him into darkness. Taking out his cell, he used the screen as a light, feeding his way into the drain. It was hot and humid, as he expected a steam drain to be, but it was so much hotter and wetter than he could have ever realized. He'd only been down there a minute and he was already soaked from head to toe. His cell wouldn't last long. He'd need to be quick or he'd get lost in the pitch black.

A double knock on the cover above was Lionel's farewell, and then Josh was alone. As quick as he wanted to be, he knew progress would be slow, especially since he had to double over to fit into the drain itself. He headed in the direction Lionel had told him, praying for his cell to hold out against the moisture long enough for him to find his exit. Breathing was hard work, and it wasn't long before he felt like he was being suffocated, while his back screamed with agony—but he couldn't stop. He had no idea what awaited him at the end of the tunnel, and every second he took was another that Edwards gained an advantage over him.

After an endless amount of time, at the point where Josh felt like the agony and the heat were going to make him pass out, his cell light caught something ahead. He could only see a meter or so in front, but even with the terrible visibility, the bright, fresh concrete stood stark against the decades-old drain it connected to. As Lionel had said, here was the drain that would lead him deep below New

York, where his destiny awaited him.

Chapter 29

If Josh had thought the crawl through the drain had been hard going up to now, it was nothing compared to the squeeze into the new pipe that led deep into the East Side Access tunnels. Shuffling forward on his hands and knees—the ground wet and peppered with debris that grazed his palms, the ceiling scraping along the arch of his spine—was slow going. He had no way of holding his cell—which had somehow lasted the duration—and so he made his progress in the dark, feeling his way along. Every shimmy forward required great effort, the narrow pipe forcing him to drag his knees forward rather than lift them. Between his aching joints and his burning flesh, added to the suffocation of both the hot, humid air and the claustrophobic space, Josh had been transported to hell.

The pipe wound down and forward for a while, before turning a corner in long, angled segments. Although Josh couldn't see how deep he was, he could feel it as he worked his way further into the ground. The pressure in his ears was slowly changing as he descended, a sensation that had become acute from his time working below the surface. Unfortunately, the feeling wasn't strong enough to know just how much longer he had to go.

In the dark, on all fours, Josh felt his crippled sense of vision give way to the heightening of his others. The pain, the heat, the sound of the loose debris littering the base of the pipe and his sodden clothes being dragged along, all echoed in his head with enormous clarity. The experience was so overwhelming, it almost seemed existential. He watched himself crawl, an animal slinking low, bleeding and bruised, into the belly of the Earth.

Something registered in his vision: a light, faint and far, but a light nonetheless. Josh redoubled his efforts, pushing himself to the end of this pain. It was the joint down to the inspection chamber Lionel had told him about. He scratched and scrabbled his way forward, the intoxicating agony making his head light. The glow grew bigger, becoming the junction down into the inspection chamber. As he reached it, light filled his eyes, washing through him with such intensity he nearly fainted. He took a moment to breathe, to let the pain ease, and then he climbed down.

Over the edge and down the short ladder, he was finally able to stand again. He took his time extending his limbs—they had become stiff almost to the point of being frozen in place—and he stifled his need to cry out. Under the light pooling through the vented access panel, he inspected his palms: they were in shreds, glistening with wet and fine gravel. He brushed them off as best he could, wincing with each wipe, then set about removing the access panel. There was a hinge on one side and a fastening on the other, which was presumably turned via a key from the outside. From the inside, however, Josh was able to turn it freely with his fingers, which he did. The panel needed a small shove to free open, and he stepped out into the tunnel.

As Lionel had said, he was between the staging area and the station at the far end of the tunnel; how far down, he did not know. But he did know which way he needed to head, and head that way he did. Although his body was still fraught with agony, walking freely upright was something of a blessing, and the air, although warm, was a cool breeze in comparison to the steam of the drain. His wet clothes cooled him quickly, soothing his joints, freeing them. Maybe five minutes of walking and he'd be there. There was no sign of Edwards and his men; with any luck, Josh could walk right in.

Remaining cautious, Josh proceeded along the tunnel as quickly as he dared, listening out for any signs of other people. As far back as this he could feel the humming energy already; the power of the portal was indeed growing. As he reached the station—which was deserted, no train there—he slowed, stepping quietly around the corner to see what awaited him.

And there it was, as he expected: the tunnel, the drill, the room. There was additional equipment there, but Josh could see no one manning it. Somehow, he had beaten Edwards. Perhaps they'd gone back to Langley first, adding precious minutes to their return journey? They could still be some time away yet. All Josh needed to do was step into that portal and it would begin all over again. He needed to get there quick; he could feel his body shutting down, exhaustion and pain finally taking over. It wouldn't be long before he fell unconscious.

Feeling exposed and struggling to hear above the swelling energy, he approached the rear of the drill, staying close to it as he made his way around. He held his breath as the freshly bored tunnel came into view, stepping quickly onto the uneven ground.

"I think that's quite far enough," a voice said from behind. Josh spun around. It was Edwards; he'd been hiding behind the drill, waiting. In his hand Josh saw a gun, glinting with silent menace. It was pointed squarely at Josh's forehead.

"Edwards…" Josh said. Edwards twitched.

"Such arrogance," he said, waving Josh to move out of the tunnel with the barrel of his weapon. Josh did as instructed. "Thinking you could just walk straight in there."

"You still need me," Josh told him. "Don't forget that."

Edwards laughed softly, shaking his head. "I do, I do…" he trilled. The smile dropped. "And yet… I don't."

Josh's stomach fell. "What do you mean?"

"You awakened the beast, Mr. Reed," Edwards said.

The creature, Josh thought. *They weren't looking for me in the helicopter, they were looking for it. If they've caught it, they have no need for me…*

"I have to thank you, really," Edwards said, pacing back and forth. In the distance, above the vibration, Josh could hear footsteps. Heavy, booted footsteps, and lots of them. He was done for. "I would have never trusted the creatures with the seed myself."

"So what are you going to do now?"

"You should know by now," Edwards said with a grin, taking the chance to revel in this newfound opportunity. "I only tell you what you need to know, and from now on, you don't need to know anything."

"You should close the portal down, before it's too late."

Edwards folded his arms. Behind him, armed agents rounded the corner. They were in no rush. "No, I don't think I'll be doing that." Circling Josh, Edwards stuck the barrel of his pistol into Josh's back. The pain was amplified by Josh's exhaustion, and he staggered forward a little. "Walk," Edwards told him.

Josh did as he was told. "What's going to happen to me?"

"You don't need to worry about that. Let's just say that you won't be doing any more traveling for a while."

Following behind the armed agents, a forklift truck came into view. On it, a crate—like the ones Josh had seen in the Langley archive—balanced on the forks. Sudden dread filled Josh. "You're not going to put me in that, are you?"

Edwards laughed. "Don't be obtuse, Mr. Reed. That's not for you."

They stopped to meet the agents. Edwards instructed the forklift truck driver to place the crate down to one side, and ordered the agents bearing arms to take position around the tunnel entrance leading to the room.

At once, Josh understood. "It's not for me," he whispered. "It's for the creature…"

Having sent his men to their respective positions, Edwards turned to Josh, weapon still dangerously aimed. "There's nothing more you need to say from now on." His grin had dropped; he was serious now.

Josh could feel his vision fading a touch. He needed to sleep so badly. "But—" he said.

"I said shut up," Edwards reminded him, jabbing him with the pistol. His attention was on the tunnel now, down where the creature would come. His radio hissed.

"It's moving down into the tunnels now," it said. "Be with you very shortly."

"Everyone ready?" Edwards asked his troops. A murmur was his confirmation. He, with Josh in tow, backed down toward the drill, taking cover behind it. From there Josh could see that the agents were spread along each side of the wall; they were going to surround the creature. It knew pain, knew the weapons they carried. It would have no chance. Surrender would be its only option.

The tunnels were so quiet that only the light whirr of ventilation could be heard, in among the occasional drop of water echoing from further down. Edwards, Josh and all the agents held their collective breaths, waiting for the creature. The air hummed with energy.

Josh felt faint. A fuzzy static blurred his vision, and the pains across his body had blended into one nauseating, rhythmic headache. He made to sit down, but Edwards jabbed him with the barrel again.

"Stand up!" he hissed.

Josh, feebly, did as he was told, but had no chance to retort as the air filled with a screech so loud that it echoed for an eternity. His tired heart beat hard once more, and Edwards took a nervous step backward.

"Ready…" he told the agents, who shouldered their weapons. They were all focused down the tunnel, toward the station, unblinking and unmoving. "Remember, only fire on my command."

A low rumble followed. It was hard to tell just how far down the tunnel the creature was, but Josh knew it wouldn't be long before it came into view. Did it have any idea what was laid out for it? It must have some concern for its own wellbeing, as it had managed to flee Edwards earlier and evade capture until now.

Josh chanced a look at Edwards. His eyes were wide open and unblinking. Josh had never seen him like this before. He was—nervous. Apprehensive. The future of his project lay in the hands of this creature, and he would do anything he could to stop it.

After this, where would he take Josh? A cell, most probably. Lock him away for the rest of his life. Make him disappear. Give Edwards long enough to crack the secrets of the portal. Suicide wouldn't be an option; Edwards would make sure of that. He'd rot there, never see his family again. And what would happen to them? The same, probably. Josh shuddered, and not because he was getting slowly colder, but because the thought of Georgie and Joseph in Edwards's grasp made him feel sick. He couldn't let that happen.

The scream came again, this time a longer, more mournful wail, and closer, too. The creature was in pain, Josh could sense it.

Edwards could too it seemed, as the corners of his mouth tipped up slightly.

"Everyone stay nice and calm and this should be easy," he reassured the waiting throng. "We'll have it back in no time."

A few moments later and Josh could hear the creak and crackle of the creature's crystalline form moving along, as well as the dull, echoing impacts of its steps. They were erratic and slow, like it was struggling. Clearly the seed had given it a burst of energy to complete its mission and close the portal, but it wasn't going to be enough. Not if it wanted to get by all these agents as well.

"Steady…" Edwards said, perhaps more to himself than to anyone else.

Josh decided he was going to have to take a chance. He couldn't watch the creature get captured and get taken away himself, where he would be unable to protect his family. The decision was made before he even realized it. He glanced at Edwards, who was still locked on to the tunnel ahead. The agents, too. All paying no attention to him. Edwards's pistol had even drifted slightly away from Josh, aimed to his left instead.

A deep rumble gave him the burst of adrenaline he needed to make his move. As the echo died down, he scrabbled away, nearly slipping as he twisted and ran into the fresh tunnel to the room. He heard Edwards react behind him, shouting something he couldn't quite make out. The ground was slippery and uneven, and Josh had to flail forward to catch himself from falling, to keep moving on. Once he was into that room, he'd be safe. He'd have made it.

Another wailing scream pierced the air, so loud and so close it felt on top of him. He could hear Edwards bellowing, but didn't listen to what he was saying. Time seemed to slow, and clarity with it, blurring and blending into one unintelligible goop. It was like he knew the past, present and future all at once. He braced himself.

There was a crack, and Josh was suddenly winded. His ears rang as he watched the walls fall away from him. He hit the ground. Heard screaming. It was him. He was screaming.

Chapter 30

There was another crack from overhead, and another. Josh flinched both times. People were running. A booming howl filled the tunnel. Pain filled him. It was white hot. His vision was blurry. His side felt wet. Blood. He could see it on his hands.

He moved, and the pain drew his vision to spots. No one was paying any attention to him now. More shots rang out, further down the tunnel. He climbed to his knees, a tearing in his side. The ground was hard beneath him.

"Don't let it get away!" Josh heard Edwards yell. Another howl followed it, masking the yells of the agents as more bullets were shed. The creature was putting up a fight, more than Edwards had expected. "The portal! It's trying to close the portal!" he screeched, in among the screams of men and the howling of the creature. "Stop it!"

Josh slowly hoisted himself to his feet, clutching his side, staggering forward. He was close to unconsciousness, he knew it. If he let it take hold of him, it would all be over.

One step, and then another. Colors swam, pain followed. The two interchanged. Heading for the room, he clawed his way along the muddy tunnel, vision blurred, head thumping. The energy cascading from the room was the only thing keeping him up. He moved away from the wails and howls, away from the gunfire, not knowing how or if he could make it. There was no other choice but to keep moving on.

Muzzle flashes lit up the tunnel as round after round was fired. There sounded to be less of them now. Less screaming. Less fighting. Edwards's voice rising in desperation.

"Kill it!" he screamed. "Kill it!"

More shots rang out, echoing around the room, ricocheting from surface to surface. Josh felt his way along the fresh, uneven schist, whole body throbbing, knees quivering. It felt like the tunnel was extending into infinity, into the blackness. But if he kept going, he just might make it. He'd go back and… try it all again.

The creature emitted a deep groan, which sounded louder and closer than ever. Multiple weapons were still being unloaded, then it was just two, and then just the one. Then there was silence. Almost silence. Just breathing.

Josh stopped. Footsteps. He turned around. A blur in the darkness, a figure, silhouetted. The tunnel behind was dim and flickering, lights destroyed by arms fire. Smoke hung in the air. Energy hummed between them. The figure breathed, long ragged breaths. The breaths of a victor.

"Mr. Reed…" the figure said. Josh's stomach dropped. He staggered, the wound hotter than fire, the agony all-consuming. He said nothing. He couldn't. "Mr. Reed…" Edwards repeated.

Through fading vision, Josh squinted at Edwards. He looked maniacal against the flickering light, his clothes and skin soaked in blood; the blood of his now silent colleagues, Josh assumed. It had been a massacre. Only Edwards was left. And the creature?

"It's destroyed," Edwards said, as if reading his mind. "Gone. Dead." He sighed, slapping his hands against his sides, as though he'd lost nothing more than a casual bet. "All that work, for nothing."

"Edwards…" Josh wheezed. His own voice sounded unfamiliar to him.

Edwards chuckled. "Mr. Reed," he said, shaking his head. "Oh, Mr. Reed. What to do with you now, hmm? After all, this *is* your fault. *You* did this." He raised his weapon. He wasn't chuckling now. "What did you think you were going to do, Mr. Reed? Close the portal? You'd come out of that room decades into the future. I'll be waiting for you, Mr. Reed.

"Or perhaps you wanted to go back again? I'd win every time. You could have been part of something big, Mr. Reed. Instead, you tore it down. You're an idiot, Mr. Reed, a fool. You can never be as dedicated as me, and that's why I'll always beat you."

"Then why don't you just kill me…" Josh said, barely audibly.

"Kill you?" Edwards repeated, incredulous. "How stupid do you think I am? No, Mr. Reed, no, no, no, no, no… I'm going to do far worse to you. You could have been looked after for the rest of your life, your family too, but now look." He held his arms up as if showing Josh what he'd been responsible for. "I'm afraid I'm going to have to punish you, and to do that I'm going to have to punish *them* as well."

"Don't you dare…" Josh wheezed. He was struggling to stay upright, but he did.

Edwards frowned. "What, are you going to stop me? I don't think so, Mr. Reed. And as for you, I am going to pull your brain apart while you watch. I'm going to dig around in there until I find out how all of this works, whether you want me to or not. By the time I'm done with you, you'll wish you'd got what your wife and your son are going to get instead." Edwards was spitting the words by the end.

Josh wanted to fight back, but his pain and his dizziness overwhelmed him. He raised a hand, but it dropped back down again, energy spent. The pulsating hum from the room seemed distant now. Everything did.

"You took away the only thing that ever mattered to me," Edwards continued, approaching Josh. He walked with a limp; he must have been injured in the fray. "So I'm going to do the same to you. You'll never see your family again." He raised his arm, ready to bring the butt of his gun down on Josh's head. Josh winced, preparing himself for the blow.

Behind Edwards, a shadow stirred.

"I worked too hard," Edwards said, arm aloft, "and got too close." He grinned, gritting his teeth, his eyes flashing white from his blood-soaked face.

The shadow whipped forward, toppling Edwards. His gun went off. Josh dropped to the ground instinctively, covering his head. The sound of tearing flesh and cracking bone resonated with wild screaming as he saw Edwards lifted clear of the ground, his left half and his right half being peeled apart down the middle by two rising columns of crystal.

And all at once the screaming stopped. Both halves of Edwards were dropped to the ground, one wet thunk after another.

The crystal retracted back into the shadow. Josh held his breath, watching, not daring to move. Above the hum, all was quiet. Then the shadow stirred again. It grew in a creaking, stuttering motion, as if struggling to keep form. It groaned, low and mournful. Josh was sure that it was fading, like he was. They would probably die together, start all over again.

It emerged again from the shadow and stumbled toward him, cracking and snapping as it tried to keep itself stable. It staggered and fell, the impact with the ground sending a splintering crash echoing all around. Josh tried to push himself away, but he hit the tunnel wall and could go no further.

The creature gathered itself up from its largest piece, lifted its shape forward again, building itself up tall before Josh. What was it going to do? Would it kill him like it did Edwards? Josh shut his eyes. Death would come swiftly, he hoped. It would be a relief.

But it didn't.

When Josh opened his eyes again, he was presented with the sight of the creature, bowed down low, offering him the seed that he had dropped. Under the creature's dim glow, he could see its crystalline form draining of color, the rippling slowing, taking on the same solidified appearance as he had seen in the creature back at Langley. One dead, another dying. Its last wish was for him to take the seed. It could not complete the journey itself. Josh reached out and took it.

With one last long groan, the creature froze up for good. The color was gone. Its shape was fragmented and splintered.

Josh knew what he had to do. Now more than ever, he knew.

He watched the swirling glow of the seed, looked deep into it, wondering about its secret. These creatures, why were they here? What had happened to them? All he knew was that he had been entrusted to perform the final ritual, to close up the portal for good.

Levering himself to his feet, standing hunched in a spattering of his own blood, Josh took a breath. In lumbering strides he staggered to the entrance, to the top of the ramp. He looked into the darkness.

The feeling of familiarity, of warmth, filled him. He made his way down the ramp, his shoes slipping with the wet of his blood, the pulse drawing him through the darkness. The seed glowed brightly, growing hot, and he forced himself to hold onto it. With every step the pain lessened as his mind and body separated, the tearing agony in his side just a distant twinge. His head was clear, his thoughts unencumbered by flesh and blood. He was at the portal. The time had come.

There were two choices available to him: the first was to take the seed into the portal and close it. Even if it worked, as Edwards had pointed out, he'd still be advanced well into the future. His family would be much older, having lived a lifetime without him.

His other choice was to drop the seed, go back in time, start again. Perhaps he could do it over in such a way that meant he could still be with Georgie and Joseph. Perhaps he could persuade Edwards to close the portal quickly, so they'd all be safe. That was what he wanted, and wanted so badly, even if he didn't believe it. He considered the seed in his hand. It wouldn't be a problem, to go around once more. If it didn't work, he could try again. And again. And again.

Thinking back, he remembered Manhattan as it was in the future, rotten and crumbling. He tried to think beyond that, to the pulsing memory of death that sat no more clearly than a fog. He'd been through the portal before, he knew that. The portal was familiar to him, comforting, like an old friend. He couldn't think of a time before its existence.

A slow, creeping horror built in him as he came to a terrible realization. How many times had he been through the portal already? Once, for sure. Twice was hazy. Three times? Four? Ten?

There was no way to know. There never could be. Had he spent eternity doing this, trying to find the ultimate solution? Trying to avoid this ultimate sacrifice?

When he had landed after his flight back from Niagara, he had called Georgie, but she had not answered. He'd worked for three days solid after that, sleeping in the office on-site, and when he'd finally returned home, Georgie was already back. She didn't mention it, not even once. It was like nothing had happened.

But everything had happened. Their relationship had been permanently damaged. A blemish, a chip that would not polish out, that looked uglier and uglier every time he saw it. Josh knew the only way was out. He had given her the divorce without a fight. He had been praying for it to come, if anything to give her peace.

He loved her, and she loved him. That was why they had to move on. But it didn't have to be like that. For years, Josh blamed his work, blamed his upbringing, even blamed Georgie, but only now did he see the truth for what it was: his life was in his control and no one else's. The blame lay squarely with him.

The decision was his; it always had been. He wished he could take it back, try again, wished the portal would transport him to the moment he took that phone call at Niagara and stepped on the plane to go back to New York, but it wouldn't. And it shouldn't. He had to take responsibility for himself, *now*. And that meant making the hard decision.

He thought of Edwards's commitment to the portal, the sacrifices he'd made. He'd described himself as dedicated. That was what Josh needed to be, but being dedicated didn't mean doing what was best for him. Being dedicated meant doing what was best for *them*.

He took a breath, and gripping hold of the seed tight, the scent of blood twitching his nostrils—he stepped in.

Chapter 31

"What makes you think you'd be suited to work below ground?"

It wasn't a question Josh had expected, but one in hindsight he really should have. "I don't know… I'm not claustrophobic or anything."

The interviewer's questioning continued in the same detached manner. "How do you know that?"

"Well, I guess I've never really had any problems squeezing into tight spaces or anything like that."

"Do you have any examples?"

Josh thought. "Yeah—last year, me and a few friends went on a potholing experience for Sam's—he's one of my friends—twenty-first birthday. I was the only one who could do the hardest course there; the others all gave up."

"And it wasn't a problem for you?"

"No. I just pushed on. Better to see it through, that's what my dad always used to say." Josh laughed nervously; the interviewer did not reciprocate.

"This is a five-year program—you think you can see that through? It's not going to be easy."

Josh shrugged. "Once I've made my mind up, there's no stopping me."

"And beyond that? This is young man's game—there's no long-term future in this for anyone."

"Management, I guess. Training. Passing on the baton."

The interviewer nodded, a seed of approval showing on his face. He scribbled on his notes.

The old makes way for the new.

"What are we going to call him?"

"Him?"

Georgie pointed at her gently rounding belly.

"Oh," Josh said, "right! It's still not quite sunk in."

"So? What are we going to call him?"

Josh put down the magazine and shuffled across to Georgie, and they snuggled together on the sofa, Josh stroking her belly. "How do you know it's going to be a him?"

"I just know."

"I'll take you up on that bet. Fifty-fifty odds, right?"

Georgie laughed. "Prepare to lose. Fifty dollars?"

"Make it a hundred."

"Confident, huh?"

"You may as well give over that hundred dollars now."

Georgie squeezed Josh's knee, making him squirm in pain. "You won't see a single cent out of me, because this bump right here is going to be a boy."

Josh, giggling and rubbing his knee, having wriggled from Georgie's death-grip, said, "You're lucky you're pregnant or I'd have you for that!"

"Oh yeah? I'm pregnant, not paralyzed. Bring it on!"

Josh pounced on her, laying himself gently on top of her. They rolled back and forth on the sofa for a minute, then Josh kissed Georgie. "I love you," he said.

"And I love you too. But you still haven't given me a name."

Sitting up and mock pouting, Josh said, "Aw, damn! I was hoping you'd forgotten."

"You're going to need to be sneakier than that to distract me. So, what's it gonna be?"

Josh felt his smile fall as he sat and thought about the baby's name. He'd purposely avoided thinking about it up to now because he knew that doing so made it real. His chest fluttered; he wasn't ready to be a dad, and he knew it. A young thing, under his care—he couldn't do it, didn't *want* to do it. Well, he did; he just didn't want to do it wrong.

"I'm waiting…" Georgie said, folding her arms.

"Hang on, I'm thinking!" Josh replied. He wondered what it was like for Georgie, actually growing the child inside of her. At its most vulnerable time, she was responsible for every part of it; she held its life within her. Yet here she was, smiling and happy, not a ball of nervousness like Josh knew he would be. How did she do it? "I don't know," he said. "I can't think of any."

Georgie looked sad, but not because she resented Josh for not picking a name, but because she sympathized with how he felt. She stroked his arm. "You'll get there," she said. "What lies ahead of us may be uncertain—may be crazy—but we have each other. We'll get through it, and it will be amazing. You'll love it, I promise. It'll be *our future*, the three of us together. Besides," she added, grinning, "if that ditzy Joan and her stupid boyfriend next door can manage it, it should be a piece of pie for us!"

Josh laughed, but felt empty. A weight hung from his shoulders.

You carry our future.

"Jesus, it's cold," Lionel said, rubbing his gloved hands together. He and Josh surveyed the landscape, or at least what they could see of it through the blizzard. "Have you ever seen such a godforsaken hell hole?"

Josh didn't mind it. In fact, he found it to be quite beautiful in a melancholic kind of way. The isolation was powerful, made him feel a very small part of a very big universe. "You're just an old New Yorker who refuses to learn new tricks," Josh said, jabbing an elbow into Lionel's ribs, making him cough.

"Damn, what was that for?" Lionel said, rubbing his side. "I'll teach you a new trick all right—it's called writing you up for being an insolent little shit. Then we'll see who's a miserable New Yorker."

Josh laughed. "I said old, not miserable, but yeah, you're that as well."

Lionel muttered something under his breath, talking into his gloves as he resumed rubbing them together.

"So where do we start?" Josh asked.

"Somewhere over there," Lionel told him, pointing. "The desalination plant is going just south of that ridge, and we're piping all the way out to the coast a mile over."

"Do we have any rough figures yet?"

"Twenty-foot diameter, reinforced concrete. Seems the right way to go. The bosses are talking about jacking the pipe in."

"Really? A twenty-foot-diameter pipe?

"That's what they're saying."

Josh peered into the landscape. Soon all that pristine white would be turned to sludgy brown as work commenced. Perhaps jacking was a good idea after all. "We'll need a hell of a hydraulic ram to push that pipe through."

"The bosses have been in talks with Grundoram; seems they've got a new ram coming out that'll do just the job."

"Oh yeah? Must be a monster."

"It's called *The Goliath* apparently."

Josh chuckled. "Really?"

Nodding, Lionel said, "Yeah, really."

"Well, there you go. We'll be pounding our way through the ground with it in no time."

"I'd actually been meaning to ask you about that," Lionel said. "The bosses want someone to be the liaison with Grundoram, work with them from the ground as a kind of advisor. I've recommended you to do it."

Josh was taken aback. "What, me? You want me to do it?"

"Yeah," Lionel said, seeming to have misinterpreted Josh's surprise as dismay. "There'll be a sizeable pay raise of course, a new job title, more time in New York. You've got the baby on the way and I thought it would be good—"

"Thank you," Josh said, taking Lionel's hand in both of his and damn near rattling it from Lionel's arm. "Thank you. I accept." He beamed. "I'm going home," he said.

"I've said it before and I'll say it again: you're a lucky bastard," Lionel said, freeing his hand from Josh's grip. "Make the most of it."

Josh looked back out at the wash of snow. Somehow he didn't feel quite so lonely any more.

You have returned.

"What? Now?"

"Yes, now!" Georgie yelled.

Josh froze in panic. He knew what he had to do, had rehearsed it in his mind over and over, but now the time had come, he couldn't get his body to move.

"So I'm getting myself to the hospital, is that—" Georgie cut herself off, wincing, clutching her abdomen.

Then, all at once, the world was real again, high definition, as clear as it had ever been. Josh shot up out of bed, threw the clothes from the pile in the corner on, and got some out for Georgie too, helping her dress. "Do you want something to eat before we go?"

"No! Get the bag!"

Nodding, Josh rushed out to the kitchen and grabbed the maternity bag, already pre-packed with just about everything anyone could ever need, or so it seemed. As he hoisted its surprising weight onto his shoulder, he remembered how he'd wanted to argue about its contents, but he'd kept his mouth shut. At least he'd not been carrying it on his front for the last nine months.

"Where are you?" Georgie called out from the bedroom.

"Coming!" He rushed back in, helping her up and out into the kitchen, where she sat at the breakfast bar.

"Have you called a cab?" she asked as she grimaced.

The cab! He'd forgotten! "I'm just doing that now."

Georgie's response was a long growl as she buried her head in her arms. Josh picked up the phone and dialed out. The phone rang, and a man answered.

"New York Best Taxis," the man said.

"I need a cab, now—my wife is going into labor!"

"Okay—where you want cab?"

"What?"

"Where? For cab."

Josh didn't understand. He couldn't understand. A panicked rage gurgled in his throat, spilling out uncontrolled and unmeasured. "It doesn't matter where I want the cab, I want it here, now—" He cut himself off as he realized that he'd made a mistake, misunderstanding the question. In fact he couldn't even figure out what he'd thought the man had been asking. It seemed so clear and obvious now. "I'm sorry," he said. "I'm—I'm stressed. Please send the cab to 82nd, number 1034."

"Okay, ten minute."

"Thank you."

The man hung up.

"Cab's on its way," Josh said.

"How long?"

"Ten minutes."

Georgie groaned. They sat in silence—Georgie's grunting aside—for the longest ten minutes of their lives, while Josh rubbed Georgie's back and Georgie remained slumped over the breakfast bar. All the things Josh had thought would happen, all the little tips and tricks he'd learned in the build up to now—all of it was moot. He was floundering, treading water, and only just staying afloat.

A horn sounded outside.

"The cab!" Josh yelled, making Georgie jump.

"Jesus, you don't have to shout," she said, looking up at him with a frown. She was pale, and sweating profusely. "I'm not deaf…"

Josh, not sure how to respond, stood there staring at her. Her frown wavered, and she smiled, then laughed. Josh did too. It was a moment he'd remember for the rest of his life, not because of what she'd just said, but because of what happened next.

"I don't feel well…" Georgie said, smile falling. She really did look pale.

"Shall I call an ambulance?"

Georgie shook her head. "No, cab's already here. It's the middle of the night. It'll be quicker to take the cab."

She was right. Josh helped her up, and his stomach lurched when he saw that the stool glistened with blood. He didn't tell her.

The cab raced through the night to the New York–Presbyterian Hospital, sparking the sound of horns as it darted through the traffic. Georgie was faint and barely talking, mumbling to herself as she grew more and more pale. Josh could only urge the driver to go faster—other than that, he was helpless. Helpless and useless.

When they arrived at the hospital, he screamed to a nurse standing outside smoking a cigarette to get help. When she saw Georgie, she stomped the cigarette out and flew off into the hospital, returning a few seconds later with a wheelchair. Together—after Josh had paid the driver and apologized for the blood on the seat— they helped Georgie into the wheelchair and pushed her inside, where more nurses met them. The group of nurses briefly exchanged a few quiet words, then rushed Georgie off. Josh had to jog to keep up. He wanted to ask what was going on, but his voice had left him.

When they arrived at the maternity ward, the administrator was just putting down the phone. Front desk must have called through, because she waved them in. "You'll have to wait here," she said to Josh. "They need to work."

"But…" Josh gasped. "My wife…"

"Please take a seat, sir. Your wife is good hands."

Josh wanted to be sick. His legs were going to give way. He needed to sit down. "Okay…" he said quietly, fumbling his way to the waiting area and collapsing onto a seat. He was the only one there. In his mind he was bursting through the doors and demanding he see his wife and be told what was happening, but the reality was that he waited in that room, exhausted and scared, staring at the poster on the opposite wall. It was sun-bleached and dog-eared, and although he stared at it for hours, he never actually read it. It had a pony on it, he remembered that, but the words he never took in.

"Mr. Reed?"

Josh looked up. A doctor stood in the doorway, addressing him. She held a clipboard.

Josh nodded. He wanted to stand; couldn't. He could already hear the words. The doctor's expression said it all.

"Mr. Reed," she said. "Your wife suffered a hemorrhage during labor."

Josh's entire body tingled with nausea. He wanted to run away. He didn't want to hear it. But he couldn't move.

"There was some bleeding, but we managed to stop it. We delivered the baby by C-section."

If Josh moved he'd be sick for sure. The room spun.

"Because you got Mrs. Reed here quickly, I'm pleased to say that everything is going to be okay. Mother and baby will need to stay here overnight so we can keep an eye on them, but you should all be able to go home together tomorrow." She smiled. "Congratulations."

Time had frozen. Josh's heart had stopped. Nothing moved. There was no sound. "A—a baby?" he said.

The doctor nodded. She was patient, and kind, Josh could tell, letting him take everything in at his own pace.

"They're both… okay?"

"Yes, Mr. Reed, they are both doing well. Keeping them overnight is just a precaution. Hemorrhaging isn't unusual, but it's better to be safe."

"Yes," Josh said, nodding. "Of course…" He swallowed, throat sticky. "Can I… can I see them?"

"Of course you can," the doctor said, gesturing for him to come through. "Right this way."

Josh stood. He wobbled, righting himself on the arm of the chair. Steady, he moved. Each step was long and unstable, like it was his first time walking. He couldn't remember how to do it. "Is the baby… is…" He couldn't finish.

"He's doing well. Come and see him."

"Him…?"

"Yes—he's a healthy baby boy."

A boy. Georgie had been right. She was always right. And now he needed a name. Where none had come to mind before, one did just now: Joseph. He would be called Joseph. He had seen the name on a poster somewhere and he liked it. A poster with a pony on it. He couldn't remember where he'd seen it.

We are birthed.

"Isn't he beautiful?" Georgie whispered, so as not to wake the baby. Josh stared at him from a distance. He didn't know what to do. "Come say hello," she added, smiling. She was still pale, but looked much better than before. IV lines ran to her hand from suspended bags, and Josh's stomach turned.

"Can I?" he said.

"He's your son; of course you can." Josh approached, cautious. "Here," Georgie said, passing him over. "Hold him like that, supporting his head. That's it, there you are."

Josh held him. He hardly weighed anything, yet he was so warm. And the smell—it was intoxicating. His vision blurred. Georgie was smiling, warmth flushing back into her cheeks.

"What are we going to call him?" she asked.

"Joseph," Josh said at once. Georgie looked surprised.

"That was fast," she said. "And I love it. Joseph. Joseph. Jo—seph." She grinned. "Joseph," she said again.

"I guess I owe you a hundred dollars," Josh said, breaking his gaze away from Joseph's sleeping face.

Georgie laughed weakly. "Yes, you do. And I'm going to hold you to it. You can put it toward the hospital bill."

"I want to get you something," Josh said. "Something to say thank you. You've done an amazing job." He looked down at Joseph again and couldn't help but grin.

"And so have you," Georgie insisted. "You've done the best job anyone could have ever done."

We are grateful.

Chapter 32

Are you here?

Yes, we are here.

Have you taken me?

We have taken you.

Will you bring me back?

We will bring you back.

Josh felt peace within him. A warmth, soft and soothing, enveloped him. Then, a coldness, a fading of vision, an onset of darkness.

I am dying.

Yes, you are dying.

You too have died.

We also have died.

But now you are whole again.

Now we are whole again.

It trickled from him, spreading thin and formless. He was powerless to stop the receding tide, could only watch as it drained into nothing.

You have made a sacrifice.

And so have you.

You sacrifice yourself to protect those you love.

And you have too. We thank you.

The image of Joseph, so young and so fragile, was still fresh in his mind. Georgie, cheeks pinking with joy, a fighter and a giver, gave him solace. She would be safe because of him. Their son would be safe because of him.

Where will you go now? Back to where you came from?

Yes, we will return.

Where did you come from? Another dimension?

Where we come from cannot be understood.

Why do you come to our world?

We must gestate our young in your world until they are strong enough to come to ours.

Is your form mortal in our world?

Yes, we can be destroyed in your world.

Is that what happened?

We were attacked, wounded.

What happened to your young?

It has been returned. You have returned it.

The seed was your young?

Yes, and we are grateful.

Chapter 33

All was quiet. All was empty. A flicker, nothing more. Josh's mortal form was slowly decaying, as life anew was drawn from him. He knew. He had known. The seed—it was not a portal. It was the child in its embryonic form. And it was he who returned it, carried it across into this dimension, to its home.

Light filled his vision.

Chapter 34

His mouth tasted like ash. The ground was hard beneath him. The quiet was loud in his ears. His bones ached with cold. Everything was black.

Rolling onto his side, Josh levered himself carefully onto his arm, then onto his knees. His joints grumbled. He let out an involuntary sigh as he fumbled in his pocket for his cell, praying that it still lived as he turned the screen on.

Relief came with the glow of light, but his battery was low. He needed to leave. Sitting up, he instinctively checked his side, feeling for blood, for pain. There was old blood, but nothing new. He lifted his shirt; the wound was healed. They had healed him. Their gratitude had been repaid.

The memory was that of a dream: broken, confused and indecipherable. There was clarity—or had been, once—but now there were only pieces. Perhaps they would form again, in time. The overwhelming sense of peace was all that was left of it.

To his feet he climbed, holding his weight carefully. His mortal being was unfamiliar, clumsy; he longed for the warmth of another world, one he could not go back to. He would hold on to that feeling as long as he might, but he knew that soon it would be nothing but dust.

Ascending the ramp, he moved from the room, turning back at the top to look into it. It was quiet, peaceful—empty. They had gone. Josh wondered if they would ever return; he guessed not. They would find a new place to grow their young, somewhere safe. Earth was no longer safe.

Ahead, the cell light caught the dull crystalline remains of the parent still frozen from death, jagged and broken. He moved on, into the darkness. The light picked out the drill, old and rusting. The air was thick with mildew. The tunnel burrowed into nothing.

He followed the decaying tracks as they went, his head feeling as empty as the room itself had become. A thought felt near, but he had neither the energy nor the effort to muster it. Instead he walked in quiet, inside and out, watching the rotten wooden ties slip by one by one.

Not far down he came across a wall. The tunnel had been blocked. It was manmade rather than any kind of collapse, presumably sealing the room away forever. Doubling back, he semi-consciously looked for the chamber in the wall he'd crawled from. It didn't take long to find it; the door was still open. With muscles aching and mind jelly, he climbed his way into it and headed back the way he had entered.

The crawl moved by as a blur. He remembered shuffling through, but not much else. The heat, the smell, the pain—he was too numb to feel it. He felt drained, thin, like his journey from this world to theirs had taken something from him, something he'd not get back for a long while, if ever.

In a blink he was looking at the inside of a manhole cover. He couldn't hear any traffic, so he heaved it up and emerged into the night. In the east, purple stained the sky. It would be morning soon. Without really paying much attention to what he was doing, he stumbled out of the drain, put the cover back, and shuffled to the nearest doorway, where he collapsed and fell straight to sleep.

Not much later, he awoke with a start. The morning sky was a little brighter, and a shadow loomed over him. He blinked. The shadow belonged to a police officer, who was pointing a flashlight at him.

"Sir, get up, please."

Groggily, shielding his eyes from the officer's flashlight, Josh did as he was told. The officer eyed his filthy, blood-stained clothes, and Josh looked down at them also.

"Sorry, officer," he said.

"Are you okay?" the officer asked, keeping Josh stable.

Josh nodded, teetering a little.

"What happened to you? Been drinking?"

"No, I'm fine," Josh said, trying his best to sound fine. "This, my clothes," he added, still looking down, "I got into a fight. I'm sorry. It's over now. It's all okay."

Uncertain, the officer considered Josh. "Can you make it home okay, get yourself cleaned up?"

Josh nodded. Clarity was coming back. "Yes, I'll be okay."

It was decided. "All right then." He backed up to his car, its panels gleaming under the eastern glow. "You take care of yourself and try not to get into any more fights." He climbed in, and pausing as he shut the door, added, "And don't let me catch you sleeping in doorways again, all right?"

Josh nodded again.

"All right." The lights on the car flashed and it pulled away silently, only the roll of its wheels whistling on the tarmac. Josh blinked.

The street, it looked normal enough. Trees hissed in the wind. A man walked his dog on the other side of the street. Another car whistled by, and then another. They looked sleek, compact under the pre-sunrise sky. Soon more people would be up, and the roads and sidewalks would start to fill. He needed to move on.

He found a twenty-four-hour mart and bought some more clothes, some food, a bottle of water, a toothbrush and some deodorant. There were no newspapers or magazines, but he found a news screen with the date on it: thirty-eight years had passed. Seeing it didn't feel real. It numbed his mind.

The clerk at the counter, backlit by an enormous screen advertising some kind of hair product, gave him a funny look. Josh paid and got out without saying a word.

He changed quickly in a back alley, and washed his face and brushed his teeth with some of the water. The label on the bottle was animated, fresh water tumbling from a depiction of whatever spring it had supposedly come from.

He ate and drank, and felt a lot better. He was clean and smelled fresh enough. He found a clock and waited until about eight-thirty, then headed to Georgie's apartment. The subway was surprisingly clean, but not all that much had changed. Mainly there was more advertising, long screens running the lengths of the walls, projecting color and sound at him as he walked to the platform. The adverts seemed to follow him, targeting him with stuff that seemed appropriate for his age and gender.

The trains themselves had been refreshed at some point, the unfamiliar carriages streaked with smears of grime from years of parading these tunnels. Josh's train approached, and he boarded.

Emerging into Queens, he made the walk to 82nd. The tree-lined street looked almost unchanged, other than the cars parked along its length. He found the apartment building he was looking for, and with his heart in his mouth, he pressed the buzzer. Then he waited. His mind was still numb.

A friendly, automated voice greeted him. "Hello. I'm afraid there's no one home right now. Would you care to leave a message, or speak to the landlord?"

Josh hesitated. "Can I speak to the landlord, please?"

"One moment." The line clicked, and then another voice followed, complete with a video feed on the panel above the buttons. It showed an older lady with big hair. "Hello?"

Josh didn't recognize the person, but no matter. "I'm looking for Georgina Reed, please."

The face on the screen scrunched in thought. "Georgina Reed? You mean Georgie?"

Josh's heart leaped. "Yes, that's right."

For a moment the lady was silent. She shuffled uncomfortably. "I'm afraid she passed away, a few years ago now. Can I help?"

Josh turned from the screen, his numb mind numbing further. Walking back to the street, the lady's voice saying, "Hello? Hello?" behind him, he stumbled away. He was walking, but he didn't really know it. Slabs were passing underfoot. He watched the cracks wander by one by one. Tinnitus screeched in his ears.

The door opened behind him and he stopped. The old lady's voice, free of digital flatness, called out to him.

"Sir?" she said.

Josh turned. "Yes?"

The old lady was there, in the doorway, hands clasped together, looking nervous. "Are you… are you Mr. Josh Reed?"

Josh's stomach turned. "I am."

A hint of a smile formed about the lady's lips. It was a saddened smile. "She spoke very highly of you," she said.

Pressure was building behind Josh's eyes. "She did?"

The lady nodded slowly. "I didn't know her that well, but she mentioned you often. She said you'd be coming back for her one day. I thought it was a flight of fancy but… but here you are."

"Here I am," Josh said.

* * *

A week had passed since Josh had emerged from the tunnel. He'd found his savings still intact—clearly Georgie hadn't drawn much from them over the years—and so he rented a small studio apartment out in the cheapest part of Brooklyn he could find. He was having a little trouble catching up with the way things worked; much was similar, but it was the little details that threw him. Cell phones consisted of a small earpiece and a contact lens, and there were no desktop computers as he was accustomed to, so doing research was tricky at first, but he got there in the end.

He found Georgie's obituary, learning that she'd died of heart failure in the summer three years prior. The insert was heartfelt and loving, and it made him smile. He was still having trouble letting himself think of her or feel anything about her; it would take a while longer before he allowed himself to inspect that wound properly.

Lionel had also passed on, an eighty-year-old man with scores of grandchildren and great-grandchildren. The eldest, he discovered, was called Josh. Josh could imagine Lionel bobbing the younger ones on his knee while the older ones—Josh included—listened to his tales. They'd all be nonsense, of course, but that was the charm of them. That was his legacy. That, and a message he'd left with a bemused younger Josh, who shared it via online messaging:

"He told me to tell you something about taking a bath when you get back out. I'm sorry, I don't know what it means."

Josh snorted. *He* knew what it meant all right. Even after thirty years, after his death, Lionel was still making him laugh.

Finding out anything about Joseph was harder, but with a little digging Josh discovered that he had moved out of the city to a small town called Pine Bush. There he'd co-founded a design firm that seemed to be doing well.

Josh had avoided calling the business number, or sending Joseph a message. He didn't want to simply jump into Joseph's life like that; it didn't seem fair. He wanted to go and check things out first. So he did. He boarded the bus at ten in the morning and arrived at Pine Bush at thirty minutes past midday. It was a Sunday, and he checked into a nice hotel and restaurant, where he planned to stay for the while he was there.

He went for a walk to clear his head, then returned to his room to shower and change for an early dinner. Entering the restaurant, he seated himself at the bar and ordered himself a drink, considering the same things he'd been considering over and over since he'd planned the journey: what would he do when he met Joseph? Would Joseph even recognize him? What if Joseph didn't want to know him? He swallowed the drink down, tipping it and his thoughts to the back of his head.

A waiter directed Josh to his table, and as he wound through the dining area, a bout of "Happy Birthday" rang out. Josh turned his attention to the table where the song was being sung, to see a birthday cake, awash with candles, being brought out to a girl who couldn't have been much older than seven. She grinned a toothy grin as the cake was laid out before her, her younger brother squealing with excitement next to her.

Her mother sang through smiling lips, clapping with the restaurant staff who sang too. Other tables around them joined the singing.

It was then Josh noticed the father. No—it couldn't be…

Josh had seen a group image on his son's website of the young company together, and he was sure this man's face was one of them. He loaded up the company page and checked again. The man, the father, he was there, one of the company. Could he be Joseph? All of a sudden, emotion overwhelmed Josh, like color filling black and white. Georgie, how he missed her, her smile, her laugh. And yet here it resonated through the laughter of the birthday girl. His son, the girl's father, was a handsome man, clapping and singing, enjoying the happiness of his children.

Josh blinked a few times, had to look away. The questions flooded in; he had so many to ask. And he would ask them, all of them, in time.

For now, he turned back to the family and sang "Happy Birthday" with them.

If you enjoyed reading New York Deep, *leave a review and you'll receive a free copy of Andrew J. Morgan's sci-fi thriller* Noah's Ark. *Once you've left your review, get in touch at* <u>*andrewjamesmorgan.com*</u> *to receive your free copy of* Noah's Ark. *Thank you, and I hope you enjoyed* New York Deep.

17961437R00199

Printed in Great Britain
by Amazon